HarperCollins books may be purchased for educational, business, or sales promotional use. For information, please email the Special Markets Department at SPsales@harpercollins.com.

FIRST EDITION

Designed by Michelle Crowe

Library of Congress Cataloging-in-Publication Data

Names: Sŏ, Mi-ae, author. | Jun, Yewon, translator.
Title: The only child : a novel / Seo Mi-Ae ; translated by Yewon Jun Other titles: Chal chayo ŏmma. English
Description: New York : Ecco, 2019.
Identifiers: LCCN 2019013861 (print) | LCCN 2019020273 (ebook) | ISBN 9780062905055 (Ebook) | ISBN 9780062905048 (hardcover) | ISBN 9780062959171 (pbk.)
Classification: LCC PL994.74.M52 (ebook) | LCC PL994.74.M52 C48 2019 (print) | DDC 895.73/5—dc23
LC record available at https://lccn.loc.gov/2019013861

ISBN 978-0-06-290504-8 (hardcover)
ISBN 978-0-06-299728-9 (international edition)

20 21 22 23 24 LSC 10 9 8 7 6 5 4 3 2 1

THE ONLY CHILD

A Novel

Mi-ae Seo

TRANSLATED BY YEWON JUNG

An Imprint of HarperCollins*Publishers*

THERE'S A VERY OLD ROOM, for instance.

The room is full of things I don't want to remember, and there's a big lock on the door.

As time passes, I gradually forget that the room is there, and in the end, I don't remember that it was ever there.

Memory is a strange thing. Something you can't possibly forget is completely removed from your mind for that very reason. It's a safety mechanism, they say, to protect you from shock. Your brain automatically eliminates it, knowing it'll break you if you keep thinking about it. So your mind remembers only what it wants to remember. It keeps only what it can handle.

I wonder from time to time: What's wrong with my mind?

Yes, I had a room like that once, too.

A room I drove into a corner because it was so terrible, and put dozens of locks on. There was a short period of time when I didn't even remember that there was a room like that. But it didn't last long. The locks came loose one day, all at once.

I shouldn't have gone in, even if the locks were open. But curiosity got the better of me and I went inside. And I realized.

That I had opened the door to hell.

PART I

1.

I T WAS 3:37 A.M. ON JUNE 17 WHEN A FIRE IN THE EUNGAM-DONG area was reported.

The report was displayed on the status board in the situation room of the fire defense headquarters in Namsan, and, simultaneously, at the West Fire Department and a nearby police station, and the fire investigation team in the forensic science investigation department at the Seoul Metropolitan Police Agency were informed of the fire.

Yi Sangwuk, a fire inspector at the fire defense headquarters who received the report, was on night duty when the report came in, and asleep in bed in the staff lounge. Sangwuk, who received the call on his cell phone, rose to his feet, rubbing his sleepy eyes. He had gone to sleep after one A.M., having finished a written report, so he had gotten only about two hours of sleep.

His eyelids kept drooping, but when he went outside and got some fresh air, he felt more awake. The cool night air swept away the last traces of sleep.

Before getting into his car in the parking lot, Sangwuk called Sergeant Yu Dongsik, his partner. A voice, still half-asleep, answered.

"I'm awake, I'm awake."

The Seoul Metropolitan Police must have called him already.

Sangwuk could picture him vividly. He must be sitting up in bed, shaking his head to keep himself from slipping back into sleep. He must be trying to drive away sleep, his eyes closed, and listening to the voice on the phone.

Sangwuk stifled a chuckle and said he was on his way to the scene.

"Hurry up and get on your way," he said.

"Wait," Sergeant Yu said.

"Huh?"

Sergeant Yu had called out urgently just as Sangwuk was about to hang up. Wondering what was wrong, Sangwuk listened.

"Where did you say it was?"

He must have heard, but he asked Sangwuk again, perhaps still half-asleep, perhaps just to make sure.

"The Eungam area. This time, it's around the Chungam High School's five-way crossing, on Baekryeonsa Street."

Having confirmed the site, Sergeant Yu heaved a sigh. Then he was quiet, probably trying to gather himself. He groaned and muttered something. It sounded like he was swearing, getting to his feet. Sangwuk understood, because he felt the same way.

"Yeah, it's driving me crazy, too," he said to the sergeant.

"All right. Let me get ready. I'll be there."

Sangwuk hung up and quickly got into the car.

He put the key into the ignition and started the engine, then checked the time. It was already past four.

There wouldn't be too much traffic since it was early in the morning. If he drove past the Sungnye Gate to Muakjae, it would take no more than twenty minutes. He rushed out of the parking lot, and tried to recall how many fires there had been in the Eungam area recently.

There had already been five cases of these fires, which had started in the spring. Now, Sangwuk felt that he would go into fits if he was told that someone was so much as lighting a match in the Eungam area.

The first case occurred near the construction site of Hills State Apartments in the Eungam Seventh District near Seoul Metropolitan Eunpyeong Hospital.

The area, with large-scale apartments under construction at the foot of Baekryeon Mountain, was cluttered with building materials and trucks that went in and out of the construction site.

Fortunately, the fire, which broke out in an empty lot that stood between Baekryeonsa Street and the construction site, was extinguished without anyone dying. Some plywood and materials for construction were burnt up, but the damage wasn't great, and the fire was put out quickly thanks to a worker who was guarding the construction site and who detected the fire early on. The fire department found nothing unusual about the fire, so it was categorized as a fire by cigarette, or an accidental fire.

But when a series of fires broke out in and around the Eungam area, the first case, which had been treated as an ordinary fire due to negligence, also became subject to reinvestigation. Because the vicinity of the construction site was closed off at night when no one was around, it was suggested that someone may have deliberately gone into the area and set the fire.

The greatest damage was caused by the third fire.

And that was when Yi Sangwuk, a fire inspector at the fire defense headquarters, and Sergeant Yu Dongsik, a fire investigator in the forensic science investigation department at the Seoul Metropolitan Police Agency, became involved with the series of fires.

The fire, which broke out near Eungam-dong Church behind Eungam Elementary School across from Baekryeonsa Street, caused serious damage, spreading to the multiplex housing with the dust from a sandstorm, burning down three homes, and killing three people who had been sleeping.

The case occurred around three in the morning, but there was a witness, since it happened in an alleyway in a residential area.

The witness was a resident in the area, and said he saw someone suspicious around the scene of the fire on his way home after working overtime. He testified that flames shot up in the residential area after the suspect disappeared into the main street, but that he couldn't tell what the person looked like because it was dark.

Sangwuk, in cooperation with Sergeant Yu, rummaged through the ashes searching for the exact place where the fire started and its cause, only to reach a dead end because the testimony of the witness did not correspond with the scene of the fire. The residents in the area said that there had been a long-held conflict between them and the construction company regarding reconstruction, and that the conflict must have had something to do with the series of fires.

As Sangwuk climbed over the Muakjae Hill and drove onto Moraenae Street from the Hongje three-way intersection, his phone rang.

"Where are you?" Sergeant Yu asked, his voice flat. "Are you there already?"

"No, I'm on my way."

"I thought you wanted to talk when we got there. . . ."

"Is this the sixth time already?"

"Yeah, it is."

There was silence for a while.

"Is there something you want to say?" Sangwuk asked Sergeant Yu, thinking the phone might be disconnected.

"I . . . had a bad dream earlier . . ." was Sergeant Yu's reply.

"A dream?"

It seemed that he felt uneasy, having received a report of fire, especially after a bad dream. Sangwuk felt disturbed, seeing Sergeant Yu in this sudden moment of weakness. Sangwuk had never seen him that way. He must be stressed out because of the series of fires.

Sangwuk and Sergeant Yu investigated scenes of fires together, but the two had different responsibilities.

What Sangwuk did was investigate the scene of the fire, the remaining traces, and the witnesses' statements, and find the starting point and the cause of the fire. On the other hand, Sergeant Yu worked with fire inspectors like Sangwuk, and based on the facts discovered through the primary investigation, or if the possibility of arson was detected, began a full-fledged investigation. He then had to find the traces of the criminal at the scene of the fire and solve the case.

Sangwuk, who worked for the fire defense headquarters, would be done with his task at the scene, but for Sergeant Yu, who worked for the Seoul Metropolitan Police, the scene was just the starting point. If there was a crime involved in the fire, Sergeant Yu would not rest until the criminal was found and the case resolved.

The two went around together, exchanging their opinions on the scene of the fire, but it was only natural that Sergeant Yu was under greater stress. On top of that, these fires that had been breaking out in the same area over just a few months must have added to the pressure for him to solve the cases as soon as possible. Normally, they wouldn't go to a scene of a fire immediately upon its report. But because of the past several cases of arson, Sangwuk and Sergeant Yu were contacted as soon as a fire in the Eungam area was reported.

Sangwuk didn't know what to say to Sergeant Yu. He just hoped that the culprit would be caught and that this case would put an end to the series of arsons.

"Do you believe in dreams and stuff?" Sergeant Yu asked.

"I do. My mother had an amazing dream before she had me. That's why I became a fire fighter, you know. Haven't I told you?"

To make Sergeant Yu feel better, Sangwuk brought up the dream his mother had before having him, being chattier than usual. But

Sergeant Yu, who had heard the story dozens of times already, hung up the phone before Sangwuk could go on.

Sangwuk chuckled, put his phone down, and began to speed up.

THE ROAD WAS CONGESTED several meters ahead of the Chungam High School five-way crossing, as if to notify onlookers that there had been a fire. It was early in the morning, but it was difficult to approach the scene because of the people who had come out to see the fire and the cars that were slowing down.

Sangwuk made his way onto the road leading to Baekryeonsa only after honking several times, even with a flashing light on the roof of his car. He parked the car off to the side, away from the on-lookers, and noted the busy movements characteristic of a fire scene as he approached.

The road was hectic with fire trucks that had been mobilized to put the fire out, as well as fire fighters, ambulances on call to transfer the injured, and police trying to bring order to the scene. In addition, there were residents from the area who had come running out at the news of the fire, stamping their feet, so there was confusion everywhere.

Out of habit, Sangwuk looked over at the flames shooting up. Fortunately, they were somewhat under control, and the rescue team was getting ready to enter the scene. Sangwuk looked around, boosting the morale of the fire fighters from West Fire Department, with whom he had become familiar through this latest series of fires.

Even among the dozens of people busily moving about, Sergeant Yu could be spotted instantly. His buzz cut, height, and sturdy frame were easily recognizable even from a distance.

Sergeant Yu was shaking his head, suppressing a yawn, as he stood behind a patrol car and watched the fire being put out.

Sangwuk reached him quickly.

"You're still not awake?" he asked the sergeant.

Sergeant Yu just frowned, watching the jet of water being sprayed by the fire fighters. He hadn't slept much and must have been exhausted running around because of the series of arsons.

"What's all this, because of some crazy son of a bitch?" the sergeant said.

"I know."

Frustrated, Sergeant Yu rubbed his face, looked around, and went up to a uniformed police officer keeping the scene under control.

The police officer gave them information about the witnesses, and what progress had been made. As Sergeant Yu and Sangwuk looked for the person who had made the report, the officer pointed to a nearby convenience store, saying he was there.

People were gathered, bustling, in front of the convenience store. They must have been there for a while as they started to make their way home one by one as the fire began to be extinguished.

Entering the convenience store, they found no one inside. Sergeant Yu went outside and looked for the person who had reported the fire when a young man in a striped T-shirt turned around with a nervous look on his face. The young man, who said he worked part-time at the convenience store, was clucking his tongue and watching the scene with others.

"I made the report," he said.

"Could you tell me what you saw at first?"

Everyone looked at the young man. He looked at Sergeant Yu for a moment, scratched his head, and then spoke.

"It was around three thirty, I think. There were no customers, and I started dozing off as I was sitting down, so I came out for a moment to get some fresh air. That's when I saw black smoke rising above the houses in the alleyway. At first I wondered what it was, but then I saw the flames shooting up among the black smoke. I wasn't sure, but then the flames suddenly grew large. I was startled, and then I called to file a report."

Looking toward the alleyway where the young man was pointing, Sergeant Yu fell into thought.

"Where does the alleyway lead to?" he asked.

"A dead end, I think."

"Did you see anyone suspicious when you made the report? Someone popping out from where the smoke was, or a stranger roaming around before the fire broke out?"

"I'm not sure, because I was at the counter."

Sergeant Yu gave the young man his card, asking him to call if he remembered anything else, and headed toward the alleyway.

From the mouth of the alleyway, the ground was messy because of all the fire hoses and the water dripping from them. As Sergeant Yu made his way through, he saw a rescue worker coming out of the alleyway where black smoke was still rising, carrying in his arms a girl who looked about ten years old.

Sergeant Yu looked over at the girl in the man's arms. For some reason, he couldn't take his eyes off her. He turned around and followed the rescue worker who was carrying the girl in his arms.

The rescue worker took the girl to an ambulance, and disappeared again into the alleyway.

The paramedic in the ambulance covered the girl with a blanket and asked her if she was hurt, but the girl didn't say anything and looked over at the alleyway. The girl, clutching a large teddy bear in her arms, looked calm, considering that she had just escaped a fire. Taking a closer look at her face, however, Sergeant Yu saw that she was actually immobilized with shock. Only her large eyes showed fear, glancing here and there from time to time. She didn't seem injured in any way.

The girl kept staring at the alleyway from which black smoke continued to leak, then came to herself and got out of the ambulance, and looked around. She seemed to be searching for someone to talk to, to ask if she should go back into the alleyway and return home, or wait where she was.

Sergeant Yu felt a pang in his heart.

It was always the victims that brought him the greatest pain at the scene of a fire.

It was a bolt out of the blue. In an instant they lost their homes, and had to send their families away. Most of the victims would shake from anxiety for a while, losing sleep due to the shock. The memory of the fire would haunt their sleep for a long time to come.

Seeing the girl look around for her family among the people, Sergeant Yu felt enraged.

When the girl began to drift away from the ambulance, Sergeant Yu quickly went up to her.

"Where are you going? It's safer to wait here. And you need to go to the hospital," he said to the girl.

She looked up at him with large, clear eyes. They were full of anxiety, guarded against strangers. Sergeant Yu wanted to put her fear to rest any way he could.

"Don't worry. When the fire fighters put the fire out, you can be with your family again," he reassured her.

At his words, the girl blinked her eyes and mumbled something, as if she finally remembered. At first, she barely moved her lips, mumbling so that he couldn't hear very well, but then she looked up at him and raised her voice.

"My dad . . ."

"Huh?"

"I want to go to my dad."

Sergeant Yu looked at the ambulance. The back door was open, but there were no victims inside. If they had been rescued earlier, they could have been transferred to the hospital in another ambulance. But if not, they could be inside a blazing house. He didn't want to consider that possibility. Sergeant Yu didn't know what to say, and looked around for someone who would help him.

The girl grasped his arm and shook it, as if to ask for help. He looked down into her eyes, and felt the sharp pain tug at his heart. The girl, growing more aware of what was happening, looked as if she would start crying any minute, her eyes brimming with tears. The longer she stayed apart from her family, the more anxious and frightened she would become.

Sergeant Yu looked around for Sangwuk.

Sangwuk was checking up on the situation, questioning the fire fighters who were putting their gear away. By finding out how the fire fighters worked at the scene and the processes involved, you could prevent errors. Sergeant Yu waited for Sangwuk to finish his task, and looked down at the girl.

Soon, Sangwuk exchanged his final words with the fire fighters, and approached Sergeant Yu.

"We should start making our way in, huh?" he asked the sergeant.

Sangwuk, who clearly wanted to start their primary investigation now that the fire was extinguished, saw the girl standing next to Sergeant Yu. Then he looked back at Sergeant Yu. His face was full of questions. Sergeant Yu pointed to the alleyway with his chin.

Sangwuk realized only then that she was a victim of the fire, and bent down to pat the girl on her head.

"You must've been very shocked. You're not hurt? Where's your mom?" he asked the girl.

There was a pause before she spoke.

"She's dead."

The tears that had barely been managing to stay in her eyes began to trickle down. Startled by the girl's answer, Sangwuk stared at Sergeant Yu, not knowing what to say.

"Is she . . . still inside?" Sergeant Yu asked the girl.

The girl shook her head fiercely, then clammed up as if to say she didn't want to talk anymore. She turned sullen after the talk of her mother, and clutched her teddy bear even tighter. Then, avoiding Sangwuk's gaze, she buried her face in the stuffed animal's face.

Sergeant Yu, who had been watching, spoke to Sangwuk in a low voice.

"Her dad must've come out. She wants us to take her to him."

"We can take her in the ambulance, then. He must be at West Hospital. Should I check to make sure?"

"My dad's at Seoul Hospital," interjected the girl, who a moment before had been reluctant to talk.

"Seoul Hospital?"

Sergeant Yu stared at the girl, then looked over at Sangwuk.

"Is there a Seoul Hospital around here?"

"I'm not sure. I've never heard of it before, either."

There were several designated hospitals to which victims of fires in the region were taken. There was no hospital named Seoul Hospital there, though. The girl, feeling frustrated, wiped away the tears on her cheeks with the back of her hand, and took out a card from her pocket and handed it to Sangwuk.

"This is my dad's phone number. Please call him," she said.

Taking the card in his hand, Sangwuk gave Sergeant Yu a puzzled look.

"What are you waiting for? Call him!" said the sergeant.

At the words, Sangwuk hurriedly took his phone out and made the call.

"Hello? Um . . . is this Mr. Yun Jaeseong?" he asked when someone picked up.

The voice on the other end of the line sounded barely awake. It seemed that the man didn't know anything about the fire. No one would be pleased to take a call so early in the morning. Gruffly, the girl's father asked what was going on.

"Your daughter is looking for you. We're in Eungam-dong. There's been a fire. . . . Yes. Yes, that's right. Around Jeongseong Villa on Dalmaji Street. Yes. . . . Don't worry. She's safe. Yes. . . . Yes."

The girl's father, alarmed at the news of the fire, confirmed the address and said he would be there soon, and hung up.

As soon as Sangwuk put his phone back in his pocket, the girl tugged at his pants. He quickly looked down at the girl. Hope and excitement shone in her eyes.

"Is he coming?" she asked eagerly.

"Yes, he'll be here soon, if you wait here."

The girl's face relaxed with relief. The fear and anxiety disappeared instantly. Sangwuk looked around to see that the ambulance was gone. Sergeant Yu and Sangwuk left the girl in the care of the police, and made their way to the scene of the fire in the alleyway.

THE RESCUE TEAM HAD LEFT, and the remaining fire fighters had broken down the burnt doors and were checking inside the house. Sergeant Yu and Sangwuk also began to look around.

It seemed that the detached house at the dead end of the street, and the apartment building next to it, had sustained the greatest damage.

Sergeant Yu and Sangwuk walked over to the house.

When they entered the gate, they saw a yard with several trees and a single-story structure. The yard was a mess from the efforts to put the fire out. Black water had leaked out of the building and formed puddles here and there. Sergeant Yu and Sangwuk turned on their flashlights and began to look around, paying careful attention to the outer wall of the building, which had turned black.

The house was almost completely burnt down, with all the windows broken, and the walls covered in black soot. The two-story apartment building next to the house was burnt as well, with the balcony windows shattered. Beyond the door the interior could be seen, all black. Electronic goods and furniture had melted in the fire and were dripping with black water. It was an appalling sight; it didn't seem possible that people once lived there. The place, swept through by red flames, had turned into hell.

Flames leave footprints on walls, in the form of soot.

Sergeant Yu and Sangwuk checked the soot-covered walls of the house and the apartment building, sidestepping the puddles.

"It looks like the flames spread from the house to the apartment."

At Sangwuk's words, Sergeant Yu nodded. Sergeant Yu went to the back of the house and checked the space where it connected to the apartment.

The wall of the house was adjacent to the outer wall of the apartment building. There must have been a lot of stuff piled up in between, for the space was filled with burnt refuse. Smoke rose occasionally from the remains, drenched in water, as if the fire weren't done with the house yet.

Sangwuk touched the debris that had turned into lumps of charcoal, then rubbed the soot with the tips of his fingers. He tapped a lump with the tip of his shoe, and sniffed it.

"I think it's a mixture of wood and chemicals. And I think there were some Styrofoam boards as well," he said.

"They must've been left over from the construction. Doors and construction materials."

"Yes, it looks like it."

If this space had been empty, the fire might not have spread to the building next door. The plywood and Styrofoam boards must have served as a stepping stone for the fire to spread from the house to the apartment building.

Sergeant Yu and Sangwuk went back out to the front yard. Fire fighters who had gone inside the house shouted that dead bodies had been found. One of the men ran outside the alleyway for a stretcher.

Sergeant Yu frowned without realizing it.

A fire breaking out early in the morning was bound to cause more deaths than usual because most people were sound asleep. The family in the house must have been killed in their sleep, not knowing there was a fire. Sergeant Yu went inside with a fire fighter, preparing for the worst.

An acrid smell stung his lungs. He put on a mask and entered the main room. The fire fighter who had been keeping watch there nodded at him. Sergeant Yu barely acknowledged him, and looked at the dead bodies in the room.

There were two of them. It seemed that they had been sleeping side by side when they died. The burnt bodies looked like those of a husband and wife. Sergeant Yu barely managed to fight off the nausea, and pressed his mask closer to his face with his hand.

Looking at the bodies and the room, Sergeant Yu instinctively sensed that something was wrong.

Something inexplicable was caught up in his brain and would not leave. He approached the dead bodies and lifted the half-burnt cotton comforter. The parts of the bodies that had been covered by the comforter must not have been touched by the flames, for they were not damaged. Sergeant Yu was shocked, but tried not to come to a rash conclusion.

Sangwuk, who had been about to come into the room, saw the dead bodies and backed out. He had been working as a fire inspector for quite some time, but still avoided seeing dead bodies if he could. Sergeant Yu left the room, asked the fire fighters not to touch anything inside for a while, and went out the gate. Sangwuk, who had been pacing around in the yard, followed him and asked, "Where are you off to?"

"To get the camera from the car."

"I have one."

"Not yours, mine. I need to take the pictures myself."

Sensing the stiffness in the sergeant's voice, Sangwuk clamped his mouth shut. By saying that he was taking the pictures himself, Sergeant Yu was implying that there was a crime involved in the fire. He needed to take detailed photographs that would identify the scene.

At that moment, the phone rang in Sangwuk's pocket. He checked the number and took the call. It was the girl's father, whom he had called earlier. He said he was almost there, and asked where his daughter was.

"There's a patrol car right at the mouth of the alleyway. That's where you should go," Sangwuk said.

"Her father must be here," he then said to Sergeant Yu.

Sergeant Yu blocked the way as Sangwuk made to follow him.

"What's the matter?" Sangwuk asked.

"I'll talk to him, so stay here and keep watch."

Sergeant Yu, worried that the scene might be compromised, left Sangwuk there and quickly headed out of the alleyway toward the patrol car on the main street.

The alleyway, which had earlier been so crowded, was quiet. All had withdrawn except for the bare minimum number of fire trucks and ambulances. There was much less of a crowd now. The fire had been put out, and it being early in the morning, people must have returned home to get some more sleep, or to get ready for work.

Sergeant Yu hurriedly got his camera from the car and approached the patrol car. He didn't see a uniformed officer. Looking around for one, he peeked into the car.

The girl was lying on the backseat, asleep.

After the shock of the fire, she must have been relieved to hear that her father was coming.

Even while sleeping, she clutched the teddy bear tightly. She coughed from time to time, frowning as if in pain. She must have inhaled smoke. But after fumbling to make sure that the teddy bear was still in her arms, she fell into deep sleep, looking relieved. Sergeant Yu felt sorry for the child, who was able to sleep soundly even after going through something so terrible. How many nights would she lie restless because of what happened that night?

"Oh, she's asleep. I bought some milk for her because she said her throat hurt."

Sergeant Yu turned around and saw a uniformed officer with milk and cookies in his hands. He must've felt sorry for the child as well.

"Where's her family?" the officer asked.

"Her father is on his way," replied Sergeant Yu.

"That's good."

Sergeant Yu looked at the girl for some time, then turned around and looked for her father.

A man parked his car and came rushing out.

He ran into the alleyway, then stopped in his tracks, startled by the sight of the fire trucks, as well as the fire fighters who were busy cleaning up. Looking at the alleyway, his face hardened with shock.

"Mr. Yun Jaeseong?" Sergeant Yu called out.

The man turned around to see the man who had called his name, then saw the sergeant and approached him. His face was trembling with fear. His voice was urgent as he asked, "Where's my daughter?"

"Don't worry. She's asleep over there. She's not hurt."

The man hurried over to the patrol car to make sure that she was safe. Finding her asleep, he heaved a sigh of relief and returned to Sergeant Yu.

"Where are my in-laws? Are they hurt? Where are they?" he asked the sergeant.

"The injured have been transferred to a nearby hospital."

Sergeant Yu was about to say that he'd confirm with the hospital, but stopped himself. He was overcome by an ominous feeling.

"Which one's their home?" he asked.

"The one at the end of the alleyway."

"Is it the detached house in front of the apartment building?"

"Yes. Why do you ask?"

The image of the couple who had been lying dead with a blanket pulled over their heads flashed through Sergeant Yu's mind. The couple must have been the child's maternal grandparents.

The man saw the look on Sergeant Yu's face and understood immediately. His mouth dropped open in disbelief. He blinked as he tried to find the right words.

"Are they both . . . dead?" he asked at last.

Sergeant Yu nodded, avoiding his eyes. He could sense the man's body go limp.

"Where . . . have their bodies been taken?" the man asked further.

"Well . . ." The sergeant hesitated.

It wasn't easy to get the words out. He couldn't really explain what had happened yet.

Things would become clearer after an investigation of the scene and an autopsy. Until then, he couldn't tell someone who was undergoing shock from losing family that the cause of death was murder, not fire. Sergeant Yu decided that it wouldn't be too late to tell him after he had overcome the initial shock.

"You should take your daughter home for now. We'll give you a call. She must be exhausted," he said.

The man remembered his daughter, and turned around and looked at the patrol car, nodding his head.

"Was your wife in the house, too?" Sergeant Yu asked.

"Huh?"

The man looked at Sergeant Yu with a startled expression on his face.

The girl had said a little earlier that her mother was dead. The house hadn't been thoroughly checked, so there might be another body inside.

"No, my wife . . . died a year ago," said the man.

"Oh . . . I'm sorry. There's been a misunderstanding."

As Sergeant Yu apologized, the man waved his hands, indicating it was all right, and went up to the patrol car.

Sergeant Yu saw the man open the car door and take the girl in his arms, then headed toward the alleyway.

As he fiddled with the camera in his hands, his mind began to speed up.

Murder, huh? We really need to look at the scene from a different angle now, he thought.

It was gradually growing light as the sun came up.

2.

WHAT'S THE OLDEST MEMORY IN YOUR HEAD?
Going to kindergarten, holding your mom's hand? No, something older than that, the first memory engraved in the inner folds of the brain.

They say that you don't remember things from when you were a baby. I don't know whether you don't remember them because they happened too long ago, or if memories that aren't that important are discarded, but in any case, I'm curious as to what people keep tucked deep within their brains as their first memories.

"What's the oldest memory in your head?"

That is the first thing I ask when I meet people. Somehow, it seems that the first memory in someone's head determines his destiny or personality. And it seems that you can tell what kind of person he is based on the memory.

The oldest memory I've ever heard of was from a man who remembered getting a bowl of seaweed soup on his first birthday.

It being his first birthday, it had been exactly a year since he was born into the world. I asked him how he remembered that, and he said that as soon as he got the bowl, he threw up in it. That's why he never forgot. I had a drink from time to time with this man who never had seaweed soup after that, and I think his habit of throwing up formed on that day.

If such a nauseating memory was my first memory, I would want to throw up, too. Still, his is better than mine.

Once in a while, I picture myself doing something.

I'm lying in a comfortable chair, and tracing my memory as the hypnotist tells me to. As you go back in time, you remember your childhood days, even your mother's womb, they say. Some people see their past lives. I don't want to find out about my past life, of course. I don't even believe in such things.

What I'd like to know is what my mom looked like when I came out through darkness into the world. I want to know what kind of look she had on her face at that moment.

Why?

I think it's because my mom told me that she hated me before I was even born.

She said she didn't look at me after I came out. The nurse handed me to her, but she set me aside, saying she didn't want to touch me, and fell asleep. She slept with her back toward me, and when she woke up and turned around without thinking, she saw me and was scared out of her wits. She said it gave her the chills to see me lying still, not crying when I had been set aside.

I wanted to know if she really didn't look at me, if she didn't smile at me, not even once. Did she really hate me, when I had been in her womb for nine months, and had come out into the world through her? Didn't she smile brightly at me, just once? Didn't she want to reach out a hand and touch those wriggling fingers, to kiss the soft, tender cheeks? I don't remember because I was too young, but I want to look in every nook and cranny of my brain to see if there had ever been such a moment.

If you could see the memories of my mom in my mind right now, you would understand.

The first memory in my mind begins with darkness.

I'm struggling because it feels as if my heart is being ripped to shreds and I can't breathe. Suddenly, the darkness lifts and my mom is looking down at me with a blank expression on her face. I finally manage to breathe again; gasping, I look at the world through my tears. When the pain in my chest finally subsides and I can breathe normally, my mom, who has been staring at me, begins to scream. She bites into the pillow she's holding in her hands, and sobs in pain. The sound is so terrifying that I, unable to hold back, start bawling as well. My mom shakes me and screams even louder, writhing. I don't know how old I was. Two? Three? Probably around that age because I could barely speak.

Yes, the first memory I have is that of struggling painfully under the pillow in my mom's hands. That's my first memory, so I'm sure you can guess the things that happened after that.

Whenever I try to picture my mom and me, I can only recall scenes in which I'm being beaten, or running or hiding from her, huddled in a corner, frightened.

She did smile at me once in a while. But that was only when she was trying to catch me, with a stick behind her back, or when she had an underlying motive. If I went up to her, fooled by the smile, her rough hand would grab my tender arm and twist it, or slap me.

I would resolve in my heart not to be deceived by her again, but would fail every time. When it became possible for me to outrun her, she shouted, cursing at me. But no curse could catch me.

But you know something?

Words can leave a deeper, more terrible wound than a slap on the cheek. Angry that she couldn't catch me, she would shout like crazy. Even when I covered up my ears, the words burrowed inside me. Those words wounded me, and the wounds festered inside. I became full of dirty blood, pus, and polluted words and thoughts.

When I was little, I couldn't even look people in the eye. I would stiffen and my heart would start beating faster if I so much as heard someone approach. If my eyes happened to meet someone else's, I would avert my gaze and run. I thought everyone in the world hated me.

I thought that my mom beat me every day because everyone hated me, that nobody wanted me in the world. I thought my very self was a horror. Only later did I find out that it was just my mom who hated me.

Do I hate my mom?

No, no. How could I? She's my mom.

I love my mom.

3.

W HEN THE LIGHTS CAME ON IN THE CLASSROOM, THE
students let out a sigh of relief, as if they'd woken up
from a nightmare. The students who had been sitting
by the window hastily drew back the curtains that were keeping the
sun out and opened the window. When sunlight and fresh air filled
the room, it became lively again. The crimes that had made the students tremble in fear seemed to vanish into the sunlight.

Seonkyeong turned off the LCD projector and turned around to
face the students.

From the way they were talking in low voices, she could sense
faint traces of fear and anxiety. But just as a nightmare could no
longer threaten the day once you were awake, the fear they felt would
soon evaporate.

The students' eyes had been sparkling with curiosity and excitement when the lecture began.

Their faces were full of anticipation, as if to say, we're finally going
to see it! It was just as someone had said: they had waited a whole
semester for it. When the slides began to appear on the screen, the
noise quickly died down. The excitement was replaced by a heavy
atmosphere.

As the photographs were shown one by one, moans of fear and

confusion could be heard here and there in the classroom. Everyone was focused on the lecture, and it was so quiet that you could hear the sound of a pen drop. The students, listening to Seonkyeong explain, looked stiff with shock.

There's nothing more frightening than reality.

The weight of an actual crime scene, like no horror movie, reveals the cold-bloodedness of humans. The student representative, who had talked big, saying it couldn't be as bad as a slasher movie, was at a loss for words. The gap between reality and fiction was greater than they could have imagined. On top of that, seeing with their own eyes how the criminals' twisted imaginations had damaged the victims, they seemed deeply disturbed by the brutality of an actual crime scene.

The special lecture Seonkyeong had given a year before had led to her post at the school, and she'd given a lot of thought as to what the final lecture should deal with. Since the course was an introduction to criminal psychology, she had no choice but to teach theories by countless psychologists with unfamiliar terms, but that wasn't the kind of class she'd wanted to teach. It wasn't the kind of class that the students wanted, either.

From the first day, the students showed great interest in Seonkyeong and had high expectations. The rumors of the special lecture, as well as her profile on the school website, had piqued their curiosity.

During her first lecture, a student gave Seonkyeong the nickname "Clarice." It was the name of the fictional FBI cadet agent who investigated a serial murder case with the help of Hannibal Lecter, a genius serial killer. The fact that Seonkyeong had been trained by the FBI, and in the Behavioral Analysis Unit at that, was of great interest to the students. Naturally, the questions poured out during the first lecture.

Seonkyeong was flustered at first. She couldn't understand why the students were asking such questions. Only afterward when she heard about her profile on the school website did she realize what had gone wrong.

"Trained in the Behavioral Analysis Unit of the FBI."

What she had mentioned in passing during her interview with the dean had been placed on her profile. Having seen that, the students imagined that Seonkyeong had been trained as an investigator like Clarice Starling in *The Silence of the Lambs*. She wanted to tell them that there had been a misunderstanding, but the students' eyes, full of curiosity and admiration, made her hesitate.

It was true that she had been trained by the FBI, but it was different from what the students imagined.

What Seonkyeong had received was a two-week training program—ten days to be exact, five days each week—provided for outstanding students of criminal psychology at a university in the eastern United States. By the time Seonkyeong became familiar enough with the vast FBI Academy to find the bathroom without getting lost, the training was over. She had seen no more than the door to the Behavioral Analysis Unit, and had only a distant view of the special agent, a master at profiling, while listening to his lecture in an auditorium. It was almost something of a publicity program for the FBI, it seemed, a cursory training.

The students, however, who had no such information, were full of admiration. Seonkyeong tried to avoid talking about it, saying it wasn't a big deal, but they wouldn't let her leave it at that. She was freed from the topic only after relating some personal anecdotes, including those belonging to someone with whom she had shared a room during the training.

She had said in passing that she would tell them about the serial killers she'd learned about at the FBI if she had a chance. The students remembered what she'd said, and waited all semester. Naturally, in the end, that became the topic of the final lecture. Seonkyeong put a lot into the preparation, thinking it was a good topic with which to wrap up the course.

She searched diligently on Google and wrote an e-mail to a friend in the States so as not to disappoint the students, who were full of anticipation. Luckily, she was able to find the images she wanted through Google searches alone, and Jessi helped her out with what little she lacked.

She figured it would be easy for Jessi, her roommate in the dorm and who was now working as a researcher at a private crime lab, to get her hands on some materials. At Seonkyeong's request, Jessi willingly got her what she needed. Jessi was able to gather a lot more material than Seonkyeong had expected, thanks to the information system of U.S. public institutions. When Seonkyeong sent an e-mail saying thank you, and mentioned that the students had nicknamed her "Clarice," Jessi replied, "Say hello for me if you ever meet the Korean Hannibal."

Seonkyeong had been packing her bag, thinking she should let Jessi know that the lecture was a success thanks to her, when someone called out, "Professor!" She turned around and saw a student sitting by the window with an arm raised.

Seonkyeong nodded her head, and the student stood up and asked a question.

"We've been hearing about the childhoods of serial killers. Does that mean that serial killers can be detected from when they're little?"

She could understand why the student was asking such a question. The material must have been overwhelming. Why had those serial killers become what they were? Dozens of questions would now begin to pour out.

"That's something psychologists were greatly concerned with all through the twentieth century. Criminal psychologists sought to find out where the root of the criminal character lay. Scholars studying genes and biological evidence thought it lay in birth, and those who observed social environment thought that the environment caused it. And those who studied photographs of criminals' brains claimed that crime was a result of brain damage."

Seonkyeong paused for a moment and looked at the students one by one.

"What do you think?"

Everyone looked at her, captivated, waiting for her next words.

It seemed that they didn't want the lecture to end yet. Feeling a sense of satisfaction, Seonkyeong thought about what to say next, and asked, "Have you heard of the McDonald's Triangle?"

"Big Mac, McMorning, and apple pie!" a student in the back quipped. The students, who had been listening in earnest, broke out in smiles. Seonkyeong smiled as well.

"That's a different McDonald you're talking about. The one I'm talking about is an American psychologist. He maintained that the three childhood characteristics of bed-wetting, arson, and cruel behavior to animals indicate whether someone will turn out to be mentally ill or normal. You've heard of these characteristics before, right?"

"They're the childhood characteristics of serial killers," a girl sitting in the front row answered.

"That's right. Serial killers have those characteristics in common. There are exceptions, of course, but most serial killers showed such behavior in their childhood. Did any of you wet your bed when you were little?"

Seonkyeong looked at the students and raised her hand.

The students looked at each other to see who raised their hands. When the student who had asked the first question raised his hand, several others did as well, laughing.

"Some of you haven't raised your hands, but it shows on your face," Seonkyeong joked, and more laughter followed.

"Now, who's ever played with fire?"

More students raised their hands this time, no longer hesitant.

"And finally, who has ever done something cruel to an animal?"

This time, no one raised their hands. Seonkyeong looked around at the students, and said, "When I was in elementary school, there was a popular game the kids played. A man came in front of the school to sell little chicks, and the boys put their money together and bought all the chicks and went up to the roof of an apartment building. And . . . you can guess what happened next, can't you?"

The girls covered their mouths, grimacing. But the guys were different. Remembering at last, they looked around at each other and nodded. Their eyes showed a secret bond of sympathy.

"Yes, just as you've guessed, the boys dropped the chicks, one by one, out of a sort of curiosity. They didn't think what they were doing was cruel—it was more like an experiment. They wanted to find out if the chicks would survive the fall. Let's say it was an experiment to measure the flying capacity of the chicks."

The look of hesitation disappeared from the guys' faces. Seonkyeong smiled and asked another question.

"Have you ever conducted an experiment on an animal to satisfy your curiosity?"

"Does dissecting a frog count?"

"Yes, I suppose, if it wasn't because you were told to, but because you wanted to see for yourself."

This time, a number of students raised their hands, including girls.

"Now, how many of you raised your hands to all three questions?"

Four students raised their hands. One of them began to raise his hand, then hastily lowered it after looking around, making everyone laugh again.

"So there are four of you here in this classroom. Are any of you a serial killer?" Seonkyeong challenged.

One of the students pointed to himself, trying to get attention, then stopped when the others told him off.

"Now you see what's wrong, don't you? Yes, an error occurs when you generalize a special circumstance. Even if these are the childhood characteristics of serial killers, not everyone who has them is a serial killer. In fact, the numbers would be extremely few," Seonkyeong said.

"Which argument do you side with? Nature or nurture?" one of the students asked.

"That's what psychology deals with. There's no one right answer. As Einstein said, the last human frontier is not the universe, but the human mind," Seonkyeong answered.

To students who were used to always getting clear answers to their questions, psychology could be an ambiguous and frustrating field. Everyone looked deep in thought, reflecting on what Seonkyeong had said. She looked at the clock on the wall. The time was up.

"Any other questions?" Seonkyeong said to wrap up.

The students packed their bags, sensing that the lecture was coming to an end, but a student wearing black horn-rimmed glasses raised her hand. Everyone stopped packing, and looked at her.

"Why did only they become serial killers, when others had the same experiences in their childhoods?"

Seonkyeong had expected the question. She always asked herself the same thing.

Why? Why did they become criminals?

There was no question, however, as difficult to answer as "Why?" Human beings were much too complex to be summed up in a word. Seonkyeong herself had much to learn. Being fairly new in the field of criminal psychology, she could not yet answer the question. When would she know?

"I can talk about how serial killers committed murders, cut up the victims, or ate them, but to be honest, I don't know why they became serial killers. Their behaviors are something that can be observed, but the question as to why can't be fully answered even by the killers themselves."

The student didn't seem satisfied by the reply. Looking at the student, Seonkyeong added, "I have asked myself, however, what kind of impact your childhood experiences—pulling wings off butterflies or dragonflies, kicking puppies, dropping chicks from a roof—leave on your mind. Once you lose interest, you stop doing those things out of curiosity. Or you are able to stop, realizing how awful and loathsome those acts are. As I said before, it's something you experience as a rite of passage in your childhood."

Seonkyeong paused to collect her thoughts.

"Some people, though, have an evolving curiosity, meaning that they move on from little insects to little animals, such as birds or mice, and then on to bigger animals. The experiences are no longer awful and loathsome, but fascinating and absorbing. Then they move on to human beings. The incomprehensible damages and marks on the victims' bodies show how their minds work."

"Do you think it's something you're born with, then?" asked the same student.

"In part, yes. But not entirely. I read a book that said that serial killers and surgeons have two things in common—a cool head and boldness. But even if they both started out from childhood curiosity, they can end up worlds apart, depending on the environment given to them or chosen by them."

The student who had asked the question nodded her head. Seonkyeong looked at the other students, who were paying close attention to her words. She felt both sad and pleased that the semester was thus coming to an end.

To wrap up what she was saying, she returned to the lectern.

"Many factors make up serial killers, just as many puzzle pieces form a picture. The factors include genetic disposition, personality traits, growth environment, current state, psychological conditions, and so on. Just as paper starts burning through a lens you hold under sunlight, focusing on one point, I believe serial killers are born when various factors are put together, creating a point of ignition."

Several students nodded.

"Paul Britton, a British psychologist, referred to himself as someone who puts puzzles together. He was right. The task of criminal psychologists is to piece together scattered materials to draw up the psychology of the criminal, like putting a puzzle together. Each of those pieces is collected during the process in which someone becomes a serial killer. If even one of the pieces is missing, we wouldn't be able to fully understand why the person evolved into a serial killer."

"Can't we just ask?" a naive-looking girl in the front row asked. Her friend sitting next to her nudged her with her elbow, as if to chide her for what she was saying.

"I mean, can't profilers and criminal psychologists ask the serial killers when they interview them?"

"Do you think they'd tell the truth?" Seonkyeong asked in reply.

The girl hesitated, then tilted her head to the side with a blank look on her face.

It didn't seem to have occurred to her that criminals would lie. How nice it would be if criminals gave honest answers to all questions, as the girl innocently thought. But Seonkyeong had never heard of such a criminal.

"They don't agree to an interview in order to tell the truth. They want to flaunt themselves and confirm their power. To that end, they tell lies, exaggerate, and talk big," she explained.

"How can you tell? Whether they're lying or talking big . . . ," the girl asked timidly.

"What's more accurate than their lies is the scene of the crime. Unfortunately, the crime scene is made up of countless codes, and deciphering them isn't an easy task. The many crime scenes we just took a look at give us clues as to where all the puzzle pieces are, and we must complete the picture by putting them together."

The girl nodded, understanding at last. Seonkyeong looked around at the students to see if they had any further questions, but most of them were closing their books or packing their bags. It seemed now that they were just waiting for the class to be over.

"Well, that's it for this semester. Good job, everyone. Good luck on the test, and have a great vacation."

As soon as Seonkyeong finished speaking, the students rose from their seats and left the classroom. When she turned around after packing up the projector, the seats were deserted.

Looking at the empty classroom, Seonkyeong heaved a sigh, relieved that the first semester had gone well. She felt a little sad and tired, in a good way. She realized how much she enjoyed teaching. Feeling a sense of satisfaction, she began to walk out of the classroom, when her bag started to shake. Her phone was vibrating.

She quickly took her phone out, checked the number, and answered.

"Hello, this is Yi Seonkyeong."

The call was from Han Dongcheol, the director of the Association of Criminal Psychology.

Seonkyeong tilted her head. She had met him once or twice at seminars, but had no personal ties to him. She wondered if he even remembered her face.

4.

I TOLD YOU ABOUT THE ROOM, DIDN'T I? THE ROOM WITH DOZENS of locks on it.

I thought I'd locked it up really tight, but the locks opened all at once. Do you know how?

It's because of a song.

If I hadn't heard the song again, the memories of my mom would have stayed five thousand meters under the earth and would never have come up again.

When I was eleven or twelve, I ran away from my mom and tried to go as far away from home as possible. I walked aimlessly along the national highway, secretly climbing onto the back of a truck now and then, going as far away as I could. I didn't get any farther because I got into an accident.

I was rummaging through trash cans in the market when I noticed a truck parked in a corner of the parking lot. Looking at the license plate, which said Gangwon, I wondered where Gangwon was, and saw the driver get off the truck. He didn't lock the door, though. He was probably coming right back. I thought it was my chance to look inside the truck for something to eat and even for some money, if I was lucky.

I quickly went to the truck and opened the door. Inside, I saw the driver's jacket. I went through the inner pocket, and found a thick wallet. Thinking I could eat my fill now, I took the wallet out and put it in my pocket when I heard someone approaching. I looked around but there was nowhere to hide, so I went to the back of the truck and ducked out of sight.

The driver must have returned, for the engine turned on and the truck started. I was going to jump if the truck slowed down even a little, but soon we were on the national highway and kept going through the darkness. I had no choice but to wait for the truck to come to a stop. I gave myself up to the rocking of the truck, and before I knew it, I was asleep.

It was a week later that I woke up.

While I was sleeping, the truck ran into a car that drove over the centerline and rolled over to the side. The driver died on the spot. I must've gone flying out of the truck and lain there with my head bleeding.

When I woke up a week later, everything had changed.

I was lying under a warm, clean hospital blanket, and a nurse came at regular intervals and asked me in a sweet voice if I was hurting anywhere. She brought me water when I was thirsty, and medicine when I frowned with a headache.

I couldn't move or speak, but I felt strangely comforted. I wondered if I had died and gone to heaven. I had nothing to regret even if I was dead, so I was happy just to lie there blinking.

I was lying by the window where the sun was pouring down, and even if I so much as knit my brows, someone came and drew the curtains. My heart felt warm for the first time. So this is what it feels like to be loved by someone. How nice it is, I thought.

As I gradually recovered and began to speak, the doctor would come and talk to me but I didn't want to talk much. Once I began to talk, he would ask who I was, find out where I lived, and call my mom. It was terrifying just to think about it. So I kept my mouth shut and pretended to think about his questions, and closed my eyes tight as if I had a headache. Finally, the doctor stopped asking questions, took some brain scans, and let me be.

The next day, the doctor said I didn't remember anything because of the accident. Oddly, when I heard those words, the memories in my mind really did become faint. A lock was fastened when I saw the face of the nurse smiling and patting me on the head, and another clicked when the other patients in the room clapped when I was able to move my hands again and clench them into fists.

The locks on the room of terrible memories were set one by one in this way, and just as the doctor said, I lost my memories. I forgot who I was, what my name was, everything.

The authorities must have thought that I was the driver's son, because his wallet was found among my clothes. The traffic police who had dealt with the accident and the insurance company contacted the driver's family and they came. The police naturally thought I was part of their family, but the wife and the kids saw me and didn't say anything.

The wife might have asked me about my relationship with her husband, but when she was told that I didn't remember anything because of the shock, she didn't inquire any further. She saw me eating, using my left hand, and merely said that her husband had been left-handed, too. I don't know why, but after her husband's funeral, she came to see me from time to time, as if to visit a sick son.

Then when I recovered enough to leave the hospital, she took me home.

I went with her because I had no other place to go, but in my mind I thought I could leave at any point if I didn't like it there. But guess what, everyone was waiting for me, welcoming me home.

There were three girls, one in middle school and another in high school, and one who was about four years younger than me.

There was an orchard with hundreds of apple trees.

The girls were waiting in the shadow of the tree in front of the gate, and when we arrived in a taxi, they all stood and opened the door for us.

One of the older girls helped me out of the car, as I was still on crutches, and the other older girl took my bag. The youngest threw herself into her mother's arms and looked at me. Her eyes weren't cold, but full of warmth and curiosity.

Even now, when I think back to that day, it feels like a dream.

The woman said I could stay till I got my memory back. I looked inside the gate, and it really did feel like home. I felt as if I had been wandering in the wrong place for a long time, and finally found my way home.

Do you know how beautiful an apple orchard is in June?

It was pleasant just to look at the green apples, still small, hanging in clusters on the branches. When I pointed at the apples, the woman smiled and said, *Wait just a little longer, when they're ripe, you can have as many as you want.*

At that moment, I flung the dark room in my heart down into the deep basement of my unconsciousness.

Yes, I can live here. Here, I can have a new life. I don't have to run anymore, I don't have to look around, trembling in fear.

I lived there for five or six years.

Just as the woman had said I could, when the apples ripened, I ate my fill, till my mouth smelled sweet. The girls gathered the fallen apples early in the morning. The others all ate the bruised or wormy apples, but I picked out the biggest, best-ripened ones from the branches. Still, the woman didn't say anything, and only looked at me with a warm smile on her face.

If it hadn't been for that song—if I hadn't heard that song—I would still be living at that orchard, watching the apples ripen, pruning, thinning out the fruits, and spraying insecticide on the trees.

THAT DAY, I'd taken out broken apple crates from the storage and was hammering at them. I was doing my part by then, earning my keep. The apple blossoms weren't in bloom yet, but we'd sold all the apples from winter storage and were putting the storage in order.

At the sound of the song streaming from the radio off to the side, my hand holding the hammer came to a stop.

The song penetrated my ears, made my heart tremble, and I felt suffocated.

At first, I didn't know why.

I wiped away cold sweat and heaved a long sigh. But the anxiety and fear didn't go away. My hand holding the hammer shook. Feeling dizzy, I turned off the radio in a hurry, but I knew that something was terribly wrong.

I dropped to the ground and saw the hammer in my hand. The song kept going around in my head. Did I tell you about the oldest memory in my mind? Yeah, that day when I nearly suffocated under the pillow. Another memory carved deep into my bones was that song.

I think it was when I'd barely started walking and could move about the room. I don't know why, but my mom was beating me severely. When I started crying, she would drag me to the bathroom, push me into the filled bathtub, and press my head under the water. It was the song she sang in a low, indifferent voice, as she watched me suffocating in pain. Even when it felt as if my heart would rip to pieces because of the water seeping in through my nose and mouth, I would listen to her singing. When the song was over, she would let go of me and go find her bottle of liquor. That happened repeatedly over a long period of time. After a few years, I got used to getting my head thrust into the bathtub.

When my mom went to look for her liquor after harassing me, I would crawl out of the bathtub, throw up, wipe away my tears, and hum the tune of the song that was going around in my head. It must have terrified me, but the song never left my head. I wanted it to stop, but couldn't make it.

I don't remember very well the times when I got beat up or was bruised. I know that I was taken to the hospital from time to time, but those memories are just a background for the music, like a music video. What pricks my heart like dozens of needles, shredding my nerves, is the song.

When the song began, I knew what was about to come. The song was like a signal for the beginning of pain.

It was that song that I was hearing again.

While I was hammering away in the storage shed of the orchard in the still-cold early spring, the locks on that room I'd forgotten about completely were opened all at once by the song.

Several years had passed, and I was completely free from my mom's hands, but when the song began, I turned back into a three- or four-year-old kid and trembled in fear, recalling the painful times when I was gasping in the bathtub, was stabbed with scissors, and had my flesh bitten off.

If I'd recognized the song from the first line, I would have turned the radio off right away, but only after the chorus did I realize it was the song my mom used to sing. I'd never heard the original song before. I didn't know what the words meant, but the song, sung by a gentle voice, was quite different from the one my mom used to sing. I couldn't believe that the background music to acts that had inflicted wounds, fractures, and scars on me was a happy song sung by such a sweet voice.

I threw the hammer down and went inside the house and, with a blanket pulled over my head, waited for the song to go away. But the song, now revived, only rang louder and louder in my head. And soon I realized that I was humming along. It gave me the chills.

One of the older girls, who heard me humming, asked me how I knew the song. I couldn't say anything. I finally managed to say that the song just kept going around in my head.

She said I might be able to recall my lost memory and, in her excitement, told me the name of the song. At my request, she even got me the lyrics later on. She said it wasn't hard to find the lyrics, even though the song was old, because it was such a famous song.

Do you know the Beatles? Yes, I'm sure you've heard of them. The band who boasted that they were a little more famous than Jesus. One of them got shot to death, right? If I'd been born a bit earlier, or if I'd had a chance to meet them, I would probably have killed them with my own hands. I would've really liked to ask them why they made a song like that.

The lyrics were for my mom. She'd chosen such a perfect song for herself. What's the song, you ask?

It's called "Maxwell's Silver Hammer."

Bang! Bang! Maxwell's silver hammer came down upon her head. . . .

Maxwell kills his girlfriend, his teacher, and even the judge.

He bangs down on everything he doesn't like with the silver hammer. Then with a clang, their heads are smashed.

Why did my mom sing this song, out of all the songs? She probably couldn't explain it herself.

The song probably just stuck to her lips the moment she heard it.

I wanted to stop the song from going around in my head. How could I stop it? I screamed and plugged up my ears, but it was no use. The gates of hell, once opened, would not close.

I stuck my head in the river by the orchard and stayed that way till I became unconscious, but underneath the dark water, the sound of my mom's singing only became clearer. Just like the voice I'd heard in the bathtub when I was little. In the end, I made the stupidest decision.

I decided to go meet the person who had carved the song into my head.

I was foolish. No, I was proud. I thought I'd grown taller and stronger not only in body, but in mind as well, in those six years.

I'm no longer what I used to be, I would no longer just cover up my face when a fist came flying at me, I can protect myself now, I can make her afraid of me if I want—that's what I thought.

That's how I stepped in through the hell gate.

That's how I returned to the place I'd taken such pains to run away from.

5.

A S SEONKYEONG PASSED BY SADANG STATION, THE WESTERN sky began to darken and, instantly, black clouds gathered all around. Suddenly, it became as dark as if there were a solar eclipse, and Seonkyeong quickly turned on her headlights.

The weather forecast that afternoon had said that there would be regional torrential rain. A short burst of rain seemed likely.

Sure enough, drops of water, so thick that they almost looked like hail, began to fall onto the hood of the car, and fierce streaks of rain began to pour down as the car went over Namtaeryeong Hill. On top of the usual heavy traffic, the rain made it even more difficult to move forward. The rain was so heavy that it was hard to make out the car that was just ahead.

Seonkyeong turned on the wipers and looked at the clock. Normally, the drive wouldn't take twenty minutes. There was half an hour until the appointed time. Despite the slight delay, she would manage to make it just in time. The sound of the rain beating down on the car hood thumped through her head.

She felt stifled all of a sudden in the car, so she lowered the window a bit.

Raindrops poured in through the crack, as if they had just been waiting for the chance, and wet her shoulders. She felt somewhat refreshed. Her head had been feeling heavy since she stepped out of the house.

The question that had arisen a few days before led to yet more questions, and her mind became more and more tangled as she neared the detention center.

On the day of her last lecture, Seonkyeong had received a phone call from Director Han.

"Yi Byeongdo wants to meet you—do you feel up to it?" he'd asked.

Seonkyeong was stunned that Yi Byeongdo had singled her out, and couldn't say anything for a while. It took some time for her to understand what Director Han was saying, as it was something that had never even occurred to her.

"He wants to meet me? Why?" Those were her immediate questions.

She'd heard that he'd refused to see anyone. And now, all of a sudden, he'd agreed to be subject to research and investigation, on the condition that he be permitted to talk to Seonkyeong. She had no personal acquaintance with him—she had never even met him.

"How does he even know me?" The question that now arose, before her previous questions had even been answered, confused her all the more.

It was another professor in the psychological association who had requested an interview with Yi Byeongdo at the detention center. He, however, had refused. Someone who never got to talk to him wouldn't have told him about Seonkyeong.

"Why?" she asked again.

"What do you mean, 'why'?" the director returned.

"Why did he single me out when I don't even know him?"

The director, of course, didn't know the reason. He advised her, however, that whatever the reason, an interview with Yi Byeongdo was vital, so she should set a date soon. Seonkyeong said she could do it anytime.

Her mind was in a daze, as if she had been hit in the head with a hammer, but once the basic data was entered, it began to work rapidly.

The semester was over, and she had only two requests for articles. As far as external circumstances were concerned, the timing couldn't be better. The doubt that had surfaced a moment before was already pushed far back into her mind.

The director said he would check up on the situation and get back to her, and hung up.

Seonkyeong stopped by the department office and exchanged greetings with the teaching assistants, and had left the building and was on her way to the parking lot when Director Han called again.

The appointment had been set for three days later.

Things proceeded swiftly. The necessary materials would be sent to her through rush delivery. Word spread fast, and phone calls from acquaintances came before the dispatch arrived. They were all stunned by the sudden news and asked how she knew Yi Byeongdo. Each time, she responded, "Why me, of all people? I don't even know him."

No one believed her, though. They asked her why he would single out someone he didn't know. When they realized she was telling the truth, they all made conjectures, but none of them could clear up the confusion. One or two of them said in jest that maybe he had gone through the list of the association members, out of boredom from being in solitary confinement. But there was no way he could have gotten his hands on the list in prison; besides, Seonkyeong's name wasn't on the list yet.

The calls died down at last when Seonkyeong returned home. After she'd set her bag down and taken a shower, the rushed dispatch arrived. There were three encyclopedias' worth of materials. As she began to browse through them, his face, which had been in newspapers and on television, came to her mind.

Yi Byeongdo.

He was a serial killer who had kidnapped and murdered thirteen women in the Seoul and Gyeonggi areas in the past three years, and had been arrested the year before. His emergence had turned the world upside down for the first time since Yu Yeongcheol and Kang Hosun, two other serial killers. He was different from the criminals of the past.

He presented himself confidently before the broadcasting company's cameras and the photojournalists who flocked to the police station. The investigation team tried to cover up his face with jackets and towels, but he flung the towels aside. Far from hiding his face, he stared straight into the cameras, smiling and looking as if he felt no sense of guilt whatsoever for what he had done.

The viewers who had been watching the news live that day were astonished.

It happened only half a day after heated arguments arose over citizens' right to know what the alleged criminal looked like versus concerns about protecting the criminal's right to privacy. Yi Byeongdo, however, took the matter into his own hands and made the dispute among the third parties a moot issue.

It wasn't just his audacity in boldly revealing his face that shocked the viewers.

Contrary to the expectations of people who had presumed that the killer's face would fit the heinous criminal acts, his soft, wavy hair, fair skin, and regular features made for a favorable impression. The slight downturn at the corners of his eyes triggered the maternal instinct. People who believed the face was an indicator of what was in the heart and had imagined him to have the face of the devil were thrown into confusion. And the confusion developed into arbitrary hypotheses on the Internet.

Some conjectured that Yi Byeongdo wasn't the real culprit, and others said that childhood wounds must have caused multiple personality disorder, leading him to commit crimes without his being aware of what he was doing; such theories, the stuff of movies, spread heedlessly. Some found personal photos of him and posted them on the Internet, and a fan club called "David" was organized on a portal site. The name came from the sculpture *David*, for his resemblance to it. Thousands joined instantly, but the club was soon shut down when it was reported in the media.

Within a year of being arrested, Yi Byeongdo was sentenced to death at his trial, and was now currently incarcerated at the Seoul Detention Center.

Now Seonkyeong reviewed the materials, and the next day met the investigators who had arrested and investigated him.

According to the investigation report, the Seoul Metropolitan Police and the Seoul Gangbuk Police had collaborated on the case, but it was the investigators from the Seoul Gangbuk Police Station, the station in charge, who had been there from the onset of the investigation to the arrest and the reenactment of the crime.

The Seoul Gangbuk Police Station was five minutes away from Suyu Station.

Seonkyeong had made a phone call in advance, so most of the serious crime division investigators who had been in charge of the case were there. They, too, were surprised that Seonkyeong was going to be interviewing Yi Byeongdo.

When Seonkyeong asked them about the series of incidents that occurred after the arrest, as well as the hypotheses on the Internet, the investigators burst out laughing at the absurdity of it all.

"Just spend a day—no, half a day—with him," one of them said.

He was the devil disguised as an angel, said another.

As shocking as it was, his angelic face must have played a crucial role in his crimes.

Just as they did with Ted Bundy, the American killer, the victims must have easily let down their guard because of his face. In that vein, the investigators' description of him was quite appropriate. An angelic face must have been a very useful tool for the devil.

But it must have been more than his appearance that drew the victims so easily to him. There must have been something else that touched the hearts of ordinary people. Just as Ted Bundy had bandaged his arm or leg and asked for assistance from women passing by, feigning disability, Yi Byeongdo, too, must have set a trap so as not to make it easy for the victims to pass him by.

Most of what the investigators told Seonkyeong had been in the report—the dates of the crimes, the names of the victims, and a long list of things he'd done in the past. What Seonkyeong really needed wasn't in it.

From the start, there were bound to be differences in the way the investigators looked at the case and the way Seonkyeong looked at it. For the investigators, Yi Byeongdo's crimes and the evidence thereof, as well as his confession, were enough.

It didn't matter to the investigators what kinds of victim he preferred, how he approached or communicated with them, what he was feeling at the moments he committed the murders, how he evolved as he repeated his criminal acts. They all looked at different parts according to their roles.

Seonkyeong asked them about the scene of the crime, but there was nothing unusual about the hill where Yi Byeongdo's house was and the victims' bodies had been found. She tried putting the question in different ways, but they all said basically the same thing. She had gone to them in the hopes of finding something, but she became bored by their rambling talk and decided she had heard enough.

At that moment, someone began to talk about something that had happened during the crime scene investigation, but about which the investigators had kept quiet.

They must have been shocked by the incident, and now they all began to talk at once. At last, Seonkyeong felt drawn to what they were saying.

It was such a big case that dozens of journalists, citizens, and family members of the victims gathered at the place where the crime scene inspection was held, causing an uproar. The investigators said that twice as many people must have been there as at the excavation site of those killed by Yu Yeongcheol.

The journalists had all pointed their cameras at Yi Byeongdo as soon as the police car transporting him arrived, and the families of the victims made a grab for him despite the police's efforts to hold them back. Three or four investigators surrounding Yi Byeongdo tried to move forward, blocking the crowd, without success.

"All those people were shouting, but he didn't even blink an eye," one of the investigators said.

No matter how brutal a serial killer was, he would probably shrink back with so many people watching. But Yi Byeongdo was much too calm. The investigators said he had nerves of steel.

"He knocked them out with a single blow," said one of the investigators, and fell into thought, probably thinking about what happened that day.

"He looked at the people who were shouting insults at him, and smiled at them. That made them even more upset. He enjoyed it. He was completely calm, but then he pointed at someone, and made a gesture of slitting his throat with a finger. The people who saw that were shocked and didn't know what to say, and just stared at him."

The investigator sitting next to him chimed in. "Yeah, I remember. Did you see the look on his face when he did that? Whoa, I had goose bumps all over my body. If we hadn't had our hands on him, he probably would've pounced on someone and done something."

A veteran investigator who had been in the violent crime division for fifteen years shook his head. He must have dealt with dozens of violent criminals, but Yi Byeongdo seemed to have left an unusual impression even on him.

"Why did he react that way all of a sudden, when he'd been so calm?" Seonkyeong asked.

"Well, I'm not sure. . . . Does anyone remember?"

All the investigators looked at one another and shook their heads.

"People were flying at him, and shouting and cursing, so who knows why he did, amid all that chaos," one of them said.

The investigators were right. But Seonkyeong regretted that they had lost an important clue that would have helped them understand Yi Byeongdo. If it was possible, she would have a drink with the investigators and make them recall everything they saw and heard that day.

What was it that made Yi Byeongdo, who had been so calm, change all of a sudden?

It may have been a word that provoked him. Or someone may have hit his sore spot. If only she could find out what it was, it would be easier to talk to him, but for now, there was no way to know.

Fortunately, though, this memory must have triggered others. As the investigators went on talking, something caught Seonkyeong's ears.

"What really got to me was when he was reenacting the crime. . . . No, it wasn't a reenactment. It was as if he was back in the moment. As if what he was doing wasn't something that had happened in the past, but it was as if he was in a trance, as if he couldn't see anything else, despite the police and citizens who were there. It was so real . . . so real that Investigator Choi over there tried to seize him by the neck, to save the mannequin. The look on his face at that moment. . . . Ugh, even now, it makes me shudder."

Seonkyeong saw fear in the eyes of the investigator as he spoke.

What was it that made even a violent crime investigator cringe?

Seonkyeong wanted to know what kind of look Yi Byeongdo had had on his face. She would never know unless she saw it herself. It couldn't be described in words, and even if hundreds of words were used in an attempt to describe it, it wouldn't be to any satisfaction, and would just leave one feeling as if one were wandering through a fog. Seonkyeong could only guess at the look on his face by the look on the investigator's face.

"We did arrest him, but I wasn't sure if we really had. I felt that even though his body was captured, his mind went on killing in a world of his own."

The investigator knew. Yi Byeongdo's dark soul still had a strong, brutal power, and he was repeatedly picturing in his mind the last moments of the victims he had killed, savoring what he had felt.

Seonkyeong tried to imagine the darkness in his heart. He is unaware of either his body, tied up with rope, or the jeers and insults from the people. He is back in time where only the victim and he existed, and reveling in the moment in which he took a human life. He is still in the moment, with the same feeling in his hands, and looking into the woman's eyes full of fear, at the face gasping out of fear.

After saying goodbye to the investigators and making her way out of the police station, Seonkyeong felt that she was getting closer to the living, breathing Yi Byeongdo, not the Yi Byeongdo trapped in the files.

As she came out, the chief of the violent crime division stopped Seonkyeong and said, "I've been trying to decide whether to ask you or not . . . but if it's all right with you, we'd like you to help us."

"Yes, of course, if I can. What is it?"

"To be honest . . . there are several more cases that remain unresolved. We found out that some of the evidence remaining at his house belonged to unidentified victims, but he wouldn't say a word about them."

"So . . . you're saying that there are more victims? But the police report said . . ."

"He wouldn't open his mouth, so we couldn't do anything about it."

So only the cases that had been confirmed through his confession had been disclosed to the world.

"I don't know if he'll speak, but you may be able to come across some clues when you talk to him. We'd like you to tell us what they are."

Seonkyeong understood what he was saying. Cold cases can't stay buried. Who knew if a victim who died at the hands of Yi Byeongdo lay abandoned on a hill somewhere? It could be one of the countless missing people whose faces covered the bulletin board hanging in front of where Seonkyeong and the chief stood.

"All right. I'll give you a call if I find out anything," she said.

"Thank you."

THE POURING RAIN CLEARED UP completely as Seonkyeong drove past the Indeokwon Intersection. Or the rain must have fallen only in the area between Sadang and Indeokwon. There were no traces of heavy rain anywhere, as if she had entered another world. The sky once again boasted a blistering sun.

The road to the detention center was so dry that dust flew everywhere.

Driving on the road in front of the detention center, flanked by gingko trees swaying in the wind, Seonkyeong recalled the conversation she'd had with Director Han in the association office. He had asked her to be sure to stop by the office before meeting Yi Byeongdo.

"So, have the materials helped at all?" he asked.

"Yes, thank you. It must've been hard to get them all of a sudden."

"The advisory committee made preparations to interview him when he was taken to the Seoul Detention Center after the trial. They're from back then."

Seonkyeong had heard that the criminal psychology analysis advisory committee, made up of psychologists, criminologists, and psychoanalyst specialists from different universities, was formed by the Laboratory Division of the National Police Agency ten years before. Some members of the criminal psychology association belonged to the advisory committee as well, and Director Han was one of them. It was the advisory committee that led the efforts to interview criminals for in-depth research and investigation into violent crimes, including serial murders.

"Considering what happened at the time of the arrest and afterward, I thought he'd have a lot to say about his crimes," the director said.

But contrary to his expectations, Yi Byeongdo didn't consent to an investigation or even an interview with anyone. But now he had singled out Seonkyeong and volunteered to be interviewed.

"There was a dispute in the advisory committee regarding this," said the director.

"Huh?"

"I'd like to ask you one more time if you're acquainted with Yi Byeongdo in any way."

"As I said on the phone the other day, all I know about him is from the media. I've never met him personally."

Director Han looked at Seonkyeong for a moment, then nodded.

"I thought so. And that's what the committee was concerned about."

Seonkyeong stared blankly back, not sure what he meant.

"You don't know him, but he knows who you are. However he knows you, the fact that he's singled you out means that he has more than an interview in mind," he explained.

Suddenly, the suspicion and anxiety she had consciously buried after his phone call resurfaced.

"What else do you think he has in mind?" she asked.

"Well . . . that's something we won't find out till you meet him, isn't it? I called you in spite of everything because this may be the only chance we have to hear about his crimes directly from him, and . . . ," the director said, rubbing his forehead with his fingers in hesitation, then went on. "If we find out why he chose you and asked for you, we'll be able to understand him better."

Seonkyeong understood what he was trying to say.

Seonkyeong didn't know Yi Byeongdo, but somehow, he knew her.

It wasn't clear what it was about her that drew his attention, but he wanted to meet her so much that he decided to open up at last. That alone was enough to indicate that Seonkyeong surely meant something to him.

"We don't know what may happen under the circumstances, but I trust that you'll handle it well. Just be careful that no matter what his intentions are, he doesn't get his way."

He looked at Seonkyeong as if he were looking at a little child by a riverside.

There was no telling what was in the river. Or how deep it was, or what kind of danger lurked beneath the surface. He could only hope that Seonkyeong would swim safely to the destination and return.

Suddenly, Seonkyeong felt afraid that she wouldn't be able to handle the task. But she knew better than anyone that she couldn't back down. It would be a tremendous opportunity to interview him. There was some risk involved, but if she watched her feet, she could avoid falling into a trap. *I can do it*, Seonkyeong repeated to herself.

After she returned from meeting the director, however, she had too much on her mind and couldn't sleep.

She lay restless until dawn, when Jaeseong woke to a phone call and left early to go to the hospital. She then got out of bed as well and went into the study and sat down.

The materials on Yi Byeongdo lay spread out on the desk as she had left them.

She wasn't familiar with the materials yet, but she didn't want to go through them in the darkness.

She began to close the files and set them aside, when a photograph fell to the floor. She picked it up and saw that it was a photograph of Yi Byeongdo from a newspaper. It looked like he was getting in a police car after a crime scene investigation.

No emotion could be read on his face as he looked back over his shoulder and directly faced the camera. His eyes seemed to be gazing far off into the distance.

What had he been looking at?

AS SEONKYEONG PICTURED the face she had seen in the photograph that morning, the front gate of the detention center presented itself before her eyes.

Seonkyeong stopped the car, took a deep breath, and lowered the window.

The guard who had been keeping watch at the checkpoint saluted and approached the car. Seonkyeong handed him her identification and told him the purpose of her visit.

As she waited for the guard to confirm her credentials, sweltering heat rushed into the car.

6.

STRANGE, ISN'T IT. I THOUGHT I'D FORGOTTEN IT COMPLETELY, but I knew exactly how to get home. Some new shops had opened, and some of the walls had disappeared, and many changes had been made in the alleyway in six years, but not so much that I couldn't find my way home.

The house I had run from was still standing in its place.

The moment I saw the house, I realized that six years had been nothing. The little kid who had run from the house hadn't grown at all. *Run!* a voice shouted in my head, but I stood frozen to the spot, staring at the house. My past took ahold of my ankles and wouldn't let me move.

For the first time, I regretted having run away.

If I had stayed at that house, and felt myself growing in power as my arms and legs grew little by little, and stood up to my mom with that power, wouldn't I have been able to make the song come to a stop? But that was a very rash thought.

Do you know something? People don't change easily. It's hard to change a relationship that's already been established. And no matter how atrocious the circumstance, people adjust and get used to it.

If you have to live in Siberia, where the temperature is forty degrees below zero, you just drink vodka and bear the cold. If you have always been beaten till you bled, ever since you were born, and scabs cover your wounds, you go on living that way. On some days nothing happens and you breathe a sigh of relief, and on other days you're beaten near to death and sleep as if you've passed out. If you break a bone, you lie down for a few days, moaning and groaning, and if you're lucky, you get up and walk again.

It didn't take a single day to wipe out my six years at the orchard. Had there really been such a time? It seemed like it had all been a dream. Sometimes I think it really was a dream.

My mom? Yeah, she was surprised to see me at first. But then one of her eyebrows rose, and she began to curse at me in an annoying voice. She hadn't changed at all in those six years. Within an hour of returning home, I once again had to put up with her slapping hands, the stick, and the kicking.

I dreaded to think that the next day, and the day after that, would go on in the same way. I wondered why she went on tormenting me, why she didn't just kill me. Yes, it was a struggle that wouldn't end till one of us died. You know how you have those dreams where you keep trying to run, but don't get any farther away from the thing chasing you? You try desperately to run, but then you just want to drop to the ground and get caught so that it would come to an end, whether the thing killed you or not.

If it hadn't been for the kitten that came into the house one day, it wouldn't have happened. No, that's just an excuse. I might just have been waiting for a chance. I would've done the same, using whatever as an excuse.

It was drizzling that day.

I found a cat that was taking shelter from the rain under the eaves. The cat was in heat and had been crying every night, getting on my nerves, and now it was in the yard, so I began to throw whatever I could get my hands on at it. But each time, it quickly dodged away, looking at me as if to mock me, and purred.

I felt angry. I felt as if the cat was looking down at me, so I looked around for something else to throw at it, and found a shovel. Yeah, you're gonna get it, I thought. I quickly got down to the yard, picked up the shovel, and threw it at the cat. It hit the mark. The cat, hit in the tail, went around the yard shrieking.

It was at that moment that a light flashed in front of my eyes.

My mom was holding a brick in one hand. Stunned, I looked from her face to the brick. Then I felt pain in the back of my head. I ran my fingers through my hair. A lukewarm liquid flowed out and wet my hand. I looked at my hand, covered in blood.

My mom called out to the cat, meowing as it went around the yard, as if she didn't care about me at all. She had a can of tuna in her hand.

Her voice was tender, a tone I'd never heard her call me with. And she had never looked anxiously for me in order to feed me. I mattered less to her than a stray cat.

I felt disoriented, with my head bleeding. I felt as if someone was leading me along. I didn't hear the rain. I was half out of it.

Strangely, the song flowed out of my mouth. The shovel I had thrown at the cat a moment before was in my hand before I knew it. My mom was startled when I began humming the song. Then she saw the shovel in my hand.

My mom, who had always been so self-assured, looked tense for the first time, and spoke in a trembling voice.

"Wh-What are you doing? Put that thing down this instant!"

I hadn't really planned on doing anything, but when I heard her orders it suddenly occurred to me that I was much taller than she was. And now I was stronger, too. And I didn't want to . . . run anymore. I was tired. I felt as if I was up against a wall in a dead-end alley.

I clutched the handle of the shovel more tightly. I could never forget the look on my mom's face as she looked from my eyes to the shovel.

"Mom, do you remember this song?"
Bang! Bang! Maxwell's silver hammer . . .

Yes, I learned the song from you, Mom. It was the song you always sang to me. Remember? You remember, don't you? This time, I'm singing it to you. You've raised me this far, so I should do something for you in return, shouldn't I? Don't worry. The song has never left my head these past dozen years or so, so I won't get it wrong.

I don't know how long I went on singing the song.

When I came to myself, I was no longer singing.

I stood in the middle of the yard, looking at the rain falling onto her face. The eyes, which had glared so coldly and fiercely at me, wouldn't close even in the rain. The mouth, which had always hurled abuses at me, was too quiet. I realized at last why I had come back to this house.

Yes, I had been waiting. For the day I would be singing that song. I had really wanted my mom to hear it. Humming the last chorus once more, I thought, this song will never again circle around in my head now, will it?

7.

A FTER SEONKYEONG DROVE PAST THE GATE, PARKED THE car in the parking lot, and entered the public service center, the prison guard who had been waiting greeted and approached her. After a brief process of identification with his guidance, she was handed a pass with the word "visitor" printed in large letters.

Seonkyeong hung the pass around her neck, and followed the guard to the building where the prisoners were held.

Visits with the prisoners in the detention center were usually held in the public service center. The visit with Yi Byeongdo, however, was to be held in a separate place assigned by the detention center.

Past the building with the confinement facility, there was an empty lot. It was a space provided for the prisoners to exercise or take walks in, but their brief hours must have come to an end, for it was empty now. There was an enormous wall across the lot, blocking the view. The place was for locking people up, but curiously, it felt like an impregnable fortress that wouldn't allow anyone near.

Seonkyeong had been there several times, and had brought her students there on a field trip a month before, but she had never come this far inside. Looking at the high wall, she turned to the guard.

"What is this place?" she asked.

"It's for condemned criminals only," the guard replied.

The building stood in the innermost part of the detention center. Beyond the high wall was a space reserved for condemned criminals. Slowly, Seonkyeong looked around at the wall.

The detention center was built in 1987. It had been more than twenty years since then, so naturally, the building looked worn. But there was a strange feeling to it that couldn't be explained by the years alone. Seonkyeong felt as if she were looking at a photograph that was neither black and white nor in color, a photograph that had faded through the years.

This world was utterly different from the world beyond the wall, one in which even time and air were locked up.

The barbed-wire fence, easily two meters high, and the watchtowers in between, were rusted by storms or had peeling paint. For a moment, Seonkyeong, overwhelmed by the old and enormous gray wall, couldn't say anything.

In the high wall that blocked Seonkyeong's view, there was an iron gate that looked as if two people could barely manage to pass through it. After the guard confirmed her identification, Seonkyeong followed another guard through the gate, and she felt as though she had entered the gate of hell, from which she could never return.

The gate closed behind her with a loud creaking noise.

Her brow automatically furrowed at the sound. It was as irritating as nails scratching a blackboard. She had been feeling increasingly tense, and felt as if the taut nerves in her mind had snapped.

An indescribable feeling overwhelmed and stifled her. It felt as if a heavy rock were pressing down on her chest. She took a deep breath, but the heavy feeling did not leave her.

Suddenly, she wanted to turn around and leave.

Calm down, there's no need to be nervous, she told herself, but it was no use. She recalled the nickname her students had given her.

Clarice Starling. A rookie FBI investigator.

Seonkyeong pictured Jodie Foster from the movie *The Silence of the Lambs*. It occurred to her that right now, she looked like Clarice as she walked step by step toward the dungeon amid strict security, flinching and tensing up at the slightest sound. Seonkyeong wasn't on her way to see Hannibal, but she realized that she was mentally overpowered by Yi Byeongdo before she even met him.

The case journal, the materials, the investigators' anecdotes, and three days of cramming seemed to have overloaded her mind. There had been no time to think and prepare calmly. Seonkyeong decided that she should forget everything she had crammed into her head before meeting him.

The Yi Byeongdo in the files or in the stories told by the investigators was merely one piece of the puzzle. Seonkyeong had to find another piece, a different side of him. The thought helped her relax a bit. The vague, childlike fear seemed to ease a little as well. To hide her remaining anxiety, she tightened her stomach. She finally felt calm enough to look around.

Following the guard walking ahead of her, Seonkyeong gazed about her. There was only a crude building with no remarkable features. She stopped for a moment and looked up at the sky.

It was June, but already an intense sun ruled the world. The clouds that had sent down heavy rain in Indeokwon were no longer to be seen. Seonkyeong took another deep breath. She could feel the heat from the ground. Her face was sweating under the blazing sun, but strangely enough, a chill ran down her spine. She turned her head and looked around, but couldn't see anything.

"Are you coming?" asked the guard.

He had come to a stop in front of the building and was looking at her. Realizing she had made him wait, Seonkyeong hurried on. She wished she could wait until the chill coursing through her body had left, but soon gathered herself. She could feel sweat on her palms.

Solitary confinement was for condemned criminals only, in the innermost part of the detention center. She approached the door of the building, cold even in the middle of summer.

"Creepy, isn't it?" the guard asked cautiously in an effort to help her relax.

"I didn't know I'd be coming this far inside."

"People usually don't. Interviews or counseling with general criminals is held in the building with the public service center, which you saw earlier."

His words didn't really explain anything to her. He must have known why Seonkyeong had been led this far inside, but seemed to have no intention of telling her the reason. The guard opened the entrance with a security card.

He said, "There were more than thirty maximums here just till last year."

"Maximums" referred to condemned criminals—those sentenced to the maximum penalty that could be handed down by the court.

"There are only about ten now, with the others transferred to prisons in different regions throughout the country."

She had heard that on the news. A condemned criminal's sentence was carried out only through execution. Thus, condemned criminals had always been treated as prisoners on trial. Then last year, a change in the law ordered that they be treated as convicted prisoners. In the end, a good number of the condemned criminals here were transferred to prisons out in the provinces, and the building was left with empty rooms where they had stayed.

As they entered the security office adjacent to the building entrance, a monitor on a wall came into view. More than ten screens showed different rooms.

CCTV cameras had been installed so that each condemned prisoner in solitary confinement could be seen at a glance.

Some were asleep on a blanket, and some paced ceaselessly around the room as if suffering from a behavioral disorder. They all seemed aware of the CCTV, for they glanced at the camera now and then, looking disgruntled, or approached the camera and cursed, with a middle finger sticking up.

Seonkyeong's eyes were automatically searching for Yi Byeongdo.

"After the last incident, all the solitary confinement rooms have been placed under a twenty-four-hour surveillance system."

Seonkyeong turned around at the sound of an unfamiliar voice, and saw a heavily built man in his mid-forties standing there. He introduced himself as the security manager at the Seoul Detention Center. Seonkyeong understood right away what he meant by the "last incident." He was referring to the suicide of Seong Kicheol, a condemned criminal.

Seonkyeong, who had written an article for a police journal on the mental state of prisoners, was relatively well-informed about the incident.

"There's going to be a lot of backlash," she said to the head, looking at the prisoners on the monitor.

People are bound to get edgy when they're under surveillance for twenty-four hours a day. Although it was an effort to prevent another suicide, it didn't seem to be a good solution. There was the possibility of human rights violations, and the condemned criminals, who were psychologically unstable, not knowing when their sentence would be carried out, would be adversely affected.

The security manager looked at the monitor with indifference, as if to say that he already knew all about her concerns.

"If they know that they're being watched around the clock, at least they won't make an attempt," he said.

Seonkyeong was about to say something, but then stopped herself. It wasn't something she should interfere with. Besides, she wasn't here to deal with that. The important thing was to see Yi Byeongdo.

"They made all that fuss because it was Seong Kicheol who

died—the papers wouldn't have made such a big deal if it had been some other guy," the manager said, shaking his head. He must have been quite harassed by the media.

"Would anyone even care what happened within these walls if something like that hadn't happened?"

Seong Kicheol committed suicide using one of the trash bags distributed throughout the prison.

Those who make up their minds to kill themselves manage to find a way somehow, no matter how strict the surveillance. They tear up what they're wearing to make a cord, or manage to find and bring back inside a jagged rock during a thirty-minute exercise break.

With the current manpower at the detention center, it wasn't an easy task to keep watch on the prisoners around the clock. If nothing happened, the prison system would have no problems, but if anything did happen, every detail of its operations would be subject to scrutiny.

It seemed that the security manager, probably having suffered a great deal of harassment because of the incident, decided that he would deal with disputes regarding violations of human rights rather than be reprimanded for negligence in managing the prisoners.

As the security manager talked, his attention focused on one of the screens. Seonkyeong followed his gaze, and saw Yi Byeongdo leaning against a wall. Upon closer look, she saw that his head was shaking lightly.

"Are you really going to go see him?" asked the security manager.

"Huh?" Seonkyeong replied blankly.

The security manager took his eyes off the monitor and looked at Seonkyeong with a serious expression on his face.

"To be honest, I wish you wouldn't go through with the interview," he said.

"If it's a matter of security . . ."

"It's not that. Whatever happens in here is thoroughly under our control."

"Then what's . . ."

"Something doesn't feel right. I thought it was strange how he singled you out, so I asked him how he knew you."

"What did he say?"

Seonkyeong had been wondering about that herself.

"He didn't say anything, just looked at me and smiled. It gave me goose bumps. He's got some kind of a hidden motive," said the manager, no longer indifferent and looking serious.

"Can't you just cancel this appointment? If you refuse to see him, there's nothing he can do about it," he added.

He seemed genuinely concerned about Seonkyeong's well-being. She looked at his eyes, tense with concern, then smiled gently.

"I'll be fine as long as you keep watch over me, won't I?" she asked.

The manager's eyebrows rose for a moment at Seonkyeong's roundabout rejection. He then nodded to the prison guard with a resigned look on his face, no longer trying to dissuade her.

The guard opened a door to one side of the office and led her out.

Leaving the office, Seonkyeong sensed the security manager shaking his head.

She knew what his concerns were. Things were already in an uproar regarding security issues, and if problems arose again, he would be in a most difficult position. It would be better to rid oneself of such possibilities in the first place than to go through the drudgery again. The manager wasn't interested in what kind of person Yi Byeongdo was, or what story he had to tell. He just wanted everything that happened in the detention center to stay under control.

Seonkyeong felt rather relieved that the security manager was sensitive to the task at hand. His fussiness insured that the external security would be thoroughly under his control. As long as the matter was in his hands, the possibility of unfortunate incidents occurring would be prevented.

Feeling more relieved, Seonkyeong became anxious to see Yi Byeongdo's face. She quickened her pace as she followed the prison guard.

It seemed that the room where she would be meeting Yi Byeongdo was a makeshift visiting area provided by the detention center. She couldn't tell what the original purpose of the room had been, but it seemed that a table and chairs had been placed in a space that had been empty. The rectangular table and the chairs were new, and looked completely off in the room. The traces of rain on the cement walls, whose paint was peeling, as well as the black mold here and there, told her that no one had been in the room for quite some time. The humidity and mustiness stung her nose. The chill of the walls could be felt even without touching them.

"Please wait a moment," the guard said.

Seonkyeong nodded and took a look around.

There wasn't a window in the room. A pane of glass the size of a human face, which was on the single door, was the only channel through which to peek outside. Seonkyeong looked up at the ceiling and saw a long tube of fluorescent light.

The room was so sealed that it seemed even air would get locked up within, and a person with claustrophobia would have felt stifled the moment he walked into the room. Seonkyeong felt as if her breath were growing quicker and shallower.

The guard who had gone to fetch Yi Byeongdo did not return promptly. Five minutes passed, turning into ten.

Seonkyeong looked anxiously at her watch and around the room, and sat down on the chair facing the door. Looking at the empty chair beyond the table, she pictured Yi Byeongdo sitting there. Then she realized that she was on the inner side of the room. If he stood and blocked the door, she would lose her only way out. She knew it was an absurd thought, and yet she stood up from her seat and walked over to the chair in front of the door.

She sat down on the chair, opened her bag, and took out a notebook to get ready for the interview. She took out the digital recorder and was pushing the record button to see if it was working properly when the door opened.

Involuntarily, she jumped to her feet and turned her head.

He was standing at the door.

8.

JAESEONG CAME OUT OF THE OPERATING ROOM AND CHANGED his clothes in a hurry, and headed straight to his office.

He opened the door cautiously, so as not to wake Hayeong, but the room was empty. He had checked to see that his daughter was there, sleeping on the sofa, before he went into the operating room. But now the sofa was empty. Only a milk carton on the table confirmed that Hayeong had been there.

He looked around the room, and went out to the corridor.

He had talked to the head nurse before going into the operating room, in case Hayeong woke up. If she awoke and wandered around the corridor, the nurses at the corner desk would have noticed.

Only Nurse Kim was at the desk at the moment.

Nurse Kim looked up at the sound of footsteps and, recognizing Jaeseong, quickly pointed inside the staff lounge. There was space behind the desk for storing equipment, as well as the staff lounge.

He looked where she was pointing and saw Hayeong with the head nurse. Hayeong, who had been shaking her head at the snack the nurse was offering her, jumped up when she saw Jaeseong and came running over. He could tell that she had been anxious, not knowing where he was.

He caught a faint whiff of something burnt as he held her in his arms. He thought he should take her home immediately and have her take a bath.

Leaving the scene of the fire, he had thought he should go home. But he changed his mind while driving. He felt that he couldn't go home to his wife with a child all of a sudden, when she had no idea what had happened. He needed time to think things over.

After a great deal of thought, he decided to take Hayeong to the hospital. He took her to the emergency room, gave her a shot of tranquilizer, and checked to see if she had sustained any external injuries. In the process, Hayeong began to doze, relaxing from the tension. He felt it would be best to let her sleep, but whenever she heard the sound of footsteps, she opened her eyes instantly and looked for him. She seemed afraid that he would disappear. In the end, he stayed at her side, holding her hand, as she lay there getting an IV. Only when it was time for the morning appointments did he go up to his office, taking along Hayeong.

Sitting on the sofa, Hayeong looked at him, her face full of fear. She seemed nervous, unable to meet his eyes as he looked at her without saying a word. As the silence drew out, she couldn't hide her anxiety and hugged her teddy bear tight.

Jaeseong felt mired in confusion as he looked at the child. He had been thinking that he would tell his wife one day when he had a chance, and bring the child home. But he felt lost and helpless at the sudden turn of events. The news early that morning had come as a shock, but he was also worried about how his wife would take it.

"Dad . . . are you mad?" Hayeong asked, looking at him with caution.

Coming out of his thoughts at last, Jaeseong shook his head. Hayeong seemed to have taken his silence in the wrong way.

"No, no, why would I be mad?" he asked.

"You . . . told me not to call."

"Well . . . that's because I'm always busy with work."

Having said that, he gazed at her for a moment and spread his arms open. Hayeong, however, did not readily fall into his embrace. She was hesitant. He felt sad, wondering how distant they had grown. He gestured again with his hands, and Hayeong, who had just been staring at him, put her teddy bear down at last and threw herself into his arms.

Hayeong shivered. She must have been more shocked than anyone else. She had been through something even adults couldn't easily handle. There was no telling what great storm was raging in her heart. He was flooded with regret that he hadn't properly seen to the child's needs, preoccupied with his own.

"You were scared, weren't you?" he asked.

Instead of an answer, there was a burst of sobbing.

"It's all right. I'm here. You have nothing to worry about now."

Hearing the words, Hayeong began to weep bitterly. How frightened she must have been amid the burning flames, among the strangers. All the emotions that had been pent up in shock and confusion seemed to explode at those words. He held her tender body close, and patted her back. He wanted to sweep away all the bitterness in her heart.

She pulled herself back only after crying so much that she was drenched in cold sweat.

"Can't I come live with you?" she asked.

He couldn't answer her right away. It wasn't for him alone to decide.

Noticing his momentary hesitation, Hayeong wiped away the remaining tears on her cheeks with the back of her hands, as if she hadn't cried at all, and returned to the sofa and sat down. Jaeseong looked at her, unable to say a word. Hayeong, waiting for his answer with her head lowered for some time, lay down sideways, saying she was sleepy.

Jaeseong quickly pulled out a little blanket from a desk drawer and draped it over her. He gazed at her, lying there with her eyes clenched shut and holding the teddy bear, and pushed back the strands of hair sticking to her neck. The child who had been sobbing a moment ago, clinging to him, was gone; Hayeong was sleeping soundlessly with her back to him.

A knock came at the door. It was time for his morning routine.

He looked at Hayeong for a while as she stayed lying there with her back to him, then got to his feet.

"I have to go in for a surgery. It won't take long, so get some sleep, okay?" he said.

The child remained still. His heart felt heavy, but he decided to think about it after the morning's work.

He kept picturing Hayeong, with her back to him, during the two hours of surgery.

Can't I come live with you?

Her voice kept going around in his mind. But her question hovered in the air, like an echo in an empty jar. He wasn't the one who could give an answer to the question.

They had been apart for only a couple of hours, but now Hayeong clung to his waist with all her might, as if to say that she wouldn't stay separated from him for another moment. The head nurse looked at her with a face full of pity.

"I heard your house was on fire! It must have been quite a shock," said the nurse.

The rumors that had started going around in the emergency room early that morning had spread through the entire hospital. Even the interns in the operating room extended words of concern. With Hayeong in Jaeseong's office, it was impossible for them not to know. But he didn't want any further exposure of his private life.

"Thank you," he said to the head nurse, to cut her interest short.

He took Hayeong's hand and rushed out to the corridor. The meal carts were already going around to the hospital rooms. He hadn't even had breakfast yet, now that he thought about it.

"Should we go get something to eat?" Jaeseong asked, and Hayeong nodded in silence.

"What do you feel like? Black bean noodles? Pork cutlet?"

Hayeong made no reply.

"Hayeong?"

"Just whatever . . . you want to eat," Hayeong said gruffly, not meeting his eyes, probably still miffed that he hadn't readily said that she could come live with him. He was just grateful that she didn't draw back her hand from his.

Jaeseong left the hospital, Hayeong in tow, and went into the pasta restaurant across the street.

There were white wooden chairs with the paint chipping off, with colorful seat cushions on them. Sitting across from him, Hayeong made a conscious effort to avoid his eyes, tracing the outlines of the flowers on a cushion with her finger. Watching her sit there against the backdrop of pink curtains, he became aware of her age, which he hadn't thought about in a while. She had turned eleven this year. They had been living apart for three years already. She had grown quite a bit in the several months he hadn't seen her.

"Cream sauce for you, right? You like cream sauce, don't you?" he asked.

Hayeong would not reply.

Jaeseong called an employee over and placed the order, and poured some water into a cup for Hayeong.

"You're going to go on, not talking to me?" he asked.

Hayeong remained silent.

"Then I won't talk, either."

Hayeong, who had just been staring at the table, looked up. Her eyes looked anxious again. He regretted what he had said. He tried to appease her, in a gentler voice.

"You're not going to stay sulking like that, when I haven't seen you in so long, are you?"

Hayeong shook her head, but it was clear that she was doing it against her will. Even as they ate, she gave only cursory answers to his questions.

Jaeseong felt bad, but in truth, she hadn't been on his mind at all in the past several months. Things hadn't been all that different when they were living together. It wasn't that he didn't like her. He was so busy at the hospital that when he went home, he most often hit the bed without even seeing her. Although they lived in the same house, he saw her only once every few days, and played with her rarely—once every few weeks.

When was the last time he had taken such a good look at her face? He sat gazing at her as she ate her spaghetti, sitting across from him.

Her big, clear eyes and thick eyebrows were like her mother's. She still had baby fat on her face, but when she grew a little older and her features became more distinct, she would look even more like her mother. Jaeseong realized that he turned cold even at the traces of her on the child's face.

He didn't want to acknowledge that there were still remaining wounds and feelings inside him that had to do with his deceased ex-wife. He hastily took his eyes off the child and finished the food on his plate.

"It's . . . because of that woman, isn't it?" Hayeong asked.

"Huh?"

Hayeong, who had been eating quietly, put her fork down and said, "I mean that woman, who lives with you . . ." She trailed off, not really knowing what to call her.

She had always been quick and perceptive. She knew quite clearly why he couldn't just take her home.

"It's all right. . . . I'll go to Grandfather's, in America."

It seemed that she had already resigned herself to the reality of the situation and thought about where she should go. But the plan she had in mind wasn't quite so feasible, either.

Jaeseong's father had gone to live in Seattle, where Jaeseong's two older brothers lived, when Hayeong was two; for the past year, though, he had been suffering from Alzheimer's and was under Jaeseong's mother's care. He couldn't load her with another burden when she was so busy nursing his father, nor could he ask his brother's family, who were tied up with work at their restaurant, to take care of Hayeong. There never had been any room to ask them in the first place. Family you couldn't see even once a year, family who called once every several months, and only when something had happened, wasn't really family at all.

Besides, he balked at the thought of sending the child so far away when she had a father.

The answer was clear, no matter how he looked at it. He was only grappling with how to make it work.

"What did I tell you earlier?" he asked Hayeong.

Hayeong looked at him, not saying anything.

"I told you not to worry. I'll take care of it," he assured her.

"So . . . that means I can live with you?"

Jaeseong nodded, and the child finally smiled, looking relieved. Seeing the smile on her face, Jaeseong made up his mind that he would tackle the problem head-on.

It had been a year since he started living with Seonkyeong; he knew what kind of person she was. She wasn't someone who would coldly refuse a child in a situation like this. She might hesitate for a little while, but in the end, she would accept Hayeong. But even as he thought that, there was another reason why he hesitated, not taking her home right away.

He didn't want to tell Seonkyeong, if possible, about what happened between his ex-wife and him. Seonkyeong wasn't someone who pried about the past, so he had never told her what happened.

If Hayeong came to live with them at the house, he would have no choice but to tell her about many things in his past that he didn't want to tell her, things he didn't want her to know. Hayeong would be spending more time with her than he would in the days ahead. There was no telling what might happen, and what Hayeong might say, when the two of them were alone without him. That was what troubled him the most.

But there was no alternative for the moment. He might end up watching them, feeling as if he were walking on a minefield every day, but he decided that he should take the child home with him.

Jaeseong wondered how much Hayeong knew about what happened that night. But it wasn't something he could talk about easily, or ask. He didn't want to stir up her memories for no good reason, either. He watched her as she focused on eating, her head lowered, and picked up his cup and drank the remaining water.

He felt as if there were something cold and hard stuck in his throat.

9.

H E WAS WEARING A BLUE PRISON UNIFORM AND HANDCUFFS, but he looked unbelievably at peace.

The fair face from the photograph was so pale, having been hidden from the sun for some time, that the capillaries showed through. The handsome face, with shapely eyebrows and soft lips, looked gentle because of the downturned eyes. The nickname "David" was quite fitting. The short hair made the face stand out even more.

It was difficult to see in that face a cold-blooded killer who had committed heinous crimes.

Standing there, Yi Byeongdo slowly looked Seonkyeong up and down. As his gaze slid down from her face to her chest, Seonkyeong felt her heart beat faster. His gaze wandered in the air for a while, then returned to her face. When his eyes met hers, wrinkles gathered around them, and he smiled quietly. If they had been meeting by chance somewhere else, her heart would have fluttered at the smile.

When the prison guard nudged his arm, Yi Byeongdo came to himself and took slow steps forward.

Sitting across from Seonkyeong, Yi Byeongdo stared at her while the guard handcuffed his arms to the chair. His eyes were certainly full of gladness, as if he were seeing someone he knew.

The guard stood beside him after he finished handcuffing him. Yi Byeongdo turned his gaze, looked up at the guard, and asked, "Are you . . . going to keep standing there?"

"It's the rule" was the guard's reply.

"I want to talk to her, just the two of us."

Rumor had it that he played the master and did as he pleased even at the detention center, and it seemed that the rumor was true.

"With things the way they are, I can't say what I need to say, don't you agree, ma'am?" Yi Byeongdo asked, turning around to look at Seonkyeong. As long as there were safety measures in place, Seonkyeong, too, would prefer an environment in which he could talk frankly.

"You can't talk to him without a guard present," the guard said firmly even before Seonkyeong opened her mouth.

She could sense that both the security manager, whom she'd just met, and the prison guard were not pleased with this special visit. The guard couldn't break the rules because of the prisoner. In the end, Seonkyeong suggested a compromise.

"Like you said, rules are rules. If it's all right with you, would you sit by the door over there? This might take a while."

The guard looked from Yi Byeongdo to Seonkyeong, and reluctantly conceded. As long as he was in the room, he would be able to hear the conversation between the two. But it would irritate Yi Byeongdo to have him so close to his side. Spatial distance would make him feel relaxed, which would work to Seonkyeong's advantage as well. Everyone would win without breaking any rules. With everyone being flexible, they could all sit down in their chairs.

Yi Byeongdo checked to make sure that the guard sat down, then turned his gaze toward Seonkyeong. He seemed to be in a better mood after the arrangement. Smiling gently, he looked at Seonkyeong, and slowly began to speak.

"You were curious, weren't you?"

Seonkyeong looked at him, wondering what he was talking about.

"How does this person know me? Why me, of all people? You asked those questions, didn't you?"

His eyes, directed at Seonkyeong, were laughing. She felt flustered, feeling as if he were seeing right through her. But she didn't want to pretend that he was wrong. She felt that she had to open up to him for the interview to go well. She looked at his face and saw a peculiar chill in his seemingly good-natured eyes. Even his smile couldn't hide that chill.

"Yes, I did. I was very curious for several days. Will you tell me why?" she asked.

Instead of answering, however, he stared at her, and leaned back and relaxed in his chair. He seemed pleased that he had control over the situation. He asked another question.

"What's the oldest memory in your head?"

"What?"

The question threw her off. The oldest memory? Is he saying that he knows all about my childhood, or that he wants to know more about me? Seonkyeong thought. She felt at a loss, as if she had studied all night for a test only to find out that it covered a completely different topic from the one she had prepared for.

The right corner of his mouth lifted. Watching him wait for her reaction with sparkling eyes, Seonkyeong thought she shouldn't let him call the shots again.

Seonkyeong chuckled and calmly opened her notebook, saying, "Let's talk about something else."

Yi Byeongdo never answered her first question, either. There was no reason why she should answer his. An invisible struggle between the two was creating tension. How will he react this time?

"Why are you avoiding the subject? Bad memories?" he asked.

"I'm not here to talk, I'm here to listen."

"Is that all? It seems to me that there's something you don't want to remember."

Seonkyeong said nothing in reply.

"Just as you want to hear my story, I want to hear yours. It's tedious, very tedious in here."

Déjà vu. She had seen this before. Then she remembered. Damned Clarice Starling. Hannibal Lecter said the same words to Agent Starling in *The Silence of the Lambs*.

"If you want to hear my story, you should tell yours," said Yi Byeongdo.

"Are you trying to reenact the movie?"

Yi Byeongdo snickered and said, "I don't know what you're talking about, but it's a common deal that even a child knows. You give one, you take one. It's only fair."

Someone who had taken the lives of at least thirteen people was talking about fairness. Seonkyeong wanted to ask him what he had given each and every time he took a life.

"I'm not sure because I haven't thought about it," she said.

"Think about it. There's plenty of time."

Seonkyeong put her pen down and looked at him. Just as she expected, he didn't want to lose. She decided to give in a little, so that he would open up. She lowered her eyes for a moment and fell into thought, then spoke.

"Red shoes. Red shoes my mother bought me. That's my first memory."

He narrowed his eyes and looked at Seonkyeong. He was probably trying to see how truthful she was being. In a moment, he shook his head.

"I'm disappointed. I thought I'd get to hear something original," he taunted.

Seonkyeong shrugged, and picked up her pen again.

"What's your first memory?" she asked.

"My first memory? Swimming in the amniotic fluid in my mom's belly," he said, his face expressionless. His eyes, however, were twinkling, waiting for her response. Seonkyeong, about to take notes, saw his eyes and realized that he was teasing her.

"So, how did it feel?" she asked.

"Like I would suffocate. The water was filthy."

He must not have good memories of his mother. A look of hatred flashed across his face.

It occurred to Seonkyeong that most people's first memories would probably have something to do with their mother. She didn't believe that he remembered being in the womb, but she could sense that he had some intense feelings about his mother. She recalled what she'd read in the study the night before about his family. It was written that Yi Byeongdo, who had lived with just his mother when he was younger, had been on his own since he was seventeen, when she left home.

"Let's talk about your mother, shall we?" Seonkyeong said.

At those words, Yi Byeongdo leaned back in his chair, looking at her with his eyes narrowed, as if to guess at her intent in asking the question.

In a moment, Yi Byeongdo sat up. He then leaned forward, and inched close to her face.

Suddenly, he was singing a pop song in a low voice: *Bang! Bang!*

Seonkyeong stopped in her tracks at this unexpected behavior, and raised her head.

He was smiling a genuine smile. His eyes were full of mischief. She felt that he was throwing stones to trigger her curiosity. The question was, Were the stones meaningful?

The song he sang was the Beatles' "Maxwell's Silver Hammer."

As far as she knew, "Maxwell's Silver Hammer" was a song that came out in the 1960s.

If it hadn't been for Professor Klen, her psychology advisor, she wouldn't have known the song.

Professor Klen, a big fan of the Beatles, liked to have barbeque parties with his students in his backyard. The music playing in the background was always the Beatles. If someone so much as asked him the title of a song, he would spill out all sorts of stories, his eyes twinkling, including the anecdote about the day he bought his first Beatles album, and tales about different songs as well as behind-the-scenes details. The stories always ended with him saying that the Beatles died in his heart after his visit to John Lennon's grave.

Seonkyeong was somewhat surprised that Yi Byeongdo knew the song. Neither Seonkyeong nor he was of a generation that had easy access to this song. Had there been a big fan of the Beatles around him, like Professor Klen?

"That's a Beatles song. That song is your first memory?" she asked.

His eyes widened all of a sudden. He stared at Seonkyeong, then burst out laughing.

"Wow, it's great to meet someone who knows this song!" he said, his voice louder. He seemed to be in a good mood. He was probably pleased that Seonkyeong knew the song he liked. A common theme, though insignificant, could make it easier to talk to each other. Seonkyeong thanked Professor Klen in her heart, and looked at Yi Byeongdo.

"Does that song have a special meaning to you?" she asked.

His face inched even closer at the question she had thrown out casually. He looked fixedly into Seonkyeong's eyes and whispered in a low voice. Even with her ears perked up, Seonkyeong could barely hear him.

"All the women I sang this song to . . . died at my hands," he said.

Seonkyeong felt as if a piece of ice were sliding down her back. Again, she saw a chill in his eyes. His face, seemingly gentle and full of mischief, was beset with eyes that were cold and empty. Which one was his true self?

Seonkyeong could not avoid his gaze, which was fixed on her. From his expression, she could see that he was telling the truth.

He didn't hum this song just because he had happened to hear it and liked it. If he sang it to each of the women he killed, it must be some kind of a symbol. It meant something that was his and his alone. Seonkyeong realized at last that the stones he had thrown were puzzle pieces that would lead her to understand him.

With satisfaction, he looked at the shock in Seonkyeong's eyes, and the furrows forming in her forehead, as if he didn't want to miss a single effect his words were having on her. It was as if he had thrown a rock into a lake to watch the ripples spread out.

Still watching Seonkyeong, he slowly licked his lips. They glistened with moisture. Seonkyeong watched his movements as if hypnotized. Smiling with satisfaction, he slowly took his eyes off her.

In a loud voice, different from that of a moment before, he called to the prison guard.

"The interview is over."

It hadn't even been ten minutes. Puzzled by this abrupt change in attitude, Seonkyeong rose awkwardly to her feet.

The guard seemed used to Yi Byeongdo's whims. He was sitting in front of the door, but rose quickly and undid the handcuffs on his hands and the chair. Then the guard put his hands together, handcuffed him again, and brought him to his feet.

Yi Byeongdo walked slowly to the door. He didn't even look at Seonkyeong. In haste, Seonkyeong blocked his way.

"Hey, wait . . . we haven't really talked yet," she said.

"I think it wasn't too bad for our first meeting, don't you?" was his reply.

Seonkyeong was at a loss for words.

He was like a chameleon that kept changing.

Just a short while ago he had looked genuinely happy to meet her, but now he had changed colors, turning cold, as if he no longer wanted to deal with her. He walked past her and stood at the door. The guard turned and glanced at Seonkyeong, then opened the door and led Yi Byeongdo out.

Stunned, Seonkyeong simply stood there for a while, then rushed out after him.

She had driven no less than an hour from Seoul. She couldn't let the interview end in vain like this.

"Do you not want to have this interview?" Seonkyeong shouted at Yi Byeongdo, who was already quite a distance away. At her words, he came to a stop. He stood there for a moment, then turned his head and looked at her.

"That's it for today. Let's meet again in two days. At the same hour. Oh, and from now on, when you come see me, bring me an apple. One that's very big and fresh, and satisfying to the bone when you take a bite."

With those words, he turned around, leaving Seonkyeong feeling flustered. He returned to his cell, as majestically as a master being escorted by a servant.

Seonkyeong was dumbfounded. She felt humiliated. Angry, she began stamping her feet when the security manager approached her from the corridor across from her.

"Didn't I tell you? Wouldn't it have been better not to meet him?" the security manager asked.

There must be a CCTV camera installed somewhere in the room.

"He was supposed to have an interview once with a producer from a broadcasting company. The producer thought he was getting a big scoop and showed up all excited on the appointed day with a camera. Do you know what happened?"

Seonkyeong couldn't imagine.

"He made him wait three hours and, in the end, refused to see him. The producer must've gone home spewing out every curse word he knew."

Was Seonkyeong supposed to take comfort in knowing that she had at least done better than him? She laughed in spite of herself. She had anticipated that it wouldn't be easy. But she hadn't realized that she wouldn't be given even the minimum time required for an interview. She hadn't had a chance to ask the questions she had prepared.

"You wouldn't have gotten that much out of it anyway. Think how bored he must be, living the same day over and over again in solitary confinement, with no one visiting him. So he wants someone to play with him for a little while. It's better to stop here. It's a waste of time. Are you going to be his plaything?"

The manager's sarcastic remarks actually made her feel better.

Listening to his words, she thought back on the short visit she'd had with Yi Byeongdo, and realized it hadn't been fruitless.

His attitude, his movements, his gaze while looking at her, his reactions, his questions, and even the Beatles song he offered—all this was information that couldn't be obtained from three encyclopedias' worth of materials. With this much gained, there was no reason to feel dejected. Her anxiety lifted. Seonkyeong made a point of smiling cheerfully at the security manager.

"See you in two days," she said.

Seeing the manager's face start to contort, Seonkyeong headed back to the visitors' room to get her briefcase. She heard the manager's voice behind her. He was mumbling as if to himself, but his voice was loud enough for her to hear.

"What good can come of getting involved with a bastard like that? You'll regret it in the end."

10.

SEONKYEONG PARKED HER CAR IN FRONT OF THE HOUSE AND turned off the engine.

Her body was as heavy as wet cotton. She heaved a sigh. Overcome by sudden fatigue, she wanted to go inside and immerse herself in a hot bath. She wanted to relieve her nerves that were exhausted from meeting Yi Byeongdo. She wanted to relax her body and mind, take a cold shower, and look back on everything that had been said with a refreshed mind. Contrary to her wishes, however, something unexpected was awaiting her at home.

As she opened the front door and entered the house, she noticed a child's pair of sneakers next to Jaeseong's shoes.

She entered the living room, wondering whose shoes they were, and saw a girl, about ten years old, sitting vacantly on the sofa without even noticing her come in.

Seonkyeong took a cautious look around. She saw that the door to the main bedroom was open, and recalled seeing Jaeseong's shoes by the front door.

He must've brought the girl, she thought.

Seonkyeong knew that Jaeseong had had a child with his ex-wife. But she had never imagined that she would end up meeting her in this way. He had said that his ex-wife wouldn't allow him to see the child. So after the divorce, he never saw her.

So why was she sitting there on Seonkyeong's sofa now?

Slowly, Seonkyeong approached the child.

The child, who had been looking straight ahead in a daze, finally sensed that someone was watching her, and turned her head and looked at Seonkyeong.

The child wasn't surprised to see her. No emotion whatsoever could be detected on her face.

Even at a glance, the child's fair skin and large eyes had the power to draw one in. Long, thick lashes covered her eyes, which, under the shadow of the lashes, had a plaintive quality about them. Her mouth, firmly closed, hinted that she was shrewd beyond her age.

The child looked quietly at Seonkyeong for a moment, then turned her gaze back to the living room window, as if to say she wasn't interested. A grassy yard and the gate could be seen through the window. The child must have been watching Seonkyeong as she came in through the gate.

Seonkyeong was about to say something to her when she heard someone approaching behind her.

"Oh, you're home?"

Jaeseong's voice was shaky and unstable, which was unusual; he must not have expected her to come home early.

"Say hello, Hayeong," he said to his daughter.

He rushed over to the sofa and got the child up on her feet. Only then did Seonkyeong notice the teddy bear in her hand.

The bear was tattered and grimy, so dirty that you could hardly tell what color it had been in the first place. Jaeseong had pulled the child to her feet, but she was still just staring at Seonkyeong with those clear eyes.

"Say hello," Jaeseong repeated, but the child remained silent, her mouth firmly closed. He put his hand on her head and tried to make her bow.

"Don't. You don't have to make her if she doesn't want to," Seonkyeong said.

Jaeseong shook his head, thrown off by the child's attitude.

"What's going on?" Seonkyeong asked.

"Stay here. I'm going to go talk to the lady," Jaeseong said, sitting the child back down on the sofa. Then he took Seonkyeong's arm and headed toward the main bedroom. Seonkyeong felt uncomfortable. She was tired as it was, and felt on edge because Jaeseong was flustered, which wasn't like him.

Once in the bedroom, he checked to make sure that the child was sitting on the sofa, and quietly closed the door. But he hesitated, avoiding Seonkyeong's gaze, and paced around the room.

Seonkyeong spoke first, unable to wait any longer. "What's going on?" she asked.

He sat down on a corner of the bed, as if he had been waiting for those words, and looked at her, combing his hand through his hair. Deep wrinkles, usually not there, had formed around his eyes.

"I don't know where to start explaining. And I don't know how you'll take it . . . ," he began.

"What on earth is this about? Tell me," Seonkyeong said.

"Remember that phone call early this morning?"

"It said that there was an urgent patient . . ."

Seonkyeong stared at him, not finishing her sentence. He had gone to work, not even properly dressed, after getting that phone call.

"It was about her," Seonkyeong said.

"It was the police. Telling me to take the child, Hayeong, home."

"What . . . do you mean? Didn't you say that she was with her mom?"

"I didn't tell you, but . . . not too long after you and I got married, her mom passed away. Hayeong has been in the care of her grandparents since."

It was almost a year since they had gotten married. For some reason, Seonkyeong felt a chill in her heart.

"When did you find out?" she asked.

"I got a phone call and went to the funeral. I couldn't . . . tell you. It hadn't even been that long since we got married, and I couldn't bring up something like that."

All kinds of thoughts and emotions got mixed up together within her, and she didn't know what to say.

As Jaeseong said, it wouldn't have been easy to bring up something like that. In a way, it wasn't something that Seonkyeong had to know, even. If things had ended there, there would have been no need for him to bring it up. Still, she wished he had told her before. How much more did he have buried in his heart?

Seonkyeong blinked, trying to sort out her thoughts. After the divorce, the child's name had been transferred to her mother's side of the family register. With her mother gone, she should be with her father again. But the death had occurred a year ago. Why had he brought her here today?

"If her mother passed away, shouldn't you have brought her here a long time ago?" she asked.

"Well . . . her grandparents wouldn't let her go."

"And now they tell you to take her all of a sudden? Did they say they couldn't raise her anymore?"

Jaeseong paused. "A fire broke out at dawn and the house burnt down. My in-laws . . . that is, Hayeong's grandparents, both died in the fire."

"Oh no."

Seonkyeong looked at him, unable to go on. She could see now why those deep wrinkles had formed on his face in less than a day.

Seonkyeong looked toward the closed bedroom door as if she could see through it to the living room without realizing it. The child had lost her grandparents in a fire, not even a year after she had lost her mother. She recalled how the child had been sitting vacantly on the sofa, looking devastated.

The child hadn't reacted in any way even when she saw Seonkyeong.

She had lost everything in the fire the night before. The house she had lived in had burnt down, and her grandparents had died. Just as one can't hear for a while after hearing something too loud, she couldn't respond to anything because of the shock. Her heart must be empty.

How horrific it must have been. Upon learning why the child sat there expressionless, as if she didn't belong to this world, Seonkyeong felt overcome with sympathy.

"I know this is very sudden and I feel terrible, but could she . . . stay with us?" Jaeseong asked.

"What are you saying? Of course she's staying!" Seonkyeong said.

Jaeseong's eyes widened in surprise, and he looked at her. She saw his lips tremble. She could see just how much he had hesitated before bringing up the question. He seemed to find it hard to believe how easily she'd consented.

"You . . . you really mean that?" he asked, sounding baffled.

"You're her father. Of course she's staying with us," Seonkyeong repeated.

"Honey, thank you . . . and I'm sorry."

He was moved to tears. She saw his shoulders relax, on a sigh of relief. She quietly went to him and took him in her arms.

"Was it so hard to tell me?" she asked.

Seonkyeong had actually thought that something like this might happen, after he'd told her before they got married that he'd been divorced and had a child. He said he had not seen her since the divorce because his ex-wife was so adamant about it, but Seonkyeong didn't think that the tie between him and the child was severed. A parent and a child are bound to meet someday, somehow.

It was perhaps then that she had begun to prepare herself for the inevitable.

"I . . . didn't think you'd consent so easily," Jaeseong said in a congested voice. Seonkyeong patted him on the back without saying anything.

This isn't easy for me. But there's no other way. And I'd seen it coming.

Many thoughts reared their heads in her mind, but with effort, Seonkyeong suppressed them.

She couldn't say that they should send the child somewhere else when she had nowhere to go, especially when she had a father. At least, that wasn't the way Seonkyeong had been brought up. She had already pictured the scenario in her mind and had come to a conclusion about it. If it was something she was to take on, it was better to accept it quickly and adjust to it. It wouldn't be easy living with a child, but they would get used to it, she thought. That's what a family is.

Once she made up her mind about it, Seonkyeong thought of all the things that would need to be done.

"The room on the second floor would be nice, don't you think? She'll like it, with the sun streaming in. We can move the stuff in there to storage, and we can put a bed and a desk in there. Oh, and we need to hang new curtains, too," Seonkyeong said, thinking aloud.

There were more than just one or two things the child would need.

What was she going to wear right away? And was the empty room clean? Would the walls have to be redone? Seonkyeong felt overwhelmed, thinking about what should be done first. She stood with her thoughts in a flurry, when Jaeseong took her hand.

"You should go say hi to her."

Only then did Seonkyeong remember the child sitting alone on the living room sofa.

If they made her wait too long, she might misunderstand and feel hurt. Seonkyeong quickly nodded and followed him out to the living room.

The child was clutching the filthy stuffed bear to her chest, and still sitting on the sofa like a picture.

"Say hello to the lady, Hayeong. The three of us are going to be living together from now on," Jaeseong said, going up to her and embracing her shoulder. The child, who had been looking at her father, slowly turned her face toward Seonkyeong. Then she took a good look at her, unlike before. Her eyes were full of fear and anxiety.

Seonkyeong bent down and looked into her eyes.

"Your name is Hayeong, right? What a pretty name. My name is Yi Seonkyeong. This is your home from now on," she said warmly.

Hayeong, who had been staring at her, looked up at her father and said, "Dad . . . I'm sleepy."

"Oh, you are? I'll get your bed ready," he said, but then he looked helplessly at Seonkyeong.

"Let her sleep in our room tonight," Seonkyeong said without hesitation. There really was nowhere else for the child to sleep. She must have had a hard day, so they couldn't make her sleep in a room that hadn't been tidied up yet, or on the sofa.

Seonkyeong rushed to the room and drew back the blanket on the bed. The child, who came into the room holding her father's hand, crawled under the blanket without a word. She looked so fragile that it seemed she would break any minute.

"Will you hand me your teddy bear?"

Seonkyeong reached out to take the teddy bear from the child's arms. But Hayeong hugged the bear's neck tighter, and glared at

Seonkyeong with her lips clamped shut, as if to say that she wouldn't let her take it.

"Let her keep it. She always carries it with her."

The word "but" came right up to her throat, but she took a deep breath and swallowed it. She was worried that the blanket would get dirty, but it could be laundered. She didn't want to quarrel with the child over something petty. The child was exhausted as it was, and the most important thing now was to let her get some good rest.

"Sure, keep it if you want," Seonkyeong said reassuringly, and tucked the child in and beamed.

"Dad, stay with me till I fall asleep," Hayeong pleaded.

Jaeseong looked into Seonkyeong's eyes for a moment, then nodded at Hayeong and said, "Don't worry. I'll be at your side."

He sat on the bed and patted Hayeong on the head. Feeling relieved at last, the child closed her eyes. Seonkyeong left the two alone in the room, worried that she might disturb the child, and went out to the living room.

WHILE SEONKYEONG WAS SITTING at the table writing down the things Hayeong would need as well as the things that had to be purchased right away, and thinking about how she should decorate the room, Jaeseong came out of the room and carefully shut the door. The child must have fallen asleep.

"Is she sleeping already?" she asked.

"Yeah, she fell asleep quickly."

"If you went to take her early in the morning, why didn't you come right home?"

"I didn't know what to do, so I took her to the hospital. I wanted to talk to you first."

"Were you planning on going back out with her, then?"

"I was going to take her to a hotel. I needed your consent."

He looked cheerful, with a big burden off his mind. Seonkyeong knew that he was a simple man, but felt a little peeved that he looked so carefree already.

"What would you have done if I'd said no?"

"I would've worried about it then. But I thought you would consent."

Seonkyeong gave him a little sidelong glare. He gently placed his hand over hers on the table.

"I knew you'd understand how Hayeong felt better than anyone."

Seonkyeong nodded in spite of herself. She, too, had lost her mother at a young age.

"Let's not wake her. She'll get up on her own or when she feels hungry. She must be exhausted," she said.

"Yeah, it's best to sleep when you're really tired and worn out."

After losing each of her parents and after their funerals, Seonkyeong had spent her days sleeping as if dead. It was better to forget everything in the oblivion of sleep than to wake up and feel the painful reality.

When she lost her mother at the age of fifteen, it was her father who woke her up. He did so after making curry, which her mother had often made. She didn't feel like eating anything. She hated her father for waking her up to eat when her mother had passed away. She wanted to go on sleeping, but in the end, she was led by her father's hand to sit down at the table.

The smell of curry stimulated her nose, but she did not want to eat. She took a spoonful at her father's urging and swallowed it, and suddenly she felt unbearably hungry. She polished off the plate in an instant. Without a word, her father filled her plate again.

Two years ago when her father passed away, Seonkyeong had sat huddled in bed, thinking about that day. She fell asleep and woke up again and again, imagining that her father would be waiting with curry on the table when she opened her eyes. But no one called to her.

She missed the smell of the curry her father had made for her. There was no one now who would lead her by the hand to the table and give her the strength to go on again. It dawned on her at last that she was alone. She wanted to close her eyes and go where her mother and father were.

It was Jaeseong, who was her husband now, who got Seonkyeong back on her feet.

She met him in front of the operating room at the hospital. She had rushed to the hospital upon hearing that her father had collapsed due to a cerebral hemorrhage; when she got there, he was already unconscious. The doctor, who had finished taking the CT scans, diagnosed it as a ruptured aneurysm, and recommended an angiography along with an operation. The medical team said it was urgent and handed her a surgery consent form, so she signed it in a hurry and waited six hours in front of the operating room.

He'll be all right after the operation, she thought. No, it would be okay even if he wasn't all right. If he just stayed alive, Seonkyeong decided, she would be at his side at all times, and never leave him alone. She prayed, calling out to a god she had never called out to before, but the operation, conducted too late, was of no use.

Whatever had gone wrong, her father passed away during the operation, and the surgeon offered her his condolences without meeting her eyes.

As she sat dazed in a chair in front of the operating room, someone handed her a bottle of water.

That someone was Jaeseong.

She drank the cold water, and finally managed to come to herself. Jaeseong, who had just finished an operation and was coming out of another room as her father was being operated on, saw Seonkyeong and could not just pass her by.

He took care of all the funeral arrangements for Seonkyeong, who couldn't pull herself together. He even came and helped her in the morgue in the basement of the hospital.

If only her father had been taken to the hospital earlier, if only she had paid more attention when he would occasionally say that he had a splitting headache. . . . No, if only we had lived together. . . . As Seonkyeong reproached herself endlessly, Jaeseong offered genuine comfort. Seonkyeong, deep in grief, didn't even realize that he was at her side during the funeral.

Then he called her on the phone out of the blue. He said he was worried about her, and Seonkyeong asked him to take her out to eat.

They went to a curry restaurant.

When the curry was served, Seonkyeong picked up her spoon, then started crying. He was flustered. He handed her tissues as she wept bitterly.

She finally calmed down and told him about her father's curry. And as she ate curry with him, she remembered that he had always been there at her side during the past several days of the funeral process. Working at the hospital, he must have seen people like Seonkyeong, families of patients, countless times. There was no reason for him to care for someone he didn't even know.

Seonkyeong asked him why he had helped her so. He smiled, and said that he didn't know. When she saw that smile, she felt as if he were someone her father had sent, out of sympathy for his daughter who was left alone.

Taking Jaeseong's hand, Seonkyeong stepped back into the world, and married him within a year.

As she looked at his face now, she remembered that time. She decided that when Hayeong woke up, she would make her some curry.

"I'm so sorry, but I have to go back to the hospital."

"Oh, then you must go. I'll see you later."

"I'll be back soon."

He put his arm around her shoulder.

"Thank you," he said, and rushed out of the house.

Seonkyeong, sitting alone in the kitchen and looking around the living room, feeling dazed, realized then she hadn't even changed her clothes yet. Her meeting with Yi Byeongdo seemed like a dream. She felt heavy and sluggish all of a sudden, and thought she would take a warm bath and doze for a bit while the child slept.

Carefully, Seonkyeong opened the bedroom door and went inside.

The child was asleep, clutching the stuffed bear tightly in her hands as if afraid she would lose it.

Beads of sweat had formed on her forehead. Seonkyeong hastily opened the blanket chest and changed the blanket to a single-layer quilt. The child tossed and turned, then fell back into deep sleep. Seonkyeong took some clothes out of the closet and left the room.

11.

SEONKYEONG BRUSHED HER TEETH WHILE THE TUB FILLED. Staring into the mirror without thinking about it, she thought of Yi Byeongdo. She was having difficulty shaking off the words he'd said, and the way he'd looked at her. The song he'd sung kept going around in her head.

She quickly finished brushing her teeth, and sat down in the half-filled tub. The hot water felt nice against her body.

Seonkyeong had thought that meeting Yi Byeongdo would answer her first question. But he seemed to have no intention of giving her an answer. On the contrary, he seemed to enjoy keeping her in suspense. Only when the first question was answered could the next question be resolved as well.

How does he know me? Why does he want to meet me? And what is it about me that draws his attention? Seonkyeong wondered, thinking back to the moment when he entered the visitors' room— the way he'd walked in, the way he'd looked at her, the affected smile and those cold eyes, and the song he'd sung slowly in a low voice.

Seonkyeong could see why his victims had taken to him easily.

The subtle changes in his expression appealed to the maternal instinct. One minute, Yi Byeongdo would look intensely into your eyes; the next, he would look away, revealing his vulnerability. He feigned composure, but he was anxious about the way people responded to him. Seonkyeong felt that he was like a child.

He was quite different from what she'd imagined, after reading materials on him for the past several days. If not for his prison garb, he would look like an ordinary man in his thirties, who was somewhat fragile and sensitive. It was when she'd asked him about the meaning of the song, and when he was with other people, that she noticed something unusual about him.

When the prison guard was away, Yi Byeongdo focused solely on Seonkyeong. He probably displayed extraordinary powers of concentration when it came to things he wanted to accomplish. She recalled how the investigators had said that he'd focused entirely on himself during the reenactment, oblivious to his surroundings. When it came to things that did not concern himself or what he wanted to accomplish, however, he was astonishingly indifferent and selfish.

When the guard approached him, he began to show off, to conceal his vulnerability, in a power struggle to take control of the situation. The guard seemed used to this attitude.

The hot water, now reaching above Seonkyeong's shoulders, eased the tension in her body and lulled her eyelids shut. Feeling her mind grow dim, she lowered herself deeper into the tub.

With her body relaxing in hot water, Seonkyeong thought about what Yi Byeongdo had said. She huddled up, pulling her knees to her chest. Although she couldn't remember, she imagined that if her physical senses remembered the time when she was still in her mother's womb, she must have felt as warm and comfortable as she did now. One by one, she recalled the memories of the days when she'd fallen asleep in her mother's warm embrace. She felt a surge of longing in her heart. She hadn't thought about her mother for some time.

She must have fallen asleep; her shoulders felt cold all of a sudden. She could feel the tub against her back and neck.

Someone had opened the bathroom door and was looking in. She could feel it, even with her eyes closed. She wanted to open her eyes and see who it was, but her eyelids were heavy. She could not open her eyes.

The water was cold—a long time must have passed. The water, which had warmed up her body, was now taking heat away from her. She was trembling all over. The person who had been standing by the open door entered slowly. She heard the footsteps, approaching nearer and nearer. She had to open her eyes, but couldn't. She tried to move her hands and grab the edge of the tub, but could not move at all. Her feet felt numb as well.

The person, who was now by the tub, was looking down at Seon-kyeong.

The person's face was so close to her own that she could feel breath on her forehead. Then the face grew distant. And then the hands came. The hands pressed down on her head. Her head sank down into the tub. The water, which had come up to her shoulders, was now up to her neck. She reached out a hand in an effort to get up. No matter how she struggled, though, there was nothing to grab onto. Her body kept slipping. The hands that had pushed her head down were gone, but she couldn't get to her feet. She felt frightened. What if she ended up drowning?

Suddenly, the tub felt as big as an indoor swimming pool. No matter how she flailed her arms and legs, nothing came into contact. Her body kept sinking under the water. The water now came up to her chin. Her mouth became submerged, and water came in through her nostrils. She burst into a fit of coughing. She couldn't hold out any longer, and opened her eyes in desperation.

There were corpses floating all around her—corpses of women with long, loose hair. The women, their faces pale, were all reaching out their arms toward her. She couldn't hear them, but she felt their cries for help. She screamed silently, and writhed to escape their hands. Frantically flailing her arms and legs, she barely managed to free herself of them. Finding her bearings with difficulty, she headed for the surface, when the women clutched her ankles. Cold, slippery hands pulled her down.

She screamed and struggled; then she came to herself and saw that she was lying in the tub.

Her legs had gone numb, it seemed, as she dozed. Her cold body was covered in goose bumps. Her chin trembled. Her entire body was shaking, because of either the women in the dream, or the chill in her body.

Quickly, she got to her feet, pulled the bathtub plug, and turned on the shower. The water in the tub drained swiftly and hot water rained on her. She stood under the pouring water for a while so that her cold body would warm up again.

She turned off the shower, stepped out of the tub, and opened the cabinet. She took out a large towel and dried herself off. The touch of soft cotton eased her heart, tense from the nightmare. She lowered her head to shake her hair dry. When she raised her head, the child was standing before her.

She was so startled that she nearly slipped and fell. She barely managed to grab the sink and find her balance.

"Hayeong, when did you wake up?" she asked, hastily covering herself with the towel and looking at the child.

The child looked at her with sleep still in her eyes, mumbling something.

"What did you say?" Seonkyeong asked.

"Bathroom," said the child.

She must have woken up to go to the bathroom.

"There's a bathroom in the main bedroom, too. . . . Well, all right. I'll be right out," Seonkyeong said, and immediately left the bathroom, with just the towel covering her body.

Drops of water fell from her hair. She went into the main bedroom to get some fresh clothes, after realizing that she'd left her clothes in the bathroom. She put on the clothes and gave her hair a quick dry. Hayeong opened the door and stared at her. She was wide awake now, her eyes clear.

"What is it? Do you need something? Are you hungry?" Seonkyeong asked.

"Where's my dad?"

"Oh, he's back at the hospital."

A look of disappointment flitted across the child's face, then vanished.

"Do you want to go back to sleep? Or are you awake now?" Seonkyeong asked.

Hayeong looked at Seonkyeong, and realizing that her hand was empty, she promptly picked up the teddy bear on the bed and went out of the room.

"Where are you going?" Seonkyeong asked, following Hayeong, but there was no answer. Seonkyeong went to the living room and found her putting on her shoes at the front door.

"Hayeong?" Seonkyeong called out, reaching out her arms to take hold of the child. Hayeong, however, shook Seonkyeong off violently, and shoved her hard with both hands. Seonkyeong fell straight on her back. She tried to get to her feet, but the floor was slippery from her hair, which wasn't completely dry. Sitting on the floor, she looked at the child in surprise.

Hayeong picked up her teddy bear from the floor and glared at her, mumbling quietly, "It's your fault my mom's dead."

Her cold gaze, directed at Seonkyeong, was full of threat and resentment.

"What?" Seonkyeong cried.

She felt dazed. She couldn't understand why the child would

say such a thing. It was only a few hours ago that Seonkyeong had learned of her death. And now the child was saying that it was Seonkyeong's fault. It was the coldness in her eyes, more than her baffling words, that stabbed at Seonkyeong's heart. A chill pierced her. She was thrown off by the hostility displayed by the child, who bared her teeth and growled at her. It seemed that the child had been harboring the hostility for a long time.

Hayeong stood there glaring at her, then opened the front door and stomped out. The unexpected blow confounded Seonkyeong.

Why had the child said such a thing?

Seonkyeong found herself wondering how the child's mother had died. She had been young, not even forty. Jaeseong had never told her how she'd died. Whether it was through illness or accident, her death must have been difficult for the child to accept.

The mother was dead, and the father was not at the child's side. She may have wanted to blame someone, hold someone responsible. Looking around, she may have thought Seonkyeong was that someone. But the hostility she had shown was not just vague anger or resentment.

For the first time, Seonkyeong felt that it wouldn't be easy living with the child.

She attempted to get to her feet, with her hands on the floor, and felt pain in her wrists. She must have hurt them when she fell. Rubbing her wrists, she went out to the yard. The gate was open.

Worried, Seonkyeong ran out the gate at once.

The child was nowhere to be seen in the alley, which was just a row of single houses and was usually pretty secluded. Seonkyeong ran in the direction of the main street. She ran into a woman, a shop owner, who happened to be sitting under a parasol fanning herself.

"Have you seen a little girl, about this tall, passing through?" she asked, gesturing with her hand.

"A little girl? With a filthy stuffed animal in her hand?" the woman asked in reply.

"Yes," Seonkyeong said.

To her relief, the woman had seen Hayeong running off and, pointing to the road, said she had just passed through.

Hayeong was pacing up and down by the road where cars were passing by, not knowing where to go. Seonkyeong ran over to her and took hold of her arm. Hayeong tried to shake her off, but this time, it wasn't so easy. Seonkyeong pulled her arm with all her might.

"Let's go home and talk," she said.

"No, I'm not going. I'm going to my dad," Hayeong said.

"He'll be home soon. He said he'd come home after he was done at the hospital."

"Let go, let go of me!" Hayeong cried, nearly screaming.

Seonkyeong let go of the child's arm, in spite of herself. She couldn't take Hayeong by force, and even if she did, it wouldn't be a good start to their relationship.

"Do as you please. But what will he say if he sees you acting this way? Do you think he'll be happy?" she asked.

Hayeong's face stiffened at Seonkyeong's words. She hadn't thought it through. Her face twitched—she didn't want to give in yet.

"You went to the hospital with him today, so you should know how busy he is," Seonkyeong said.

Hayeong didn't say anything.

"I'm going back home now."

Still, Hayeong remained silent.

"It's up to you whether you go to the hospital or come home," Seonkyeong declared, and turned around to go home.

Every nerve in her body pulled her toward the child, but feigning indifference, she headed home. As she walked away, taking slow steps, she heard the sound of dragging feet behind her.

Upon arriving home, she turned around and saw Hayeong with her teddy bear in her arms, standing with her head lowered.

Seonkyeong opened the gate and stood aside.

After a moment's hesitation, Hayeong went inside, keeping her distance from Seonkyeong lest they should brush against each other.

Staring after Hayeong as she stepped into the yard, Seonkyeong heaved an unwitting sigh. Following the child into the house, she hoped with all her heart that she wouldn't end up regretting her decision to live with her.

PART 2

12.

JAESEONG CAME HOME LATER THAN EXPECTED. TO TOP IT OFF, he smelled of liquor.

"You . . . had a drink?" Seonkyeong asked.

"Where's Hayeong?" was his reply as he entered through the front door without so much as a hello.

"She's upstairs in her room," Seonkyeong said.

After all the commotion during the day, Seonkyeong had cleaned a room on the second floor in haste and made it up for the child, filling it with a bed and a desk from a furniture store nearby.

"Has she eaten dinner?" Jaeseong asked.

Seonkyeong shook her head. She didn't want to talk about how her plans to cook curry and have dinner with Hayeong had gone wrong. The child didn't take a single bite, saying she hated curry. In the end, she had gone upstairs to her room, and Seonkyeong had eaten by herself.

Seonkyeong called out to Jaeseong, who was on his way up to Hayeong's room.

"We need to talk," she said.

"Let's talk after I see her," he said, and went upstairs.

Seonkyeong heard him open the door, calling out to his daughter. She felt strange, listening to the sound from afar.

After a long while, he came into their bedroom. Seonkyeong, who had been sitting at her dressing table after washing her face, saw him and turned around.

"What's she doing?" she asked.

"What happened to your arm?" he asked without answering her question, seeing the pain relief patch on her wrist.

She couldn't tell the truth about what had happened during the day. She rubbed her wrist and said casually, feigning indifference, "It's nothing. I put my hand down the wrong way."

"Don't you think it's too much, fighting with her on her first day here?" Jaeseong asked.

Seonkyeong could not believe her ears. She stared at him, gaping in astonishment, and found that he was quite upset. Hayeong must have said something to cause some great misunderstanding.

"What did she say?" Seonkyeong asked.

"Her arms were swollen red. What was the fight about?" Jaeseong asked, jumping to conclusions without bothering to ask what had really taken place, which upset her.

"Fight? What do you think I am? A little child?" she snapped.

Jaeseong did not reply.

"She woke up and insisted on going off to see you, so I brought her back inside. That's all."

"But Hayeong . . . ," Jaeseong began, then shut his mouth. It seemed that Hayeong had told a different story.

"What did she tell you?" Seonkyeong asked.

"No. That's enough."

"Enough? Tell me, what did she say? Why are you blaming this on me?"

"Honey, you know what a difficult time she's been having. Can't you be a little more understanding, and just let it go? She woke up and didn't see her dad—can't you see why she acted that way?" he blurted abruptly. He had never raised his voice with her like that.

"If she was looking for me, you could have called me," he went on.

"There was no time to call you. What was I supposed to do, when she just up and ran outside?" Seonkyeong retorted.

Jaeseong was stumped for words, and she continued.

"Don't you think you should at least hear me out? If you were so worried about your daughter, why did you stay late to have dinner with your colleagues? And now you're blaming me?"

"All right. It's my fault. Enough of this."

Seonkyeong said no more, sensing that there was no point arguing any longer, as they would only hurt each other's feelings. There were things she wanted to ask him, but she wasn't in the mood to talk to him now. Looking into the mirror, she brushed her hair with rough strokes, and hastened to her feet.

"Where are you going?" Jaeseong called after her, but she just stepped out, shutting the bedroom door and leaving him behind.

Even in the study, however, she felt ill at ease. It wasn't as if they had never argued before. But she had never gone off by herself with her feelings unresolved. If something upset her, she dealt with it promptly on the spot.

After the wedding, they had both been so busy that they could see each other only when it came time for dinner. Wanting to make the most of their brief time together, they treated each other with utmost consideration, being as pleasant as they could. Their only arguments were over trivial things, like why someone had thrown socks and underwear together in the washer, or hadn't called to say that they were having dinner out. She had never truly been angry and hurt.

She could understand well enough that he was concerned about his daughter, but she could not bear to have him blaming things on her without even listening to her side of the story.

Feeling upset, she couldn't concentrate on what she was reading. She kept reading the same sentence over and over, and in the end gave up, snapping the book shut.

She took out the digital tape recorder and notepad from her bag. She would listen to the recording of her interview with Yi Byeongdo, she thought. She put on her earphones and pushed the play button. The clarity was good, and she could hear even the sound of his footsteps as he entered the visitors' room, and the sound of the handcuffs closing.

She heard a low voice singing. The song he had sung. She turned up the volume to the max.

It occurred to her that the song might have a different meaning she wasn't aware of, and she e-mailed Professor Klen. He would be delighted at her interest in the Beatles, and give her a lengthy discourse on the song. The melody was so easy that anyone could sing along, as long as they didn't mind not getting all the words right. As did most Beatles hits, this song, too, had a very sweet melody.

The song Yi Byeongdo had sung was dark and grim, with none of the signature upbeat sound of a Beatles song. It was partly because he had sung it much more slowly than originally intended, but mostly because of the words he had uttered afterward: "All the women I sang this song to . . . died at my hands."

Music had been a major issue after the Yu Yeongcheol murders as well.

Yu Yeongcheol said that he had the theme song of the movie *1492: Conquest of Paradise* playing while he was in the bathroom taking care of the bodies of the women he had killed. It was unknown whether the song had inspired him, or he had listened to the music simply because he liked it.

What did this music mean to Yi Byeongdo?

Seonkyeong sang the chorus, lowering her voice. She recalled the gaze he had fixed on her in the visitors' room. It had felt as if he were looking not at her face, but into her very soul.

At that moment, someone hugged her from behind and she almost let out a scream. Startled, she drew herself forward and turned around. Jaeseong stood there, looking apologetic. She took out her earphones and turned off the recorder.

"You scared me," she said.

"I'm sorry. I didn't know," he said.

"Didn't know what?" Seonkyeong asked, still with an edge to her voice. She didn't want to forgive him that easily.

He took her hand in his. Caressing the back of it, he said in a tender voice, "You must be so angry. I was rash. She wouldn't leave my mind all day. And when I saw her, on the verge of tears as soon as she saw me, I just . . . and when I know what kind of person you are, too."

The hand that had been caressing hers was now touching her face.

"You have no idea how grateful I am to you. Thank you . . . so much," he said from his heart, and Seonkyeong's own heart softened.

Still, there were some things that stayed unresolved in her mind. She took his hand in hers, and sat facing him.

"There's something I want to ask you," she said.

"Go on, ask me," he said.

"Today, Hayeong . . . said it was my fault that her mother died."

Jaeseong's face grew pale. Seeing his eyes waver, she wasn't sure if she should go on with the question. But she did, thinking that she couldn't keep it buried forever.

"Did . . . something happen, to make her think that?" she asked.

He put her hand down, and rubbed his face with his hands. He looked as if he didn't know how to tell her.

"It's all right. You can tell me anything. Just tell me what happened," Seonkyeong prodded gently, and finally, he spoke.

"A little after our honeymoon, I got a phone call saying that Hayeong was hurt. There was a message saying that she was in critical condition, and I ran to her, half out of my mind. But it turned out that the critical condition consisted of scraped elbows and knees.

She had fallen somewhere, it seemed. I lashed out at her mother. I told her not to call me again with something like this, that I was married to someone else now. I yelled at her, saying that I was sick and tired of her calling me on the pretext of the child's interests, and that I would never come again," he said.

He had never spoken of this. He had only told Seonkyeong that their relationship was completely over, and that she wouldn't even let him see the child. According to him, Hayeong's mother had lied to him often, saying that the child was ill, in order to see him. But if that had been the problem, Seonkyeong wasn't to blame.

"What does it mean, it's my fault that her mother died?" she asked.

He looked away, saying nothing. Seonkyeong pressed, grasping his arm and shaking it.

"There must be a reason she thinks that, don't you think?"

"Her mother took something that night. She pushed Hayeong down from the second floor, breaking her leg, then called me. I told her I wasn't coming, and she went into her room and . . ."

Seonkyeong could guess the rest.

His ex-wife, though divorced from him, had never really parted with him.

The woman, who in her heart couldn't let her husband go, dragged her daughter in to keep her husband, who kept his distance from her, within reach of her grasp. Then at last she realized that they were indeed divorced, yet could not acknowledge the fact that he had left her. Seeing that her only weapon, her own child, no longer served as a threat, she must have taken something on impulse, in despair.

"I don't know what took place between Hayeong and her mother that night, but Hayeong refused to see me after that. Her mother probably said some harsh things to her," he said.

A daughter takes her mother's pain and despair to heart. Even if the mother pushes her and breaks her leg, the child sees the situation through the eyes of the mother, who is the weak party. It followed that for Hayeong, the one to blame was the person who took her father away from her and her mother.

"I see what you're saying," Seonkyeong said.

She felt exhausted. Her relationship with the child wouldn't have been easy to begin with, without any preconceived ideas, but Hayeong was full of hatred and resentment toward her. Things wouldn't be easy, no matter the effort she made.

Jaeseong raised his head and looked at her. Hiding the anxiety welling up in her heart, she smiled to reassure him, saying, "Don't worry. Living together will clear up the misunderstanding, and then she'll open up to me."

"Thanks, honey."

"Promise me something, though."

Jaeseong looked at her with inquiring eyes.

"That you'll trust me no matter what happens."

He gazed at her for a moment, then nodded. He drew her toward himself and held her in his arms. There was a lot more that she wanted to say, but she decided not to rush.

"Do you . . . have more work to do?" he whispered in her ear.

Seonkyeong shook her head, took his hand in hers, and got up from her chair. She put the interview file and the recorder away in a drawer, and turned off the light in the study.

They were about to enter the bedroom, when they heard a scream from the second floor.

He dropped her hand and ran upstairs. Seonkyeong rushed after him, wondering what was going on.

Hayeong was sitting up in bed, crying, and threw her arms around his neck when he went in. He hugged her and patted her on the back.

"What's the matter? Did you have a bad dream?" he asked.

"Dad, I'm scared. Don't go. Don't go," the child said.

"All right. I'm not going anywhere, so don't worry and go back to sleep."

He went on patting her, and she quieted down.

Seonkyeong's and Jaeseong's eyes met, with the child in between. She could sense how awkward he was feeling. She gave a light sigh, and forced a smile.

"I'll be downstairs. Come down when she's asleep," she said.

"Okay."

Out in the hall, she felt empty inside somehow.

She was about to head to the stairs when she heard the two whispering to each other. The child seemed completely awake now. She wondered what they were talking about, but she didn't want to be in their way, so she quietly made her way downstairs.

She didn't feel like reading, so she headed straight to the bedroom. She turned off the lights, save for the little lamp, and turned in to bed. She lay restless for quite some time, listening for his footsteps, but they never came.

Then she fell asleep without realizing it, and when she opened her eyes it was morning.

No one was at her side.

THERE WAS NO TELLING what Jaeseong had said to her the night before, but Hayeong's attitude had softened considerably. Breakfast was curry from the day before. Seonkyeong scooped up some plain white rice in a bowl just for Hayeong.

Without picking up her spoon, Hayeong sat staring at the bowl of rice in front of her.

"What's wrong? Is it too much?" Seonkyeong asked.

"I . . . want some curry, too," Hayeong said, her voice barely audible.

Hearing the words, Seonkyeong glanced at Jaeseong. He gave her a furtive wink. It seemed that he had said something to Hayeong about the curry.

Seonkyeong took the bowl of rice, put the rice on a plate and poured curry over it, and set the plate down in front of Hayeong. It felt strange somehow to watch Hayeong take a careful bite of the curry.

"It's good, isn't it?" Jaeseong said, and Hayeong nodded, shyly avoiding Seonkyeong's gaze.

"I asked her, and it turns out that she's never had curry before," he said to Seonkyeong.

Seonkyeong saw now why Hayeong had hesitated the night before, with the plate of curry in front of her. She felt bad for the misunderstanding. On the other hand, she found it odd that the child had never had curry before. What had her mother cooked for her?

Jaeseong seemed touched by their sitting down at the table and having breakfast together, something that was just a part of everyday life for many families. He sat there gaping at Hayeong as she ate, and whenever his eyes met Seonkyeong's, he took his eyes off the child and smiled sheepishly. He pushed the side dishes closer to Hayeong, urging her to eat more.

"Here, try this. Vegetables make you healthy," he said, making the child more and more uncomfortable with each comment, which he didn't seem to notice.

"Don't push her, let her eat in peace. You need to finish eating and get ready for work. You're going to be late," Seonkyeong said.

"Huh? Oh . . . am I bothering you?" he asked Hayeong. She shook her head, but kept her eyes down, focusing on the food.

"See? She doesn't mind. You're worried about nothing," he said, sounding like a child himself.

Seonkyeong said no more, not wanting to nag. He kept on fussing over the child, then saw the time and rushed to his feet.

"Hayeong, you'll be all right by yourself?" he asked.

Hayeong barely nodded.

"She needs to change schools, and there's probably a lot of other things to be taken care of as well. Thank you, darling," he said to Seonkyeong.

"Sure, don't worry about it. I'll see you later," Seonkyeong said, seeing him off, and returned to the kitchen.

Hayeong finished the rest of her food, and got up to put her plate away.

"It's all right, you can just leave it. I'll put them away after I'm finished," Seonkyeong said.

Hayeong sat back down and waited for Seonkyeong to finish eating. For a moment, there was only the sound of utensils clinking against the dishes. As she ate, she noticed that Hayeong was staring intently at her.

"What is it?" Seonkyeong asked.

"My dad told me" was Hayeong's reply.

"Told you what?"

"That you don't have a mom, either."

It had been twenty years already since her mother passed away. She had never thought, however, that she didn't have a mother.

"She's just not with me now. That doesn't mean that I don't have a mom," she said.

"How did your mom die?"

"It's better to say 'passed away.' She passed away through a car accident."

"Does your mom come to you in your dreams, too?"

The child must have dreams about her mother from time to time. Seonkyeong envied her. She had never had a dream about her mother since her death. She missed her so much that she wanted to see her, if only in her dreams, but her wish had never come true.

"So you see your mom in your dreams," she said.

"Yes. I get so scared," said the child, shivering. The look on her face startled Seonkyeong, and she remembered what Jaeseong had said the night before.

The day she killed herself, the woman had pushed her child down from the second floor, making her break a leg.

Seonkyeong wondered what kind of person she had been. It didn't matter that she had been in deep despair. How could she do that to her own child, and then kill herself?

"Are you afraid of . . . your mom?" Seonkyeong asked with caution.

Hayeong shut her mouth. Her face stiffened as it had the day before, and she looked at Seonkyeong with cold eyes.

"I . . . don't want to talk about her," she said.

"Oh, I'm sorry. I shouldn't have asked," Seonkyeong said.

Looking at Hayeong, Seonkyeong fell into thought.

The child seemed to miss her mother a lot, given the way she had blamed Seonkyeong the day before, but now she seemed afraid of her mother. She talked about her, but then clammed up when asked questions about her. She seemed to have mixed feelings about her mother—she both missed her and resented her.

Seonkyeong could guess how Hayeong's mother must have acted around her. She must have been very unstable, to use her child in an attempt to win her husband back after the divorce. Hayeong must have lived in fear and anxiety, always trying to see what kind of mood her mother was in. Living with a mother who could explode any minute must have been overwhelming for little Hayeong.

"It's okay because they're only dreams . . . because she's dead," Hayeong said, gazing into the distance with cold eyes. They were much too cold to be the eyes of a child. Seonkyeong felt a chill at the back of her neck.

Her mother must have tormented her so much, for her to say such a thing. It had been only a day, but Seonkyeong could feel how difficult Hayeong's life must have been. What the child needed now was to forget the difficult times and regain stability. Living a new life with her father, she would forget those painful days and her hatred of her mother.

"Now, what shall we do today? Shall we go shopping?" Seonkyeong asked in a cheerful voice, to change Hayeong's mood. At her words, Hayeong turned her head to look at Seonkyeong and nodded, smiling for the first time. The cold expression on her face had turned into one that was childlike.

13.

IRECTOR HAN CALLED BEFORE SEONKYEONG'S SECOND interview with Yi Byeongdo.

She had meant to call him after her visit to the prison, but she'd been so preoccupied with Hayeong that she had forgotten.

He asked her about the interview, and she told him about the ridiculously short time she'd been given and about Yi Byeongdo's attitude. The director said that anyone who interviewed a criminal for the first time was bound to get tangled up in a power struggle with him, and advised her not to let him drag her into one. He also asked if there was anything else that had made her uncomfortable, so she told him that the people at the prison security department hadn't seemed too happy with the conducting of the interviews.

After listening to Seonkyeong, the director said that he would ask for cooperation from the national police agency and the prosecution through an advisory body, and that she should let him know if there was anything she needed at any time.

The phone call made Seonkyeong realize once again that there was a lot of attention focused on these interviews. It seemed that the police, as well as the director, were waiting for a clue that would help solve the cold case. They would throw questions at her after each interview. Seonkyeong had a headache from these thoughts swirling around in her head.

Naturally, she didn't feel at ease as she went to see Yi Byeongdo again three days later.

He must have sensed that from her, since he was more cooperative than he had been during the previous interview. To get it over with, Seonkyeong handed him the questionnaire she received at a seminar. But he just stared at her, without so much as moving a finger. She decided to take the bull by the horns, to avoid a power struggle, as the director had advised, and not wanting the interview to be an ordeal.

"Are you going to make it difficult again?" she blurted out, her palm on her forehead, not hiding her irritation.

Without a word, Yi Byeongdo reached his hands out toward her. Seonkyeong looked at him in silence.

"Didn't I tell you to bring me a big, ripe apple? I think I can ask for that much, for telling you my story—don't you think?" he said, sounding as if he meant it.

Seonkyeong, who had stopped by the market before coming to the prison, took out an apple from her bag and handed it to him. He reached out his cuffed hands and took the apple.

He lifted it into the air and studied it for a moment, like a sommelier raising a wineglass and observing the color of the wine. The apple was big, a whole handful, just as he had wanted.

"This one's been in storage. Well, I guess it's too early for freshly harvested apples," he said, and bit into it without reserve. It seemed that he hadn't had an apple in a long time—he closed his eyes, slowly moving his chin as he savored the taste. He tilted his head back, enjoying the apple, then began to take big, crunchy bites. He finished it off in an instant, as if he had been starving for a long time. He even ate the skin and the seeds, and only the juice from the apple remained on his hand. His mouth was wet all around with the juice. Seonkyeong recalled what the investigators had said.

Focus. He focused his attention completely, even when it came to eating an apple. Seonkyeong could almost see him in the act of committing one of his murders. He smiled, looking at her with satisfaction.

"I can tell what kind of person you are, from the apple you picked out," he said.

His eyes looked playful for a second as he watched her, wiping his mouth with his sleeve. As the security manager had said, he was enjoying this. The moment she said anything in reply, he would seize control of the situation.

As Seonkyeong hesitated, he went on speaking.

"Did you know that apples aren't as sweet when they're big? They have to be the right size to be good," he said.

"I'll get you a smaller one next time," Seonkyeong said.

"No, I like big apples. I've always eaten big ones."

His gaze was roaming somewhere over Seonkyeong's shoulders. The apple, it seemed, meant something more than just a fruit to him. The look on his face was not one of satisfaction after eating an apple, but that of someone recalling some distant memory of an apple.

Seonkyeong quickly handed him the questionnaire. He seemed pleased with the apple he had just eaten, and calmly filled out the questionnaire like an obedient student.

The questionnaire consisted of basic questions whose answers would be used for various materials, such as criminal statistics. Providing one's age, native province, academic background, occupation, address, age at the time of the first offense, and so on didn't require much thought. It didn't mean, though, that the information wasn't important. The interview would be based on such fundamental facts.

Answering the questions without hesitation, he handed the questionnaire back to Seonkyeong. With the paper before her, she began to ask the real questions.

"We talked about our first memories last time, didn't we?" she began.

"Red shoes," he said, repeating what Seonkyeong had said.

"Yes, my mother bought them for me. Should we start with the memories of our mothers, then?"

"Did you like those red shoes?"

"I must have liked them a lot, since I still remember them."

"Or maybe you remember them because your mom got you a color you don't even like."

Looking at him, Seonkyeong tried to see if there could be an ulterior motive to his words.

"I have both good and bad memories of my mother, of course. But luckily, I have more good ones than bad. How about you? What kind of memories do you have about your mother?" she asked.

Yi Byeongdo, who had looked as if he would start humming just a moment before, stiffened up. But then he smiled, and began to talk.

"My mother . . . I haven't thought about her in a long time. I don't remember her very well, actually. I never saw her after she left home, when I was seventeen or eighteen."

"She left home for good?"

He made no reply.

"Do you remember the reason why?" Seonkyeong probed.

"The reason? Oh, you mean the reason why she left home. No, I never thought about the reason."

Yi Byeongdo seemed to be tracing back his memories, so Seonkyeong quietly waited for him to go on speaking.

"The reason why she left home . . . could have been the cat. The cat that used to come to our house. It was black, with yellow eyes. My mom loved that cat. She even bought cans of food to feed the cat. When she left home, it stopped coming. It must have known she was gone."

"What does the cat have to do with your mother leaving home?"

"I'm just saying . . . that the cat never came back after that."

His words didn't add up. He was saying that his mother, who loved cats, left home because of a cat. Why was he saying something that didn't make any logical sense? Studying his face closely, she noticed something interesting.

Whenever Yi Byeongdo said the word "cat," his eyes narrowed. It was clear that "cat" stimulated his memory more than "mother." Seonkyeong didn't know what they had to do with each other, but he clearly didn't want to talk about his mother leaving home.

"Do you have any other memories of your mother?" she asked.

He looked up at her, then looked away. Frowning, he searched his memory; he bit his lip, as if he didn't want to talk, but then began.

"I don't remember very well because it was so long ago, but I do recall a few things. I slipped in the tub once and drank some water, and she scooped me out and performed CPR on me; when she was feeling good, she sang to me. She sang beautifully. Whenever she sang, I ended up closing my eyes and falling asleep without even realizing it."

Song. She remembered the song he had sung the last time.

His very first memory.

It must have been the song his mother sang to him. A little speck of light had shone through the darkness. Seonkyeong decided that she would follow the little light.

"Was it the song you sang to me the last time?" she asked.

Startled, he stared at her, and nodded.

"I don't remember her face, but I . . . do recall that song sometimes," he said.

His mother left home when he was seventeen. He must remember her face.

He was lying. He had no reason to lie, and yet he was saying that he didn't remember his mother's face. He didn't remember his mother's face, but he remembered the color of the cat she'd looked after, even the color of its eyes.

Or perhaps he wasn't lying. It could be that he really didn't remember her face. Why was his brain, then, trying to erase her face? The fact that his memory was distorted meant that a key lay there.

Seonkyeong wrote down the words, "mother," "song," "leaving home," and "cat," and asked him another question.

"Don't you miss her? Haven't you ever looked for her?"

"I don't miss her, and I don't want to look for her."

Seonkyeong looked at him inquiringly.

"She was the same way. She never looked for me, and she never missed me," he mumbled, staring off into space as if his mother were standing before his eyes. His eyes and lips were smiling, but only to mask his anger. The string on the mask was so near to breaking that it looked as if the mask would drop any minute. No, it was already broken on one side, starting to reveal his real face.

"'You're a filthy bastard. You should never have been born into this world. You're cursed.' These are the words my mom said to me ever since I was born. You've never heard such words in your life, have you?" Yi Byeongdo asked, looking earnestly at Seonkyeong.

She looked straight into his eyes for a moment, then shook her head.

"Those were the only things I ever heard growing up. To her, I was . . . Do you think that, too? Am I such an awful monster?" he asked.

"It doesn't matter what I think."

"No, it's important. It's . . . very important!"

"Why? What does it matter what I think?"

"Because . . . you can change me."

His words seeped into her heart, staining it with pain, like dye coloring a piece of cloth. Strangely, she didn't feel that he was lying.

She didn't know him well, but as she sat looking into his eyes and listening to his voice, he seemed like someone she'd known for a long time.

"So you want me to talk about my mom? You want to hear about my childhood?" he asked.

She watched his face, then put down her pen and closed her notebook. She wanted to focus on his trembling voice. She wanted to listen carefully to what he had to say. It was a strange feeling. She could sense herself focusing on his soul.

"My childhood . . ." He paused and fell into deep thought, his head lowered. He sat still for a while, then lifted his prison garb and showed her his body. Faint traces of old wounds remained. The wounds were everywhere.

"This is my childhood," he said.

If his mother left home when he was seventeen, it had been more than fifteen years. Even after all those years, his body was scarred with the terrible things she had done to him. His memory couldn't be any different from his body. The wounds on his mind could have left deeper scars than the traces of violence inflicted on his body.

When he had been talking about the memories of his mother, she had sensed soon enough that they weren't happy memories for him. The memory he recalled was not of warm, happy days with his mother, but the day he nearly drowned in the bathtub, struggling in pain. She began to understand why the song his mother had sung to him had become the theme song for his crimes.

She realized why she had come to focus on him completely. He had shed himself of everything and bared himself to her. His honesty had touched her.

Unable to say a word, Seonkyeong just watched his face. His fleeting expressions revealed what he was thinking. Suddenly, she sensed deep pain in his face.

"Damn it, I don't want to talk about this! I don't want to remember her!" he shouted, slapping the table with his cuffed hands over and over again.

The prison guard who had been sitting by the door got to his feet in surprise. Seonkyeong raised her hand and kept him at bay. Yi Byeongdo needed this time to express his feelings. His true face, revealed through his emotions, not through a power struggle or calculated behavior, would give her the information necessary to understand him.

"If she was going to raise me that way, she should have just strangled me or abandoned me. Why did she treat me so terribly, why? She . . . never should've had me," he mumbled, his voice trembling. He shook his head, then held his face in his hands. He sat still with his head bent low. It seemed that he didn't want to be seen crying.

He must have been unwelcome, even by his mother, ever since he was born. He grew up under a mother who constantly cursed him and abused him. Seonkyeong felt disturbed, hearing him cry that he didn't have any good memories, that he didn't want to remember anything because it was so awful. She didn't know why, but his mother had left all her problems for her child to handle, and poured out her anger and pain on him in the form of physical abuse. Things might have been different if there had been anyone else around, but there hadn't been.

Why did his mother say that he was filthy, that he should never have been born?

"Why did she treat you that way?" she asked, waiting for him to start talking again, but he just sat there, his face still in his hands, for a long time. The silence stretched on.

"Mr. Yi?" Seonkyeong said.

He didn't even raise his head. Perhaps he was angry at Seonkyeong for opening old wounds and making him think about them.

After sitting in silence for a long time, he looked up.

"What's the statute of limitations on murder?" he asked.

Seonkyeong was momentarily thrown off by the unexpected question. What surprised her even more, though, was the peaceful look on his face; she had expected red-rimmed eyes, after his emotional outburst. His voice was calm as well. The changes in his mood were like summer showers. He was no longer agitated, and the faint smile had returned to his face. A mask was covering his face again. Seonkyeong sighed, feeling drained.

"There's no statute of limitations on murder," she said.

"I see. Well, let's say . . ." He paused midsentence, glanced over at the prison guard, then cupped his mouth and spoke in a lowered voice. Seonkyeong had to lean forward because his voice was so low.

"Let's say that I killed my mom. Would I be sentenced to death? Or life imprisonment?" were his words.

Seonkyeong stared at him in shock. She peered into his eyes, trying to see what he really meant. He grinned at her, got up from his seat, and shouted to the prison guard that he wanted to return to his cell.

Seonkyeong could neither get up nor call out to him.

At the word "mother," he'd shown her his scarred body. He said his childhood had been hell. He said his mother left home when he was seventeen, but Seonkyeong knew intuitively that it wasn't true. Had he killed his mother, then?

If so, his first act of murder had been committed a long time ago.

Leaving the room, he didn't say a word to Seonkyeong. She didn't take her eyes off him. He was now expressionless, but he had shown her his true face, with the mask off. The shock kept her from moving for a while.

She could not begin to guess what it must have been like to be under constant abuse, physical and verbal, by a mother who was your only family, ever since you were born. Just thinking about how such an environment must have broken his soul overwhelmed her.

Collecting her notebook and recorder in silence, she thought of Hayeong.

Hayeong came to the house on the day Seonkyeong had interviewed Yi Byeongdo for the first time. She hadn't realized it then, but Hayeong's eyes were strangely similar to his. Both Hayeong and Yi Byeongdo pretended to be strong but were infinitely vulnerable, and the sharp, cold gaze betrayed loneliness.

Yi Byeongdo's cold eyes sometimes made Seonkyeong want to take him into her arms and heal his wounds. In this thirty-four-year-old man was a child who had never grown up. Perhaps he made her think of Hayeong because she saw a wounded child in his eyes.

Little Hayeong, too, had been repeatedly hurt by her mother.

How had those memories affected her? What would she be like as she grew up? Finding herself thinking such thoughts, Seonkyeong was startled, and shook her head. She felt terrible for equating Hayeong with Yi Byeongdo.

Hayeong was different from Yi Byeongdo. Her father was at her side, protecting her; and her grandparents, though they passed away in a fire, had cared for her with love. And now, a new environment awaited to help her heal from her past shock and pain. Hayeong had plenty of time to recover from her wounds. If someone kept watch over her, helping the festering wounds mend and new flesh grow in their place, she would grow up healthy.

Hayeong was different from Yi Byeongdo.

14.

SEONKYEONG WAS BUSY ALL MORNING WITH HAYEONG'S transfer procedures.

Ever since Hayeong moved in, all the tasks concerning her, big and small, had fallen to Seonkyeong.

She had a lot more discretionary time compared to Jaeseong, who was often tied up at work; besides, the semester was over, and she didn't really have to go anywhere. So naturally, she had come to take care of Hayeong's affairs. It was Seonkyeong who decorated her room, and bought her clothes and other necessities. She had expected this work to fall on her, but doing it all on her own, she felt somewhat unhappy that Jaeseong didn't seem to care much. Compared to Hayeong's disappointment, however, her own feelings of unhappiness were nothing.

Hayeong followed her father around until he went off to work, chattering and clinging to him, playing the baby. He coddled her and was quite responsive for the first few days, but being busy getting ready for work, he soon began to respond half-heartedly, or not at all. The research paper he had long been working on also kept him from paying her sufficient attention, but this excuse did not satisfy Hayeong.

Sensing his distance, she began to talk less and less to her father, and didn't cling to him as much. This morning, she hadn't even come downstairs.

While getting ready to go to school to apply for Hayeong's transfer, Seonkyeong went up to the second floor. She knocked and opened the door, and found Hayeong in bed. Hayeong, who had expected her father to come cheer her up before he went to work, sulked through breakfast. It seemed that her mood hadn't lifted.

"I'm going to the school you'll be attending, Hayeong. Why don't you come with me?" Seonkyeong said, not wanting to leave Hayeong alone in an unfamiliar house, and thinking it wasn't a bad idea for her to see the school.

Seonkyeong waited for a while, but no answer came.

"Don't you want to see what the school's like?" she asked again.

Still no response. Without pressing further, Seonkyeong stepped out of the room. She couldn't force her to come if she didn't want to.

When Seonkyeong left her bedroom a short while later, ready to go out, she found Hayeong by the front door, already dressed. She didn't want to stay alone in an empty house, it seemed.

Taking Hayeong with her, Seonkyeong stopped at the community service center for a copy of a resident registration certificate for Hayeong. Submitting the certificate at the school would complete the transfer process. The school wasn't even ten minutes away from home, so there wouldn't be a problem with her commuting to school by herself.

To help cheer her up, Seonkyeong tried to talk to her all the way to the school.

She asked what her old school had been like, and if she had friends there she could call, but Hayeong didn't say anything. She didn't seem curious about her new neighborhood, either. It was as if it didn't matter to her where she was; she wasn't interested in her external surroundings. She was like a turtle inside its hard shell. Like a mimosa that shrank at external stimuli, Hayeong seemed to have closed her heart to everything.

She wasn't opening up to Seonkyeong, either. They didn't know each other well, and Hayeong didn't seem to want to get to know her. She was just tolerating her, since she was someone who lived with her father. For them to get to know and understand each other, they needed time and opportunity, but the person who should be mediating between the two was too busy with work to do so.

Seonkyeong could feel that Hayeong, who was putting up with her and following her around, was shrinking further and further inside. Seonkyeong stopped asking questions. As she made up her mind to tell Jaeseong to pay more attention to the child when he came home, the school came into view.

Walking into the schoolyard with Hayeong and seeing the charming school building, Seonkyeong felt a faint longing in her heart.

She had never been to an elementary school after graduation. The school wasn't the one she had attended, but it didn't look unfamiliar. The little buildings, four stories high, were painted in different colors, and the schoolyard was on the small side. She heard children running and chattering away during gym class. Seonkyeong had had such days as well, but they seemed more than a hundred years ago, and she couldn't remember clearly.

It had been a week since Hayeong's arrival. The feeling of suddenly finding herself a school parent wasn't something she could put into words. Her friends who had gotten married early on had long since become such, but for Seonkyeong, who wasn't even used to being married yet, being parent to a schoolchild was as strange and awkward as wearing someone else's clothes. There had been no time at all for her to prepare; it was no wonder that she felt clumsy and awkward.

She felt the same way about the transfer. She had no idea who to go to with her questions. In the end, she had searched the Internet and prepared all the papers herself. It wasn't as difficult as she'd imagined, but she realized for the first time that being a parent required a lot of knowledge she didn't have.

Walking through the schoolyard, Seonkyeong felt nervous and afraid, as if she were the one transferring to a new school. This moment signaled a new beginning for Seonkyeong as well. She took a deep breath in spite of herself, and felt for Hayeong's hand.

She was about to take the child's hand, but Hayeong shook her off. Regardless of Seonkyeong's feelings, the child was glaring at the school, her mouth firmly closed. It seemed that she was still in a bad mood, either because of what had happened that morning, or because she was nervous about being in a strange new school.

While Seonkyeong met with the registrar to complete the transfer process, Hayeong sat quietly in a corner of the teachers' room. It wasn't as difficult as she'd imagined. As soon as the resident registration certificate was submitted, Hayeong was assigned to a class.

The registrar got to his feet, saying that Hayeong could meet her homeroom teacher.

"Your homeroom teacher will be here soon. Come on, let's say hello," Seonkyeong said.

Hayeong, however, shook her head and went outside. Seonkyeong rushed after her, but she was running off in the distance. The registrar came down the staircase off to the side of the hallway, with a teacher, a woman in her mid-thirties.

"This is Ms. Im Eunsil, Hayeong's homeroom teacher. And this is the mother of Yun Hayeong, who is transferring to this school," introduced the registrar.

"How do you do? And I'm sorry, but she's run off that way," Seonkyeong said.

"Oh, it's all right. She probably wanted to look around the school," the registrar said, quite unconcerned, and guided Seonkyeong back to the teachers' room.

The homeroom teacher made a list of things Hayeong would need, and handed it to Seonkyeong. The textbooks would be provided by the school. The teacher made a good impression on Seonkyeong, speaking calmly and looking exactly like an elementary school teacher. Worried about Hayeong, Seonkyeong could not really focus on talking to her.

Seonkyeong asked the teacher to take good care of Hayeong, and handed her a business card. She thought she should be in close touch with the teacher while Hayeong adjusted to her new school. She felt somewhat relieved, hearing the teacher tell her not to worry, that she would watch Hayeong. Seonkyeong wondered if she should tell the teacher about Hayeong's situation, but decided against it, not wanting to plant preconceptions in her mind. It was decided that Hayeong would start coming to school the next day, and they said goodbye.

Outside, Seonkyeong looked around for Hayeong. She wasn't in the schoolyard. Only after she had looked around two school buildings, as well as the storage shed, did she find the child.

Hayeong was at the nature study area at the foot of the mountain behind the school. There was a vegetable patch, off to the side behind the storage shed, with a fence around it. Lettuce, peppers, and tomatoes grew there, and little pickets with class numbers on them were planted here and there among the vegetables; it seemed that each class was in charge of a different section. Next to the vegetable patch was an animal farm, surrounded by a wire fence.

Hayeong was sitting in front of the wire fence, watching the rabbits. Seonkyeong felt relieved at last.

"So here you are. Are you watching the bunnies?" she asked.

Standing by Hayeong, she looked through the fence and saw that there were all kinds of animals, just as there had been all kinds of vegetables in the vegetable patch. There were rabbits, chickens, and ducks, each in their section, and a number of birdcages in another area.

Hayeong, who had been quietly watching the rabbits, got to her feet, having lost interest. She didn't leave the farm, though, and went toward the birdcages. She looked around for something to feed the birds, and plucked a lettuce leaf from the vegetable patch and placed it in a cage.

The birds seemed used to children, and came near the lettuce with no sign of fear. As one or two began to peck at the lettuce, others came down and followed suit. Hayeong, who had been watching them for a while, suddenly opened the cage door and attempted to grab a bird. The birds, which had fled her hand, squeezed out through the open door into the sky.

Seonkyeong rushed over, pulled Hayeong's hand out, and closed the cage door. Some birds had already flown away without a trace.

"What are you doing? All the birds are flying away," Seonkyeong scolded.

Hayeong looked at her with clear eyes, then turned her head as if she had lost interest, and bent her steps toward the schoolyard. Seonkyeong could neither rebuke nor nag her. She sighed in spite of herself.

On the way back home, she stopped at the market and bought some clothes, underwear, and socks for Hayeong. She also bought school supplies at a stationery shop. There was a ton of things to buy for her, since she had lost everything in the fire. Seonkyeong had been buying things ever since Hayeong moved in, whenever something crossed her mind, but she continued to see things that the child would need. She went to a curtain shop and ordered new curtains, and bought an extra blanket as well. Her hands full of shopping bags, she kept thinking of things she had to buy still.

While she picked out things to buy and paid for them, Hayeong followed quietly. She showed some response when Seonkyeong held out articles of clothing, since she was the one who would be wearing them. She didn't say no, but Seonkyeong could tell by the look on her face. She seemed to like some of the clothes, as she readily took a shopping bag from Seonkyeong and kept looking inside.

Seonkyeong's mood changed depending on Hayeong's. She wondered if she was concerning herself too much with the child, but she thought that for now, the child needed the attention. She wouldn't have to worry about every little thing once she adjusted to her new environment and settled in, she thought.

They hadn't been out too long, but by the time they got home, Seonkyeong was completely exhausted. Taking care of a child wasn't as easy as she'd thought.

THE NEXT DAY, while Hayeong was at school, Seonkyeong had a mountain of tasks to accomplish. She bought more clothes for Hayeong, having left out some items the day before, and ordered books and a dresser for her room as well. She also had to do the grocery shopping. She came home to meet the delivery time for the furniture and the groceries, and the truck was already at the gate, waiting for her.

She hastened to open the gate, and led the movers to Hayeong's room on the second floor. She had cleaned the room before going out, so the furniture was promptly put in place. Once the furniture was set up, everything followed smoothly.

Seonkyeong had given Hayeong her things to take upstairs the day before, telling her to put them away herself since they were hers, but opening the wardrobe now, she found them still in their packages. She took the bedspread and the blanket out of their packages and put them on the bed, and hung the clothes on hangers and put them in the wardrobe. The underwear and the socks, she folded and put in the new dresser. She placed the bag and the stationery on the desk, and realized it was past lunchtime.

She went down to the first floor, got herself some water from the fridge, and thought for a moment to see if she had left anything out. The first thing that came to her mind was a computer. She should get Hayeong a laptop, she thought. She would need one, since even elementary school children used the Internet. She thought she should leave that to Jaeseong, though. Going shopping together on his day off would appease Hayeong's mood.

Catching her breath at last, she went into the living room, and thought of the teddy bear in Hayeong's room.

Because the bear was dirty, she had taken out the blanket Hayeong had used to be washed. She decided that the bear should be washed as well. She went back upstairs and brought the stuffed animal down.

She filled the tub with water. She put some detergent in the water and worked up a lather, and put the stuffed animal into the tub. As she squeezed it with her hands, dirty water oozed from it. It hadn't been washed in so long that no matter how many times she rinsed it, the water that came out was still murky. The original white color of the stuffed animal was restored only after she had struggled with it for an hour.

She put the stuffed animal in the washer for a spin cycle, and collapsed on the sofa, utterly worn out. She felt good despite her exhaustion.

She happily pictured Hayeong, pleased with her new furniture, new blanket, and her clean teddy bear. She looked at the clock and saw that it was almost two already. She rushed to her feet and began to prepare a snack for Hayeong. Only then did she realize that she hadn't eaten lunch. She could imagine how busy her friends with kids must be all day.

Time passed too quickly, and the tasks were endless.

The washer beeped, signaling the end of the cycle. The stuffed animal was as fluffy as new and smelled nice. Seonkyeong hung the laundry to dry and was going into the living room when Jaeseong called. He said he was leaving work early, which he hadn't been able to do in a while, and told her to get ready to go out as soon as Hayeong came home. She had told him the night before to pay some attention to Hayeong because she was sad, and he seemed to have taken it to heart.

Hayeong came home around two thirty. There were a lot of things Seonkyeong wanted to ask her, since it had been her first day at school.

"How was school? Did you make any friends?" she asked.

Hayeong seemed tired, and went upstairs without an answer.

"Your dad will be home soon. Get some rest, then get changed and come downstairs," Seonkyeong said.

Thinking the heat must have wiped her out on her way home, Seonkyeong quickly went into the kitchen and opened the fridge. If they went out as soon as Jaeseong came home, they would probably have lunch together, so she didn't take out the snack she had prepared. She took out some cold juice instead and poured it into a glass. She put the juice bottle back in the fridge and turned around, just as Hayeong came stomping down the stairs, looking as if she were about to pounce on Seonkyeong.

"Did you go into my room?" she demanded.

"Huh?"

Seonkyeong wondered what was wrong. Of course she had, to set up the new furniture, and put things in order. She felt bewildered, not knowing what the problem was.

"Where is it?" Hayeong demanded again.

"Where's what?"

"My teddy bear."

Relaxing, Seonkyeong smiled and said, "I washed it, because it was quite dirty."

"Where is it, I asked!" Hayeong screamed, before Seonkyeong had even finished speaking. Glaring at her, Hayeong looked more fierce than Seonkyeong could have imagined her to be. Stunned, Seonkyeong couldn't say a word.

Hayeong stood there glaring at her for a moment, then ran outside. Seonkyeong's mind went blank. Hayeong's face, screaming at her, haunted her.

Hayeong, who had been to the veranda, was holding the teddy bear in her hand. Without even glancing at Seonkyeong, she stomped back upstairs. Seonkyeong felt confounded. She had been so happy, running around all day getting things done for Hayeong, but the feelings of happiness had vanished into thin air. She couldn't, however, return anger for anger. She took a deep breath, calming herself, and called out to Hayeong in her usual voice.

"It's not dry yet, Hayeong. Bring it down."

It would take at least three days for the stuffed animal to dry completely. But the child neither came down nor answered. Seonkyeong listened carefully, but she couldn't hear anything from upstairs. She called out again, but to no avail. Having no choice, she went upstairs.

She opened the door and was about to go in, but then stopped. To her shock, the room was in complete chaos. Strewn all over the floor were torn fabric, lumps of cotton filling, and little Styrofoam balls.

"What . . . what are you doing?" she asked in horror.

Hayeong was cutting up the teddy bear's belly with scissors. Having trouble doing so, she hurled the scissors aside and ripped the fabric with her hands, and dug out the animal's insides. Having emptied the belly, she picked up the scissors again and attacked the bear's head. The scissors punctured the fabric without a hitch and penetrated deep inside. She didn't even seem to notice Seonkyeong.

"What are you doing? Stop it this instant!" Seonkyeong shouted, running over and grabbing her arm. Hayeong shook her hands off violently.

"I said, stop it!" Seonkyeong repeated.

She held out her hands again, and the child lifted the scissors high in the air, glaring at her. She looked as if she would lunge at her, scissors in hand, at any minute. Her eyes were ablaze. Seonkyeong had never seen anyone look so furious. She wondered if Hayeong was indeed an eleven-year-old child.

Frozen to her spot, Seonkyeong stared at her, speechless.

The scissors, still in Hayeong's hand, glittered in the sun. The glittering light flew swiftly toward Seonkyeong. She shut her eyes tight and turned aside just in time, barely preventing the blades from hitting her face. She felt a sting in her arm, though, and turned her head to see a red line on it. Blood seeped from the cut.

"What do you think you're doing?" Seonkyeong asked.

"Get out!" Hayeong shouted.

Seonkyeong's words didn't even make her blink. On the contrary, she glared at her with cold eyes, her expression unchanging, and screamed, "Get out of my room! Get out!"

From her mouth poured out curse words Seonkyeong had never even heard before. Looking at the child hurling abuses right before her eyes, Seonkyeong lifted a hand without realizing it. Rage overshadowed reason. She felt blinded.

She slapped her on the cheek, and Hayeong froze. Seonkyeong was just as shocked. She finally came to herself; she could not believe she had slapped the child. They had engaged in a war of nerves since day one, but Seonkyeong had never gotten so worked up. She looked at Hayeong, who had gone pale.

Hayeong dropped the scissors.

"Ha-Hayeong, are you all right?" Seonkyeong asked stammeringly, and went to the stunned child and felt her cheek. Hayeong's stiff face turned back into that of a child, and she burst out crying. Her eyes instantly welled up, and shed big drops of tears. Seeing her expression change in a single moment, Seonkyeong felt dumbfounded.

The child, her hands outstretched, walked past Seonkyeong toward the door, and cried, "Dad!"

Startled, Seonkyeong turned around and saw Jaeseong at the door.

She didn't know when he had come home, but by the look on his face, she guessed that he had seen her hitting the child. Holding Hayeong in his arms and comforting her, he looked at Seonkyeong with a stony face. His cold eyes showed his disappointment in her.

She understood why Hayeong's expression had changed in an instant. She felt goose bumps rise all over her body. She could not believe the child's cunning performance. Her chest felt heavy.

Jaeseong's reaction wasn't the problem. She could talk to him later and resolve the misunderstanding. What she found disturbing was the instant change in Hayeong's facial expression. It wasn't that of a child, stunned at being slapped on the cheek, seeing her dad, and crying with pent up emotion. The momentary change had been one of reason, not of emotion. She had seen the child's true intention in her eyes as she ran to her father. Her action had been calculated.

Hayeong knew what kind of feelings she would stir up in people by acting a certain way, and acted accordingly. How was she able to do that in such a brief moment? Seonkyeong was astonished at her cleverness, and wondered again what kind of environment she had grown up in.

After watching Hayeong bawl in her father's arms for a while, Seonkyeong left the room without a word. This required serious discussion with Jaeseong. But first, some time had to be allowed for him to placate Hayeong.

Seonkyeong went into the study and calmed herself. She didn't know how she should act toward Hayeong from now on. She was also worried about how Jaeseong would react, having seen his daughter getting slapped before his very eyes. No excuse could pardon what she had done, not even in her own mind.

Just as she had expected, he was quite upset with her. He soon came into the study, and stood silently looking out the window for a long time. Then he brought a chair over and sat facing her.

"Will you explain what happened?" he asked, sounding calmer than she had expected.

The calm voice, however, made Seonkyeong feel more nervous. He was someone who became quiet when he was angry.

"It was . . . yes, it was my fault that I hit her. I must have gone crazy at that moment. I . . . I couldn't put up with her screaming and cursing at me," she said.

"Why did she scream and curse at you?"

"I don't know why she became so furious."

"Something must have happened."

"It was just her teddy bear. You saw how dirty it was. All I did was wash it."

"That's all?"

"Nothing else besides that. She looked for the teddy bear as soon as she came home, so I told her I'd washed it, and . . . she took it upstairs when it was still wet, and tore it up like that."

Seonkyeong felt goose bumps rise again, thinking of Hayeong tearing up her cherished teddy bear to pieces. Where had such rage come from? Her face, as she cut up the teddy bear and glared at her, had almost made Seonkyeong's heart stop. She didn't want to admit it, but honestly, she felt afraid. She was afraid of the child. The fear had made her slap Hayeong's cheek.

Jaeseong wouldn't understand. How could she tell him that she was afraid of his daughter?

Something has to be done. Some kind of a measure has to be taken, she thought.

15.

A FTER HER DAD WENT OUT OF THE ROOM, HAYEONG WENT limp and dropped to the floor.

Something awful might have happened if he hadn't come in time. Looking at the scissors on the floor, Hayeong thought of Seonkyeong's face. She had really wanted to stab her. She couldn't understand, no matter how she thought about it. How could Seonkyeong touch someone else's belongings? Thinking about her, Hayeong felt angry again.

She grabbed and hurled whatever came into her hand, screaming. Then it occurred to her that her dad might come up if she went on screaming like that. She didn't want to listen to him nagging again. She had to be quiet.

On her first day here, he'd taken her into his arms and whispered, "If you want to live here with me, you have to listen to her."

Because of his words, she'd put up with everything, no matter how much she disliked something.

She didn't complain, even when Seonkyeong picked out old-fashioned clothes. Kids her age didn't wear stuff like that. As if playing dolls, Seonkyeong had taken her shopping, making her try on one thing after another, when she herself was the only one who was enjoying it. Hayeong was hungry and her legs hurt, but she'd put up with it because of what her father had said.

There was a pink blanket on the bed. The moment she came home and saw the blanket, she felt like puking. She didn't let on because Seonkyeong was at her side, but she got the creeps thinking she had to sleep under a pink blanket from now on. On top of that, the curtains were made of pink-and-yellow-green-checked fabric. When she came into her room, she felt sick to her stomach because of all the crazy colors. Pink was the color she hated the most in the world. But she hadn't complained about it.

She'd kept quiet because of what her dad had said, but grown-ups never listened to you anyway. They just made you do what they wanted you to do. If you ever spoke your mind, they scolded you, calling you impertinent. Living with her grandparents, Hayeong had learned that it was better not to speak at all. It hadn't been all that different living with her mom, either. She wouldn't even let her say "Mom."

Even when Hayeong broke an arm and was hospitalized, her mom wouldn't let her answer any questions from her dad or the doctor. If she so much as moved her mouth, her mom pressed down hard on her arm, which she was holding. She pressed so hard that Hayeong's eyes welled up with tears, preventing her from talking. Then her mom would speak for her. She felt unhappy thinking about her mom. She quickly shook her head to get her off her mind.

She didn't like this house, but it was a hundred times better than living with her grandmother in Eungam-dong.

From the moment she opened her eyes in the morning until she went to bed at night, her grandmother would nag incessantly, even when Hayeong was asleep. When Hayeong came into the house wearing socks, she would nag at her for not shaking the dust off; when she came in barefoot, she would make a fuss about her leaving footprints on the wooden floor. She nagged at her for eating too fast, and then for eating too slow.

Her grandmother seemed to like nothing about her—she followed her around, slapping her on the back and scolding her. Once, Hayeong made up her mind, and, sobbing, asked her grandmother to let her go live with her dad. She just snorted at her. She picked up a rod, and told her never to say such a thing again, and that he didn't care about Hayeong at all, because he had a new wife now.

Hayeong had known for some time that her grandmother was lying. Her dad did want her to live with him. But her grandmother wouldn't let her go, because her grandparents lived on the money he gave them every month for taking care of Hayeong. Hearing them fight one day, Hayeong had learned why her grandmother wouldn't let her go live with her dad, even though she hated her so much.

Because of her grandmother, it became harder and harder for Hayeong to call her dad on the phone as well. She worried that she'd never get to see him again. If not for the fire, her grandmother would still be slapping her on the back, nagging at her.

The best thing about this house was that it was quiet. When she lay in her room alone, she couldn't hear a thing. She couldn't see the awful pink, either, if she closed her eyes. Seonkyeong was in the house, but she rarely came out of the study. As a result, Hayeong had a lot of time to think things over by herself.

Just as her dad had said, she had to listen to Seonkyeong in order to live with him in this house. He was much too obliging to Seonkyeong. He did whatever she suggested, without a word. Hayeong felt angry that, sometimes, he seemed to believe Seonkyeong's words more than he did hers, but she decided to ignore this.

As time passed, she saw less of her dad, but that was all right. Her dream had come true, she was living in the same house with him.

That's why she did what Seonkyeong told her to do without complaint. She was even putting up with the color pink.

She wouldn't have cared what Seonkyeong did, whatever it was, if she hadn't laid her hands on the teddy bear.

When Hayeong came home from school and went into her room to find that her teddy bear was gone from her bed, she thought she'd go crazy. She ransacked the room, but it was nowhere to be found. She saw that Seonkyeong had touched the things in her room without asking her. Realizing that it was Seonkyeong who had taken the teddy bear, she frantically ran downstairs. She feared that Seonkyeong had thrown it away. To her relief, it was still in the house.

This was no time for her to sit and cry. She wiped away the tears on her face with the back of her hand, and began to gather up the teddy bear fabric and cotton fillings that were scattered on the floor. In a corner of a dresser drawer, she saw the plastic bag that had held the blanket. She took the bag out and swept up the torn fabric, cotton fillings, and Styrofoam into it. She took out all the cotton inside the bear's belly, but what she was looking for wasn't there.

It has to be in there, she thought.

She double-checked the cotton fillings as well. She felt more and more anxious. She could not lose it. It was a gift from her dad, and the only memento of her mom.

Nearly all the cotton on the floor had been gathered. She looked around to see if there was any remaining. She saw the bear's head under the desk. She pulled it out by an ear. She stuck her hand inside the head and poked around. She felt something hard. She had found it!

She took her hand out of the head and spread it open. It was what she'd been looking for.

Relieved, she heaved a sigh. She put the rest of the trash in the plastic bag and put it outside. She locked the door and sat down on the bed, and looked at the thing in her hand. The brown bottle sparkled in the sunlight.

Hayeong decided to hide it well, so that no one would be able to lay a finger on it. She didn't want anyone else to touch it ever again. As she looked around, a smile rose on her face.

She had thought of a place that no one else would find out about.

16.

THE NIGHTS GREW LONG AGAIN. THE NIGHTMARES YI Byeongdo had driven away long ago started visiting him once again.

He shouldn't have asked Seonkyeong for an apple. He shouldn't have smelled it. He shouldn't have eaten it. The moment he did, everything began to go wrong.

When he picked up the apple and took a bite, the hunger he had long kept at bay came over him all at once. It was because of the apple, too, that he'd been so shaken up by the interview with Seonkyeong. The apple that went down his throat spread through his body, bringing back, one by one, decade-old memories.

Memories of a place he could never return to, memories he had sealed off, ate slowly away at his sleep.

When Yi Byeongdo lay down on the cool wooden floor with his eyes closed, he could feel the chill from the apple storage.

The apples, filling hundreds of crates, were sold throughout the winter, and the remaining apples began to rot, giving off a sweet smell, as the weather began to thaw. When the sun grew warm, the woman and the girls began to pick out the rotten apples, and he put them in a crate and threw them away in a river by the orchard.

Watching the apples flowing down the river, or getting stuck midway, he thought he was like a rotten apple. No one had noticed yet, but hearing his mother's song again, his mind began to rot little by little. He fell asleep, shivering with anxiety, and was startled awake by the sound of wind or branches shaking.

You need to check them carefully. One rotten apple can make all the other apples in the box go bad.

The woman even picked out apples that still looked fine. He didn't see it, but she couldn't be fooled. It was she who first noticed that he wasn't the same as before.

What's wrong?

He acted no differently, but she saw the change in him. He didn't speak or eat any less than before, but she sensed the chill in his heart. He couldn't say anything in reply. He shook his head, indicating that there was nothing wrong, but she smiled, trying to hide the look of pity in her eyes.

You can always talk to me if you want.

He wanted to gouge it out. He wanted to gouge out the rot in his mind, and live as if nothing was wrong indeed, as he'd told her. But he couldn't. The memories of his mother, which had already spread through his body, contaminated his blood, flesh, and bones. Feeling himself rapidly rotting away, he threw himself into the river.

Yi Byeongdo learned that day in the bone-chilling cold that he had to go away. He was no different from the rotten apples dumped in the river. If he stayed, he would only give off a rotten smell and harm the woman and the girls.

And he never went back.

The day he buried his mother, he thought of the orchard house. He recalled the big, sturdy apple tree whose apples he'd always eaten. It must still bear apples that would ease his hunger. But he shook his head. He couldn't turn back the time that had gone flowing down the river. He'd left the place behind; he couldn't return.

He had thus removed the dreamy years at the orchard from his mind.

If he hadn't met Seonkyeong, he'd be going to the chair with those memories forever under lock.

In prison, he had filled the slowly passing hours, thinking back on the dozens of murders he'd committed. There were about a dozen murders he hadn't told the police about—ones he kept hidden in his memory, and thought about in secret. There were no sweet-smelling apples, but neither was there anything that got in his way. And he no longer heard his mother's song in his head. He had thought it wasn't so bad, waiting for death like that. Until he met Seonkyeong.

YI BYEONGDO WASN'T in a good mood that day.

He was chasing a cat on an empty plain, with no people or buildings in sight. He didn't know where the cat had come from; the cat, with gray fur and yellow eyes, had been hovering around him, mewling like a baby. At first he just kept walking, ignoring it. But the cat got on his nerves, stopping when their eyes met, and running when he started going after it. The cat stopped only when he had chased it into a shabby, deserted house.

It was the house where he had buried his mother. The cat had vanished, and there was a thick overgrowth of grass, untouched by human hands. There was also a rusty, discarded shovel that looked as if it were about to crumble to pieces, and one of the walls had collapsed, looking quite hideous. When he realized where he was, goose bumps began to rise from the tips of his toes. In his haste, he tried to run out the gate. But the gate, which had seemed within his reach, grew more and more distant, and the solid ground dragged his feet down like a swamp. The more he struggled, the deeper he got sucked into the mire.

His hands flailing, he felt for something to grab onto. Grasping a handful of grass, he was just about to get out, when something clutched his ankle. He turned his head and saw a bony hand clenching his foot. He kicked as hard as he could, but it was no use. His body began to fall back into the ground. It was like an antlion's pit. Again, he tried to grasp the grass around him, but everything in the yard began to sink into the swamp along with him.

"Meow!"

The cat that had led him there was sitting on the wooden floor of the house, watching him sink slowly underground. Screaming at the cat, Yi Byeongdo woke up.

The strange dream troubled him. That day, he was to see the public defender, who visited him once a month. He wanted to refuse the visit, but something told him not to. In the end, he decided to keep his feelings under control, and was on his way to the visitors' room to see him.

He was about to enter the building where the visitors' room was, when he saw a group of students beyond the glass door. Their faces were full of tension and excitement as they passed through, wearing visitor's badges.

The guard stopped him. It seemed that he would let Yi Byeongdo in after the students had passed through. So he stood there for a moment, waiting, when he saw a woman near the end of the line. Seeing her face, he felt as if he had been struck by lightning.

In that moment, everything else vanished from his view. He didn't see the prison building or the guard. There was only the woman, and himself.

It couldn't be possible. Yi Byeongdo doubted his own eyes.

The woman had come walking out of his memories, so old that they had turned into fossils, and passed right by him. The way she swept up the fallen strand of hair on her forehead reminded him of someone.

The woman at the orchard house had a habit of sweeping up falling strands of hair with the back of her hand as she picked apples, carrying a basket on a shoulder. She would wipe away the beads of sweat on her nose with the back of her hand as well, turning around to smile at him. When she smiled, her nose crinkled up.

The woman who was passing by looked like her, the way she had looked the first time he saw her at the hospital. He threw a quick glance at the name tag hanging from her neck.

VISITOR: YI SEONKYEONG

He felt somehow that the dream he'd had the night before was a sign. It seemed that something had led him to come out, despite the terrible mood he was in, so that he would meet her. She passed right by him and walked toward the group of students. She didn't notice him watching her at all.

On his way to the visitors' room, he talked to the guard and dug up some information on the students and the woman who were visiting. All he managed to find out was that they were from the department of criminology at some university, but that was enough.

As he began to wake up from nightmares more and more often, he kept thinking back to that day. He shouldn't have gone to the visitors' room, when he was feeling so disturbed. Then he would never have met her. He had destroyed his own peace.

Hundreds, thousands of rotten apples had gone down the river by the orchard. The trees, loaded with clusters of apples, had broken or died, with only withered branches remaining. It was all because of his greed. His desire to go back to the orchard house, to see the woman just one more time, had tainted the purity of the place. It couldn't be undone.

Awake, he thought in the darkness, his eyes gleaming: What is it that I want? What is it that I want to find out, so much that I wait for her like this? Seonkyeong was not the orchard woman. He had reminded himself of the fact over and over again, but he kept forgetting.

He began to grow more and more uneasy. He sensed the sound of his mom singing approaching little by little, from very far away.

When he reopened the room sealing up the memories, it was no longer paradise.

17.

BEFORE GOING TO THE HOSPITAL, SEONKYEONG CALLED
Heeju, who ran a child psychology clinic.
Heeju was a friend she had studied psychology with in col-
lege. They'd lost touch when Seonkyeong went abroad to study, but
Heeju had come to her wedding the year before, surprising her. After
a round of photos with Seonkyeong's other friends in the bridal wait-
ing room, Heeju said to Seonkyeong when they were alone together:
To be honest, I don't like him that much.

Heeju had a habit of beginning her remarks with the phrase "to
be honest." True to the words, she always told you in honesty what
others couldn't bring themselves to say. There were times when her
excessive frankness made Seonkyeong uncomfortable, or hurt her
feelings, but thanks to Heeju's honesty, the two had become close
friends who shared their innermost thoughts.

Heeju said that she had seen the groom, greeting the guests outside the ceremonial hall.

What don't you like about him?

That he's your husband.

Seonkyeong's thoughts were interrupted by a staff member at the
clinic picking up the call and connecting Seonkyeong to Heeju.

"An eleven-year-old child? And you're raising her?" Heeju asked, her voice escalating, after listening to Seonkyeong. It wasn't completely unexpected, but her reaction made Seonkyeong feel drained before she had even gone in for a counseling session. Heeju must have sensed it, as she didn't go any further than that.

"I guess the situation is what it is. Tell me what it was that made you call me," she said.

Now that she was ready to listen, Seonkyeong wasn't sure how to begin.

After a moment's thought, Seonkyeong began by telling her about the day Hayeong moved in. Heeju listened without interrupting. But when she got to the part about the stuffed animal, she jumped in and said, "Wait a sec, so you're saying you took away her stuffed animal, when she'd lost everything in a fire?"

"What do you mean? I just washed it for her."

"How can you talk like that, when you studied psychology?"

Seonkyeong couldn't say anything in response.

"Have you considered what the stuffed animal meant to her? You should've guessed, if she managed to bring it out with her in the confusion of a fire. What if it smelled of her mother? It would mean that you've erased her memories of her mom," Heeju said.

Seonkyeong understood at last.

She'd had a similar experience.

After her mother's funeral, she went home and opened her mother's wardrobe; she went inside, took down all the clothes from the hangers, and smelled them. There was no trace of her mother's smell, but she buried her face deeper in the clothes, thinking a little had to remain somewhere. When her father found her after hours of looking, worrying himself to death, she'd thrust her mother's scarf at him, saying, "Dad, this smells like Mom."

She didn't remember how he'd looked in that moment. She'd felt flustered, as he clutched her to his chest and began to weep, his shoulders shaking, before she even had a chance to see his face.

Soon after that day, he said that they had to gather up her mother's things and burn them, and Seonkyeong didn't speak to him for a while. She was angry that he was trying to remove her mother from his mind so soon.

She tried to put herself in Hayeong's shoes.

The woman who had pushed Hayeong's mother aside and taken possession of her father was now trying to remove all traces of her mother. It was only natural that the child resisted. On top of that, the woman slapped her. No wonder she flew into such a rage.

Seonkyeong thought back to what happened in the morning at breakfast.

Hayeong didn't even look at Seonkyeong, or answer Jaeseong's questions. She said she didn't want breakfast and her father made her sit at the table anyway, but she couldn't be forced to eat. She swung at the bowl of rice in front of her with her hand. Her father scolded her, but she didn't even blink an eye. An oppressive silence hung over the table.

"Are you listening to me?" Heeju asked, breaking into Seonkyeong's thoughts.

"Huh? Oh . . . yes, go on," Seonkyeong said.

"I'll just say one thing. At that age, she isn't as young as you think. A child that age can figure out in a second what kind of situation she's in, cause-and-effect relationships, and who holds the reins in the house. Just as you're watching her, she's watching you, sizing you up."

Seonkyeong hadn't thought of that. How distant had the child grown from her because of the incident the day before?

"Don't worry too much. It's not going to happen right away, but when she regains emotional stability and feels that she can trust you, she'll forget about what happened yesterday," Heeju said.

As Seonkyeong reflected on what happened the day before, she heard Heeju talking to someone at the other end of the line.

"I'm sorry, but I have to go in for the next session," Heeju said to Seonkyeong.

"Oh, of course. Thank you."

"Call me if you have any questions or problems."

During the brief conversation, Heeju had thrown light on an important point Seonkyeong had failed to see. Seonkyeong had judged the situation from her own point of view. She had overlooked the fact that though old and dirty, the stuffed animal meant something to the child. She had washed it and removed the only remaining traces of the child's mother with soap and suds. She saw at last what a great mistake she had made, and understood the rage Hayeong had displayed the night before.

Seonkyeong had to learn more about Hayeong before she made an even greater mistake. She had a lot of questions to ask Jaeseong in order to understand the child better.

She left the house in haste.

"WHY ARE YOU ASKING all of a sudden?" Jaeseong asked, his voice turning stiff, when Seonkyeong asked him about what had happened between his ex-wife and Hayeong. He gulped down his coffee, which he'd gotten from the vending machine in the staff lounge, and violently crushed up the paper cup.

He was puzzled that Seonkyeong had shown up at the hospital without calling him, but when she said she wanted to talk to him about Hayeong, he willingly set aside some time for her. He had just finished an appointment, and said they could have lunch together. He, too, seemed to want to talk about his daughter. But his attitude changed somewhat when she asked him about his wife as well. Seonkyeong had heard vaguely about what had happened between him and his wife, but it seemed to have wounded him deeply, as it had Hayeong.

"You must've guessed, by what I told you last time," he said.

"For me to understand how Hayeong is feeling now, I have to know what kind of relationship she had with her mother, and what happened between them," Seonkyeong insisted.

Turning his gaze out the window, he looked up at the sky in silence for a while; then at last, he began to talk, his voice thick, about what happened between them.

"She always seemed to thirst for more. When I gave her one thing, she wanted two; when I gave her two, she demanded three, she demanded ten. She always wanted me to be at her side, and cared for nothing but me. And she wanted me to care for nothing but her. She couldn't bear it when all my attention wasn't focused on her. It wasn't love; it was obsession. I felt suffocated. The more she clung to me, the further I ran. After the divorce I thought I was free, but things got worse," he said.

When they had begun to grow apart, what his ex-wife did was use their child to keep him close as he became less and less interested in her. She realized that he answered right away when it came to calls about Hayeong, whereas he usually ignored her other phone calls or text messages. Then she began reporting to Jaeseong that Hayeong was frequently sick or wounded because she knew he would respond.

"Have you . . . heard of something called MBP?" he asked Seonkyeong.

Seonkyeong nodded. The term had crossed her mind when she heard about Hayeong.

"At first it didn't occur to me. But after I realized that Hayeong was hurting herself or being hospitalized much too often, I asked her about it. She didn't know what was happening to her. Of course she didn't—how could she even have imagined that her mother was hurting her on purpose? But she did begin to sense it vaguely as time passed, often getting sick after eating something her mother had given her, and getting into accidents when they were together," he said.

MBP stood for "Munchausen by proxy," a disorder in which someone abused and hurt their child or pet to attract attention. Hayeong's mother had put her own daughter in danger to receive her husband's attention.

Seonkyeong had taken an interest in the subject while studying psychology and still had some materials that she had saved on the topic.

Munchausen syndrome was a psychological disorder in which people feigned illness for attention. They lied about being sick to gain sympathy and concern, and when the attention ebbed, they came up with a different illness.

Munchausen by proxy was a more serious disorder in which a caregiver feigned the illness of someone else, harming them intentionally, to receive attention as a "guardian" attending to the patient.

"So on that day, too, when your ex-wife died?" Seonkyeong asked.

"I think so. I'd told her I wouldn't go, even when she told me that Hayeong was hurt. I was so tired of it. She must have fallen into despair, realizing that even using Hayeong wouldn't work anymore."

He had said that Hayeong broke a leg the day his ex-wife killed herself. From what Hayeong had said, that she was afraid of her mother who appeared in her dreams, Seonkyeong knew that she was still having a hard time because of the memories. All victims of MBP were placed under threat by someone they loved and depended on. Hayeong must have been confused as to which side of her mother was real.

"I went to see Hayeong a few times after her mother died," he said.

Hayeong's maternal grandparents, who were looking after her, discouraged him from coming. They'd decided it was better for them to raise her, instead of sending her to live with him when he'd remarried. Having started a new family, he must have thought their advice seemed reasonable.

But how had Hayeong felt about it? She was already in shock after her mother's death; the adults' decision could have served as another blow. It seemed that she thought her father had abandoned her—for a while, she refused to see him.

Seonkyeong wanted to comment that Jaeseong's choice had been selfish, but couldn't. Needless to say, she must have been part of the reason why he had accepted such a decision. If misfortune hadn't fallen on Hayeong's grandparents, her life would have remained separate from the child's.

Driving home after the visit, Seonkyeong continued to think about Hayeong and her mother.

Hayeong had lost her mother at ten. Although her mother had abused and hurt her, a mother was an absolute figure to a child. Could she have known at ten? Could she have understood a mother who sacrificed her own child because she craved someone's love and attention? Hayeong missed her mother, who had done exactly that. She flew into a rage, screaming, when her mother's scent was removed from the stuffed animal.

Seonkyeong sighed, thinking of the stuffed animal. She realized again how high-handed she'd been. She hadn't even considered waiting until Hayeong came home to ask her. It wasn't just the stuffed animal—she'd decorated Hayeong's room, and bought clothes for her, based on her own tastes and judgments. She'd picked out the curtains and the blanket, without even knowing what colors the child liked. She did ask for Hayeong's opinion a few times while shopping for clothes, but she'd made the decisions before even hearing her answers. Looking back on the past several days, she saw that she had fed her, clothed her, and put her to bed the way she, not the child, wanted.

She realized that she had been cornering her.

Seonkyeong recalled what Heeju had said, that just as Seonkyeong was watching Hayeong, the child was watching her, sizing her up. She didn't even want to imagine how she must look in the child's eyes. She had been simple and indifferent. She had been rash and inconsiderate. She had to acknowledge that she wasn't ready to raise a child.

Seonkyeong reproached herself over and over again. She felt sad thinking that she had hurt the child when the child had already been hurt so much. Her heart felt heavy, full of regret.

Things couldn't go on the same way. She needed to ask Heeju for help in finding a way to approach the child. She also wanted to help her forget the wounds inflicted by her mother. It wouldn't happen overnight. It required small daily efforts.

Driving home, she was thus absorbed in thinking about Hayeong, and found herself looking at the signpost leading to Hayeong's school. It struck her as a sign.

Impulsively, she turned the wheel and headed to the school.

18.

L OOKING AT THE TIME, SEONKYEONG SAW THAT SCHOOL would let out soon, and decided to wait outside.

The bell rang, and shortly there came the sound of children chattering in the buildings and the schoolyard. One by one, they started coming out through the gate. Seonkyeong, who had been sitting in the car, came out in case she missed Hayeong.

Looking at the children spilling out, she kept her eyes peeled for Hayeong. She needn't have worried, as in a few minutes Hayeong came into view. A girl around her age was chatting incessantly to her, and Hayeong was walking quietly, listening.

"Hayeong," Seonkyeong called out to her, waving her hand. Hayeong raised her head and looked around, and found her. Her eyes opened wide in surprise. Seonkyeong hurried over to her.

"Who is this? A friend?" Seonkyeong asked.

"We sit together. My name is Choe Kaeun," the other girl said.

"Oh, it's nice to meet you. So you guys sit together. Hayeong doesn't have many friends yet, so please be a good friend to her," Seonkyeong said.

"Of course. All my friends are Hayeong's friends. Is that your car? Wow, it's so cool!"

Even as Kaeun chattered on, Hayeong remained silent, ignoring Seonkyeong. Seonkyeong quickly took Hayeong's schoolbag from her.

"You must be hungry. Shall we go have something to eat? Would you like to come, too?" she said, turning to Kaeun.

"Oh, for real?" Kaeun asked.

"You should go home," Hayeong said to the girl.

"But . . ."

"I'm just going to go home, too. All right?"

Puzzled, Kaeun stared at Hayeong, who was suddenly snapping at her, and turned to look at Seonkyeong.

"Oh, I'm sorry. It seems that Hayeong wants to go home. I'll treat you next time, Kaeun. I guess it's goodbye for now," Seonkyeong said.

"Okay, goodbye. Bye, Hayeong," Kaeun said, waving and heading toward the road. She was a friendly girl. Kids who were bright and cheerful like that made everyone else around them feel the same. Seonkyeong felt relieved that Hayeong had someone like that by her side.

Pretending that nothing had happened, Seonkyeong gave Hayeong's shoulder a pat and said, "Shall we go, then?"

Hayeong said nothing in reply.

Seonkyeong began walking toward the car, but Hayeong stood fixed to her spot.

Seonkyeong turned around to look at Hayeong, who shut her lips tightly and came up to Seonkyeong, and thrust out her hand.

"Give me my bag," she said.

"Let's drive home together."

"No. I want to walk."

"Hayeong, please."

Clutching the bag in Seonkyeong's hand, Hayeong wouldn't even look at her. Giving up, Seonkyeong took hold of her arm and said, "There's something I want to say before I give you the bag."

Hayeong didn't reply, and Seonkyeong continued.

"I'm sorry about what happened yesterday. It was my fault. I should've asked you first, but I did as I pleased. I'm sorry. I didn't know how important it was to you."

Hayeong didn't say a word.

"And I'm sorry I got angry at you and slapped you on the cheek. It'll never happen again," Seonkyeong added.

Hayeong still wouldn't look at her, but Seonkyeong could sense her listening to her words. Seonkyeong bent down and looked Hayeong in the eyes.

"I don't know anything. I have only grown-ups around me, and I've never learned how to make friends with someone as young as you," she said, and added when Hayeong didn't say anything, "I want to be friends with you. . . . Will you teach me how?"

Hayeong hesitated for a moment, staring at her, then gave a slight nod.

"Thank you," Seonkyeong said.

"Um . . . ," Hayeong began, and Seonkyeong tensed up momentarily. "I'm thirsty. I want some water," she finished.

Seonkyeong felt disappointed, but a bit relieved as well. It was the first time Hayeong had asked for something. Seonkyeong looked around. There was a convenience store nearby.

"Wait here, I'll be right back," she said, making Hayeong wait in the car while she went to the store. When she returned, however, the child wasn't there. Worried, she looked around, and found Hayeong pressed against a shop window, completely absorbed in looking inside.

Seonkyeong went up to her and handed her the water, and took a look herself.

What Hayeong was looking at, her eyes sparkling, was a puppy.

The pet shop in front of the school seemed a great attraction for kids on their way home—a number of kids besides Hayeong were clinging to the glass window, looking at the puppies or waving at them.

"Do you like puppies?" Hayeong asked, after gaping at the puppies for a while.

"Why? Do you want one?" Seonkyeong asked, and Hayeong whirled her head around and looked at her. She didn't have to say anything; her eyes were overflowing with longing for a puppy. Seonkyeong had never considered keeping a dog, but felt it would be all right, if it would help Hayeong settle down in her new environment and find stability.

Seonkyeong looked at her, and stretched out a hand. The child promptly took it. Her soft little hand fit right in Seonkyeong's own. The temperature of her hand made her feel overwhelmed for some reason. It had taken a week for her to hold the child's hand.

Seonkyeong hurried inside with Hayeong.

Puppies of various kinds—Shih Tzus, Beagles, and Maltese—were waiting in separate boxes for someone to take them home. Hayeong's heart seemed set on one already; she picked up a puppy at once. It was a white Shih Tzu, with brown eyes and ears.

"You like that one?" Seonkyeong asked.

Hayeong nodded and patted the puppy in her arms on the head. The puppy, with someone to take it home now, licked Hayeong's hand in return and dug deep into her embrace.

Seonkyeong paid for the puppy and the necessary goods, which included a crate, dog food, bath supplies, and toys, and couldn't be carried all at once.

When Hayeong came out holding her puppy, the kids who had been clinging to the shop window flocked around her. They reached out, wanting to touch it.

"No, don't touch my puppy!" Hayeong shouted.

Leaving the envious kids behind, Hayeong quickly ran to the car.

Seonkyeong loaded the trunk with the things and got in the driver's seat; she turned around and saw Hayeong holding the puppy in her arms, feeding it a snack they had just bought.

"Don't feed it too much. They said only a few a day, right?" Seonkyeong said.

Hayeong seemed much too absorbed in the puppy to even hear what she said. Seonkyeong watched her face for a moment, then started the car. She felt lighthearted, just for the fact that Hayeong had brightened up.

When they came home, a little squabble took place between them over where to put the crate.

Hayeong wanted the puppy by her bed. Seonkyeong tried to persuade her to keep the puppy downstairs, since it was still young and would have a hard time going up and down the steps. At her words, Hayeong picked up the puppy and said she'd carry it around. She even got scolded for eating with the puppy in her arms at dinner, but she wouldn't put it down. With the dog around, though, things felt more relaxed. Hayeong made no mention of the stuffed animal, and stayed in the living room for a while after dinner, playing with the puppy.

Feeling comfortable and at ease, Seonkyeong waited for Jaeseong to come home. She was eager to show him how things had changed since morning, when there had been a chill in the air. She felt relieved, thinking they'd grow more accustomed to and comfortable with each other as they continued to make little adjustments.

Seonkyeong called Jaeseong, as he showed no signs of coming home even when his work hours were over.

He said he was in a meeting. He was to present his thesis at a colloquium, to be held in a month in Washington, D.C. It seemed that he was staying late after work to prepare for it with the people at the lab.

He finally came home when it was nearing ten o'clock. He looked exhausted as he entered the house. He took off his suit jacket and handed it to Seonkyeong; on his way to the bathroom, he began to sneeze.

Hayeong came downstairs with the puppy.

"Look, Dad, I have a puppy now. The name is . . . ," Hayeong began, holding the puppy out to him. But instead of taking the puppy into his arms, he stepped back in fright. His sneezing continued.

"Get that away from me," he said.

"Are you allergic to dogs?" Seonkyeong asked.

"Why a puppy, all of a sudden? You should've discussed it with me," he snapped, angrier than necessary. Hayeong, who had wanted to show off to her father, stepped back as well, dejected, holding the puppy in her arms.

"Go return it right away," he said, looking irritated, and stormed off into the bathroom.

So Jaeseong was allergic to dogs. Seonkyeong had never imagined things would turn out this way. Not knowing what to do, she looked at Hayeong. Her face was dark with disappointment and sorrow. Seeing that, Seonkyeong felt angry with Jaeseong for flaring up and going off.

As Hayeong stood in silence, her eyes welled with tears, about to drop any second. She held the Shih Tzu closer in an effort to push back the tears. Seonkyeong hurried over to her, took her in her arms, and patted her on the head.

"Don't worry. I'll talk him into it," she said.

"You will?" Hayeong asked, looking up at her. When she blinked, the tears that had been filling up her eyes streamed down. Quickly, Seonkyeong wiped the tears away.

"Of course. Trust me," she said.

"What if he says no?"

He was home only at night, and for a little time in the morning. He spent only two or three hours with his family at home, not counting the hours they were in bed. If left in Hayeong's room for those two or three hours, the puppy wouldn't cause serious problems, even if he was allergic to dogs. Seonkyeong couldn't answer right away, though, not knowing if he would be convinced.

Waiting for an answer, Hayeong clung to her arm. Seonkyeong looked down and saw the eyes of both the puppy and the girl, at her disposal.

"Just wait awhile. I'll do my best to convince him," she said.

Hayeong brightened up immediately. She nodded, her eyes sparkling.

Hayeong went up to her room carrying the puppy. Seonkyeong brought out some fresh clothes for Jaeseong to change into, and sat on the sofa and waited, staring at the bathroom door.

When the shower came to a stop, she knocked on the door.

The door opened, and she handed him the clothes. He seemed to have forgotten all about the incident as he took the clothes and went into the bedroom. Seonkyeong followed him.

"Would you like a beer?" she asked.

"No, I'm tired. I think I'll go straight to bed."

"The puppy . . . ," Seonkyeong began.

"You . . . ," Jaeseong began at the same time.

"You seem to have grown closer to Hayeong. What happened?" he finished.

"It's all thanks to the puppy, which you seem to think is so awful," Seonkyeong said.

"I hate dogs."

"Didn't you see how happy she was, with the puppy in her arms?"

He just stared at her.

"So you're saying we should keep it?" he asked.

"It's already here. It's the first thing she's ever asked for. Do you know how disappointed she was, with you yelling at her? She waited all evening for you to come home," she said.

He scratched his head, realizing that he had gone overboard. But he wouldn't back down when it came to the puppy.

"I'm extremely allergic to dogs. I can't stop sneezing, and I itch all over," he said.

"We can keep the puppy upstairs when you're home."

"There will be dog hair all over the house. . . . Why did you have to go and buy her a puppy?" he kept grumbling.

Seonkyeong began to grow angry again. Looking annoyed, she stared at him.

"What?" he said.

"Take some pills. You're a doctor, aren't you? There must be something you can take for a dog allergy," she said.

He seemed quite taken aback to see that Seonkyeong was seriously angry. His eyes wide with surprise, he stared at her, looking dazed.

"Honey?" he said.

"Can't you sacrifice just one little thing, for the sake of your daughter? How can you be so selfish? Do you have to be so cross and ruin everyone else's mood as well?" she asked, barely managing not to blurt out *She's your kid!*

How often would she be tempted to say that in the days ahead?

She had been growing increasingly angry at Jaeseong for being more and more negligent with his child as the days passed. No matter how busy he was, he shouldn't be so indifferent when he knew what an unstable state Hayeong was in. Even after their talk during the day, he'd come home late. On top of that, he'd shouted as soon as he saw her, and wouldn't give an inch about the puppy.

Seonkyeong swallowed back the words "your kid." They were to remain taboo in the house. The moment she decided to accept the child, and to live with this man, Hayeong was no longer his child alone but theirs together.

Seeing the angry look on her face, Jaeseong, who had been grumbling, seemed quite flustered. Looking dejected, he scratched his head and tried to read her face, saying, "Okay, okay. Why are you so angry?"

"I'm fine. Just go to bed," Seonkyeong said coldly.

He came up to her, trying to make her feel better, but she stepped out of the bedroom, leaving him behind.

She was about to go into the study, but changed her mind and headed upstairs to Hayeong's room. She saw a faint streak of light through the crack in the door.

"Hayeong," she called out as she opened the door. The child was asleep. The puppy was wiggling around, digging into her arms. Seonkyeong put the puppy in its crate and placed a toy inside. Watching the face of the sleeping child, she searched for resemblances to Jaeseong. She didn't take much after her father. Considering how fitfully she had slept on her first night, waking up with a scream, the shock seemed to have lifted substantially. Her wounds would gradually heal as the days went by, Seonkyeong thought.

Gently stroking the child's hair, Seonkyeong thought back to the time when her own mother had passed away.

She had been much older than Hayeong, but things were hard for her for a very long time. She knew what a large, deep hole the loss of your mother created in your heart. Nothing could fill that hole. Whenever she felt as if a fathomless darkness lay at her feet, its mouth wide open, Seonkyeong wanted to throw herself into the hole.

Thanks to her father, she had been able to turn her back on the hole and come out where she could see the light. Thinking that the child had a hole just as deep and dark, Seonkyeong felt terribly sorry for her. She resolved that she would take her hand and guide her, just as her father had done for her.

19.

SEONKYEONG OPENED THE GATE AND STEPPED OUT, AND SAW two men, both strangers, standing there.

The man standing in front had a crew cut and a stocky build, and was dressed in a black suit. Beads of sweat had formed on his forehead, as it was a hot day. The man standing behind him, in a checked shirt, was sweating as well; his hair was all wet, and he was constantly wiping his face with a handkerchief.

"Is this Mr. Yun Jaeseong's residence?" one of the men asked.

"Yes, but . . ." Seonkyeong trailed off.

"We are investigators and we have a few questions regarding the fire that took place at the home of Mr. Pak Yongseok," the man said.

Pak Yongseok? Who was Pak Yongseok? Seonkyeong wondered, but the mention of a fire brought Hayeong to her mind.

"My husband isn't home right now."

"Actually, we came to see his daughter, Yun Hayeong."

"Oh . . . well, come on in," Seonkyeong said after a moment's hesitation, and opened the gate.

Hayeong would be coming home soon. And Seonkyeong couldn't make these men, drenched in sweat on such a hot day, go on standing in the scorching sun.

"Would you like something cool to drink?" she asked as they stepped in through the front door, and the man in the checked shirt jumped at the chance and asked for some water.

Seonkyeong led them to the living room sofa, and quickly went to the kitchen and got some cold water from the fridge. The two men took their cups and gulped the water down, as if they had just been waiting for it. The man in the checked shirt, who had been sweating profusely, poured himself some more water from the pitcher. Wiping away the sweat running down the back of his neck with the crumpled handkerchief in his hand, he mumbled an excuse, "The sun was so strong, it cooked my head as I walked into the alley."

Smiling and nodding, Seonkyeong got to her feet and turned on the air conditioner in the living room, and brought a fan over and turned that on as well.

"Oh, thank you so much. That feels so much better. Heat really gets to me," the man said.

Unlike the other man, the man with the crew cut wasn't sweating much, and didn't seem too bothered by the heat. He looked irritably at his colleague, who was making a great fuss, flapping his shirt in front of the fan to get some air into it. He pulled out a business card from his suit pocket and handed it to Seonkyeong.

Sergeant Yu Dongsik

Fire Investigation Team, Forensic Science Investigation Department

SEOUL METROPOLITAN POLICE AGENCY

Seeing the other man hand Seonkyeong the card, the man in the checked shirt promptly took his own card from his pocket and handed it to her as well. Unlike Sergeant Yu, he was a fire inspector in the fire defense headquarters.

Yi Sangwuk

FIRE INSPECTOR

Seonkyeong had heard that there was a fire investigation team in the forensic science investigation department at the police agency, but she had never met a fire inspector before. She hadn't known that they worked as a team with fire inspectors from the fire defense headquarters, either.

"You two are from different organizations?" Seonkyeong asked.

Taken aback by her question, they chuckled, looking at each other. The way they did so hinted that they had worked together for a long time—they seemed quite comfortable with each other.

"You're very sharp. Most people think we're both fire inspectors," said Yi Sangwuk, the fire inspector, who seemed quite talkative.

"Fire identification used to be under the jurisdiction of the fire defense headquarters. But the process of fire suppression necessitates police intervention at times, which is why the two organizations have come to cooperate," he explained.

"Oh, I see," Seonkyeong replied, and examined the two cards on the table.

According to her knowledge, fire inspectors generally examined the scene as the fire was being put out; they also talked to witnesses on the spot. Why had they come after so many days had passed?

The air had cooled, and Seonkyeong hugged her shoulders without realizing it. Sergeant Yu picked up the remote control and turned off the air conditioner.

Seonkyeong looked up, and Sergeant Yu put the remote control down, saying a fan was enough.

She realized that he was a very attentive man who was mindful of details. She felt a bit nervous, sensing his gaze resting on her. She spoke to break the awkward silence.

"As far as I know, fire identification takes place at the scene. Is there a reason why you came out of your way to see Hayeong here?" she asked.

This time, Sergeant Yu spoke. The two men seemed to have clearly divided roles.

"We were quite preoccupied that day, and on top of that, the child had a hard time talking, probably because of the shock. She was the only witness, but we didn't get to hear what she had to say. We figured out the situation that day as much as we could, but there was something we wanted to ask her in person," he said.

"I see," Seonkyeong said, nodding, and glanced at her watch.

I hope she doesn't come home late, Seonkyeong thought, feeling anxious for no reason. She couldn't help but feel nervous with two men, whom she didn't know very well, sitting in her living room. In addition, Sergeant Yu wouldn't take his eyes off her face. Inspector Yi sensed her discomfort and said with a smile, "Please don't worry about us and do what you need to do. We can just sit here and wait."

Seonkyeong, however, couldn't do as he said. She found her gaze falling repeatedly on the yard out the window.

"Um, excuse me, but . . . ," Sergeant Yu said.

Seonkyeong turned her head to face Sergeant Yu, who was staring intently at her. "Yes?" she said, tilting her head as she spoke.

"Are you in this line of work, by chance? Something to do with the police?"

"You could say that. I'm in criminal psychology."

Hearing her answer, he tapped himself on the forehead, trying to recall something. Sangwuk looked from Sergeant Yu to Seonkyeong, looking puzzled.

"What, you know her?" he asked.

"Didn't you come to the criminal psychology seminar held at the National Forensic Service last winter?" Sergeant Yu asked.

"Yes, I did, in January," Seonkyeong replied.

It had been five months. She had attended an academic seminar on scientific investigation and criminal psychology, conducted by the National Forensic Service. It seemed that the sergeant, too, had been there, and seen her.

"I thought I'd seen you somewhere," he said.

Seonkyeong finally understood why he'd looked so intently at her, making her uncomfortable. Sergeant Yu, who had been looking at her for quite some time, unable to recall the memory, now turned his gaze away, looking as if he had solved a difficult problem. She felt relieved that he had seen her before. The awkwardness lifted, and she felt more at ease.

"You have a good eye. How did you remember that?" she asked.

"Sergeant Yu remembers all beautiful women," Sangwuk said lightly, and the inspector poked him in the waist.

"I apologize, this guy has no manners. Something you said that day stayed with me, actually," he said.

"Huh? What did I . . . ," Seonkyeong asked, not recalling talking in front of people. She hadn't make a presentation, or even gotten up from her seat to ask a question. She found it odd that he should remember something she'd said.

"Didn't you say that wounds turn a man into a monster?" asked Sergeant Yu.

She felt perplexed, hearing words she didn't remember saying. Had they even talked that day?

Waving his hands, Sergeant Yu said, "You didn't say it directly to me—I was sitting in the row in front of you. I heard you talking to someone next to you during a break in the seminar. You were talking about Yu Yeongcheol."

"Oh!" Seonkyeong exclaimed, vividly remembering that day all of a sudden.

A colleague had invited her to the seminar, and introduced her to someone who wrote freelance for a police journal. He had a knack for telling stories, probably because he made a living writing, and they talked at length, never an awkward moment in that first meeting.

Hearing that Seonkyeong had studied criminal psychology in the States, he asked her questions about profiling, and talked about the childhood of Yu Yeongcheol, which he had covered in his writing. The conclusion the reporter had drawn afterward was that the wounds his parents had inflicted on him had traumatized him terribly.

The freelance reporter quoted from Robert Ressler, saying that no one lived a normal life and then had a dramatic change in personality in their thirties that led them to become a murderer; he agreed with Ressler that behaviors that foreshadow murder develop during early childhood.

During the conversation with the freelance reporter, Seonkyeong had said, in talking about the meaning of the word "trauma," "Wounds turn a man into a monster."

"You're the kind of person I fear the most," Seonkyeong said.

"Huh?" said Sergeant Yu.

"I have a friend like you. She'll remember what I was wearing during a lunch with her ten years ago, what we ate and talked about, and even the music that was playing at the café. It's a little scary, to be honest."

"Haha, that's exactly Sergeant Yu. He remembers the most trivial things," Sangwuk said.

Sergeant Yu laughed along, and said he'd been that way since he was a child.

To Seonkyeong's relief, Hayeong came home on time.

Seonkyeong looked up at the sound of the gate opening, and saw her walk into the yard.

"There she is," Seonkyeong said, and Sergeant Yu and Sangwuk looked up as well, and watched Hayeong as she came inside.

Hayeong, who had opened the front door and was stepping inside, stiffened when she saw the two men.

"Hayeong, do you remember them? They're fire inspectors. They have a few questions to ask you," Seonkyeong said.

Hesitant, Hayeong looked from one man to the other, then went to sit down on the sofa when Seonkyeong asked her to. She looked quite nervous. Feeling bad for her, Seonkyeong held her by the shoulder and tried to put her at ease.

"It's all right, you don't need to be scared. Just tell them what you remember," she said, but Hayeong wouldn't let her guard down.

Sergeant Yu looked intently at Hayeong, then began to ask her questions when Sangwuk nudged him.

"Do you remember me?" he asked.

Hayeong nodded.

"You must've been quite shocked that day. Are you okay now?" he went on.

"Yes," Hayeong answered.

"Will you tell me in detail what happened the night of the fire?"

Hearing the question, Hayeong hesitated for a moment, then shook her head.

"I don't remember very well," she said.

Sergeant Yu, after looking straight into her eyes for a moment, pictured the structure of the house in his mind and asked another question.

"Where was your room?"

"The one next to the kitchen. When you went out through the window, there was a staircase leading to the rooftop on the second floor. Oh, and that's where I went when the fire broke out, to the rooftop. Then a fire fighter saved me," Hayeong said, seeming to remember little by little as she answered the question.

"Did you see anyone suspicious when you went out through the window?"

Hayeong shook her head and said, "I couldn't see anything because of the smoke."

"Were you sleeping by yourself?"

"Yes."

"How did you know that there was a fire?"

"I woke up because my throat hurt. The smoke, it came into the room. That's why I went out through the window."

"What else do you remember?" Sergeant Yu asked, writing down Hayeong's words and waiting for her next. Hayeong, however, seemed to have nothing more to say; she clamped her mouth shut and looked at the two men.

Seeing her response, Sergeant Yu must have decided that he couldn't pry any more out of her; he closed his notebook, put it in his pocket, and took out another business card.

"I'll leave you my card. Will you call me if you remember anything else about that night?" he asked.

Hayeong nodded.

Sergeant Yu got to his feet, and nodded lightly at Seonkyeong, saying goodbye.

Then, while putting on his shoes at the front door, he seemed to recall something all of a sudden—looking shocked, he stared down at his feet for a while. He whirled his head around to where Hayeong was sitting.

Hayeong, who had been sitting on the sofa, hastily got to her feet when their eyes met, and went off upstairs.

Sergeant Yu asked Seonkyeong, who had gone out to the gate to see them off, for her phone number. He took out his cell phone, checked her name, and saved the number on the spot.

"I'll give you a call later," he said.

"Okay. Goodbye, then," Seonkyeong said.

"By the way, does Hayeong go to bed with her socks on, or off?" he asked.

"Huh?" Seonkyeong, about to go back into the house, looked puzzled, not seeing where the question had come from.

"I'm not sure," she said.

EVEN AFTER THE GATE HAD CLOSED, Sergeant Yu stood there for quite a while. Sangwuk, standing next to him and blocking the sun with his hand, rushed him, saying, "Come on, let's go. We'll get scorched in the sun, standing here."

Beads of sweat formed on his forehead. He took out his handkerchief and began to fan himself. Sergeant Yu, however, still wouldn't budge. He stood there frowning for a while, then asked, "Don't you find something about that child strange?"

"Huh? What about her?" Sangwuk asked.

"She found out that there was a fire because the smoke came into her room. How do kids usually react when that happens?"

"They usually run in a direction where there's no smoke. Or they hide somewhere."

The most heartbreaking thing at the scene of a fire was finding dead bodies of children. Children instinctively looked for somewhere to hide when a fire broke out. They often hid in a closet, as if playing hide-and-seek with the fire, afraid it would find them. So in many cases, children died by suffocating from the smoke before the flames even touched them.

Again, Sergeant Yu pictured the structure of the house where the child had lived. The window was on the wall next to the door, just around the corner. If the child found out in the darkness that a fire had broken out, how would she have reacted? Rather than go toward the fire, she would've gone back into her room.

"Now that I think about it . . . ," Sangwuk said, his eyes wide in surprise with a thought that had just occurred to him, and looked at the sergeant.

"That day, on the day of the fire! So . . . that's why you asked her that question," he said.

Looking at him, Sergeant Yu nodded. He had finally confirmed something that had been nagging at the corner of his mind.

The child, who said she'd been sleeping when she woke up to find a fire had broken out and escaped through the window, had been wearing socks and shoes that day at the scene of the fire. Which meant that she either had known that there was going to be a fire, or had been outside before the fire broke out.

Why did she lie? Sergeant Yu thought, wondering what it was that the child was hiding. There was something else that troubled his mind.

Please call my dad, she had said, handing him her father's business card. How could she have been that calm—putting her father's business card in her pocket, putting on socks and shoes, and even remembering to take her teddy bear with her—when she was running from a fire?

A sickening hypothesis rose to his mind as he recalled seeing the child early that morning of the fire. It's not possible, he thought, but the thought that had crept its way in began to grow and spread like poison ivy.

Sergeant Yu shook his head. There was still the autopsy report. The results were ready, but the cause of death had yet to be confirmed. The autopsy lab at the National Forensic Service said they would send a report after the analysis. Things would clear up a bit when he saw the report. It wouldn't be too late to judge then.

PART 3

20.

O N THE MORNING OF HER NEXT INTERVIEW WITH YI Byeongdo, Seonkyeong called the head of the serious crime division at the Seoul Gangbuk Police Station.

She asked him if he knew about Yi Byeongdo's mother, who had gone missing.

He knew nothing more than what Yi Byeongdo had said. Seonkyeong told him that there was a possibility that she had been killed by her son, just as Yi Byeongdo had told her. He listened quietly to what Seonkyeong said, and asked if she had any other information. He seemed more interested in the evidence of the other missing people that still remained at Yi Byeongdo's house than in an old case.

Seonkyeong said that she would inquire into further crimes during the interview that day.

"And . . . I called to ask you for something," she added.

There was another reason she'd called. She had guessed why Yi Byeongdo found her important and she wanted to find out if her guess was correct.

"When you searched his house, did you ever come across a picture of his mother? If you did, I'd like to see it," she said.

He said he would ask the investigators and give her a call, and hung up.

In less than ten minutes, the crime division head called back. He said he'd found in the case record a picture of Yi Byeongdo's mother that the investigator in charge had photographed as evidence. He offered to send her a copy via text message.

The text arrived just as Seonkyeong got her bag from the study and was about to leave the house. She flipped her cell phone open and checked the picture, but the face wasn't what she'd imagined.

She'd thought that Yi Byeongdo might have allowed her to interview him and considered her special because she looked like his mother. His mother, however, looked completely different from her. He seemed to take after his mother. Seonkyeong could tell, even from the blurred photograph, that she was quite beautiful.

Seonkyeong put the phone in her bag and headed to the prison in haste.

YI BYEONGDO TOOK THE APPLE Seonkyeong handed him and placed it on the table, unlike the previous time. His face had thinned in just a few days. Sitting down in her seat, Seonkyeong realized that he was staring fixedly at her.

"Something happened, huh?" he asked.

"Why would you think that?"

"You're very different from the last time."

He examined her carefully. His soft voice would have sounded as sweet as a lover's whisper, had the situation been entirely different. Seonkyeong wondered what it was about her that was different.

"Am I?" she asked, but he let the question pass, contrary to what she'd hoped. Something had happened: Hayeong. But it wasn't something to be shared with him. She made up her mind to concentrate on the interview. He, however, seemed to have no intention of doing the same.

"You . . . have a cat now, too," he said.

"What?" Seonkyeong asked, puzzled, and looked at him. A chilly smile had replaced the one that had been on his lips. He picked up the apple and wrapped his hands around it. Unperturbed, she opened the file and turned on the recorder.

"Let's talk about the cases today, shall we? I'm curious as to what it was about the victims that drew your attention," she said.

"You want to know what it was about you that got my attention, right?" he said, once again trying to dominate the situation.

Seonkyeong wondered for a moment if she should take the stepping stones he was laying out for her; then she took a step. As Director Han had said, it could be an important key to understanding him.

"Are you . . . going to tell me today?" she asked.

"If you want me to," he said.

Seonkyeong put the pen down and sat up.

"I'd be lying if I said I wasn't interested. Tell me," she said.

"There was a baby monkey who lost its mother the moment it was born. The people who raised the monkey made two mothers for it: one made of wire, with a milk bottle hanging from it, and the other made of soft, warm fur, though without a milk bottle. Which one do you think the baby monkey chose?" he asked.

Seonkyeong had seen the documentary he was referring to.

The baby monkey clung to the wire mother monkey only when it was hungry, and spent most of its time hugging the furry one.

"Does that have anything to do with my question?" Seonkyeong asked.

He smiled ambiguously.

A baby monkey. What was it that he wanted to say? Seonkyeong wondered.

Something flashed through her mind. Was he saying that his mother, who hurt him, was the wire mother monkey, and Seonkyeong, the furry one? Or perhaps he had another mother. Someone who comforted his wounded, lonely heart.

Seonkyeong knew that her hypothesis about why he had chosen her was partly right. She was surprised, however, that he had another mother.

"You had another mother. Someone who treated you with warmth, unlike the wire mother," Seonkyeong said.

He looked at her, beaming, then shook his head.

"Too late. I'm disappointed," he said.

"You want me to understand, without telling me anything."

He made no response.

"I find it strange. Last time you talked at length about the mother you hated so much. . . . Don't you have anything to say about your other mother?"

She wanted to provoke him, but there was no telling when his mood might change. Seonkyeong took a careful step forward. He pretended not to have heard her question. It seemed that he didn't want to talk about his hidden mother.

Seonkyeong decided to ask him about his first murder, of his mother.

"Do you remember what you told me last time? That you killed your mother?" she asked.

"Is that what I said?"

He was different today. He had been frank and straightforward last time, but now he was mincing words and deflecting questions. He feigned indifference, tapping on the table, and took a long time answering questions, as though he were bent on getting on her nerves.

"Why don't you tell me about yourself today?" he asked.

He had decided not to talk at all, it seemed. She remembered what Director Han had said, to not let him take control of the situation. She turned off the recorder, closed the file, and put them in her bag. At this abrupt change in her behavior, he narrowed his eyes and glared at her.

"You don't seem to be in the mood to talk today. I'll come back in a few days," she said.

When she got to her feet, he finally surrendered.

"All right, all right. You probably won't be happy, either, leaving like this," he said, looking a bit dejected, and fumbled for a moment about what to say next.

Seonkyeong repeated the question, and he nodded, remembering at last, and recalled his memories. It took a while, but he gradually became absorbed in his own story.

"You don't know, do you? What it feels like to kill your own mother," he said.

Seonkyeong couldn't say that she did.

"You don't realize at first. It happens in an instant, like a lightning strike. You do it with your own two hands, but . . . you're nothing but an instrument. Yes, as if someone made you do it. That's why you don't realize at first. What you did," he continued.

Seonkyeong remained silent.

"It was hell when my mom was alive, but even after she died . . . I suppose it was a hell of my own creation," he added, a dark shadow over his eyes.

He had committed the act out of deep hatred, but hatred was not the only thing he felt about her. Even though she had left traces of abuse all over his body, deep in his heart, he thirsted for his mother's love. Was it possible that had led to murder?

He said that his mother left home when he was seventeen. That was when he killed someone for the first time. Then three years ago, at age thirty-two, he started killing people again. Seonkyeong wondered what got him started again, when he'd remained quiet for fifteen years after killing his mother. He had killed people without reservation. She decided to ask him what had made him do it.

"Why did you start killing people again after fifteen years? Was there something that triggered you?"

"You say that fifteen years passed, but for me, time stayed still. The day I killed my mom . . . the clock inside me stopped," he said.

Searching his memory again, he began to describe the world he lived in. When he couldn't find the right words to describe what he felt and saw, he stopped talking and fell into thought for long intervals. Seonkyeong could feel how precise he wanted to be in telling his story.

"Time doesn't always flow at the same rate. Years can pass like a moment; a minute can seem like a month, a year. I've been living my most horrific moment for an insanely long time, over and over again. . . . The day it rained, the day I got upset at the sound of the cat crying . . . the moment I sang to my mom, lying in the yard. It repeats itself endlessly in my mind. I still get angry at my mom; I still get nervous at the sound of rain. The things that happened that day, which didn't last an hour, broke down into the tiniest pieces and have been happening over and over in my mind for fifteen years— every second, every minute, every hour, three hundred and sixty-five days a year. I experience them again and again, and yet they feel like they're happening for the first time, and I feel angry as if they're happening for the first time. . . . You don't know what that feels like," he said.

Listening to him, however, Seonkyeong thought of something that had been repeating itself in her mind for a long time: her mother's funeral.

The moment when she'd stood carrying her mother's portrait on a hill where cherry blossoms were scattering in the wind always replayed itself in her mind in slow motion.

The cherry blossoms had dropped to the ground in the blink of an eye, but in Seonkyeong's mind they hovered in the air for a long, long time before falling.

After the coffin was lowered into the grave, the mourners threw chrysanthemums over it; at that moment, a sudden gust of wind swirled cherry blossoms around like flakes of snow. Seonkyeong looked up, and her gaze followed the petals in the air, slowly down to the coffin. The dazzling petals floated around in the air and fell to the ground one by one, which, though it happened in an instant, seemed to take an eternity to Seonkyeong. She remembered the shape, color, and movement of each and every petal, in terms of microseconds, the way a person in a traffic accident experiences the situation as if watching a video in slow motion, while her mind stored every moment in detail in the brain.

Whenever she thought back to the moment, she could vividly feel, as if it were happening all over again, the wind that day, which had been both chilly and warm; the portrait she had been carrying in her hands; and the grip of her father's hands on her shoulders.

She could understand, in part, the feeling Yi Byeongdo was trying to convey.

He still lived, recalling the moment he killed his mother, scene by scene.

"The only way for me to erase the memory . . . was to find someone," he said.

Seonkyeong stared at him, feeling alarmed.

"It was only when I killed someone with my two hands that I could forget. Only when I had blood on my hands could I sleep, without the song in my head," he continued.

Looking like a seventeen-year-old boy again, with his mask of arrogance off, he considered the apple on the table. After staring at it for a while, he mumbled as if to himself, with red-rimmed eyes.

"Would you . . . hug a baby monkey with such bloody hands? Could you?" he asked.

Unable to say anything, Seonkyeong looked at him.

His eyes began to well with tears. Seonkyeong felt thrown off by the sudden change in emotions. He reached out a hand to take the apple, then pulled his hand back. He looked afraid to take it.

He shook his head, as if to shake off his feelings; then he pushed his chair back and got up.

Even after he'd been gone for some time, Seonkyeong couldn't move from her spot.

His last words lingered in her ears. He'd been talking not to Seonkyeong, but to his furry monkey mother. She wondered what this person meant to him, that this ruthless killer, turning into a little child, wanted her to take him into her arms.

The apple, which had lost its luster, was still on the table.

YI BYEONGDO, HAVING RETURNED TO HIS CELL, turned on the water in the sink and stared at it as it went down the drain. The memory of the orchard, which had suddenly risen in his mind, disconcerted him as much as the unexpected tears. He had wanted to go back after killing his mother. There was never a day when he didn't think about the orchard. Whenever the seasons changed, he spent days thinking about what they must be doing at the orchard now. But he couldn't go back. He knew that even if he did, things wouldn't be the same as before. So he decided to forget about it.

When he looked up at the cold autumn sky, he felt as if he could feel apple juice spreading in his mouth. When he could no longer bear it, he bought an apple. But the apple had no taste. After buying several apples he realized at last: he was being punished. He was the one who left in search of hell; he had no right to go back.

He turned off the faucet and looked in the mirror. He knew. He knew why he was in such a rush.

The hour was approaching.

The sky looks dangerous before a typhoon. No matter how clear it is, the air feels different. There's a tension so taut that it feels as if it will break any second; then the wind starts to blow, and clouds come gathering.

His heart began to beat irregularly, as if it sensed a typhoon coming. His mood rose and fell time and again. He paced up and down in his room, angry at times, impatient at times. He felt anxiety wash over him.

The hour was approaching again. He knew now when it would come, how it would come. He began to hear a ringing in his ears, and segmented notes began to float around and gather in his mind. The same measure of notes played over and over in his ears, then vanished. Soon the song would shake his soul again.

He had to finish telling his story before he heard the song, before the song got loud. He wanted to end it now. He had tied up his own hands; he could no longer live, captive to his mother's specter. His life was no longer his own. He had never really had a life. If he couldn't free himself of her clutch in this manner, there would be no other way.

He had made up his mind to end it. That was when he saw Seonkyeong. And then he knew.

She was the only one who could end it.

21.

Hayeong's school was between a river and a mountain.

There was a path behind the school that led up to the mountain, so classes sometimes went on field trips there for nature study, and children liked to play there. The river flowed in front of the school, and children took the long trail by the river to go to school and back home.

The children in class 4-3 began to pack up as soon as the last bell of the day rang. The teacher, telling them to be careful on their way home, didn't notice some of the children exchanging meaningful glances as they rushed out of the classroom.

Kaeun, who was about to pack up and follow the boys, turned around to look at Hayeong, who was looking out the window without even packing up, and tapped her on the shoulder.

When Hayeong turned around, Kaeun whispered, so that no one around them would hear.

"Do you want to come with us?" she asked.

"Where?"

"Some of the boys and I are going up to the mountain behind the school."

Hayeong stared at her, not knowing what was going on, and Kaeun pointed out the window in frustration.

"You know, the cat that killed our bird. We're going to go catch the little thief," she explained.

Hayeong's eyes gleamed.

"Where?" she asked.

"I told you, the mountain behind the school. Kang and Sihyeon said they know where cats often go," Kaeun answered.

Feigning reluctance, Hayeong followed her.

The path leading up to the mountain was by the storage shed behind the building. A long wire fence had been installed in the area, with a door that opened to the path.

When Hayeong and Kaeun came out of the building and went around to the back, they saw the other kids sitting around the wire door. They were kicking the fence, complaining about a bad start.

"What's wrong? Aren't we going?" Kaeun asked. The boys pointed to the door. There was a lock on the door, firmly fastened.

"What, so we can't go?" Kaeun asked, sounding sulky upon hearing they couldn't go up to the mountain, when she'd gone out of her way to bring Hayeong along.

"Isn't there anywhere else we can go?" Hayeong asked the boys. They looked at one another, and shook their heads. They all just looked at one another, sorry that their plans had gone wrong, and not knowing what to do about it. If someone had said they should just go home, they probably would've gone, grumbling.

Hayeong turned her eyes to the mountain, then carefully examined the long wire fence.

"Look!" Hayeong said, pointing somewhere, and all eyes turned in the same direction. Her finger was pointing at a valley in the mountain beyond the fence.

"What about it?" someone asked.

"When it rains, the water comes down through there, right?" Hayeong asked in reply.

The boys, clinging to the wire fence, looked where she was pointing. At first glance, it was just a curved slope, but upon closer inspection it seemed that Hayeong was right. They could see exposed tree roots, and leaves that had washed down.

With a finger, Hayeong drew in the air the path of the stream that would have been there if water had been flowing. The eyes following her fingers arrived at the wire fence.

"Whoa!" Kang exclaimed, figuring it out before the others.

As the other kids stood there, puzzled, he hurled his backpack aside and went up to the wire fence. Rainwater washes dirt away. Hayeong was pointing to a gap in the slope that had formed under the wire fence, where dirt had been swept down.

"Does anyone have a stick?" Kang shouted, and the others quickly looked around. Sihyeon collected some branches and brought them over. Kang and Sihyeon began to dig under the fence with the branches. There were only leaves on the other side of the fence, so a dog hole was dug up in no time, with little effort.

Kang was the first to crawl in, head first. If Kang, who was the biggest of them all, made it through, the others would have no problem. His shoulder got stuck for a second in the fence, but he gave himself a little twist and made it through without difficulty.

Seeing him get out through the fence, everyone cheered.

"You're incredible. How did you know?" Kaeun asked in surprise, but Hayeong watched in silence as the others passed through to the other side of the fence.

"Come on," Kaeun said, when all the boys had done it. She pulled Hayeong by her hand, heading to the hole.

"You go ahead," Kaeun said.

"Wait, my backpack!" Kang cried, realizing he had left his backpack behind.

Kaeun picked up the backpack, shoved it through the hole, and stuck her head in as well.

When everyone, including Kaeun, had passed through, the kids began to climb the mountain slope, holding on to the little branches around them. Once they climbed the slope, they could take the path, which wasn't difficult to do.

"Where are we going, though?" Kaeun asked, huffing as she climbed up.

Kang and Sihyeon, who had come up with the plan in the first place, looked at each other, grinning.

"You'll see when we get there" was the reply.

Without joining in the conversation, Hayeong walked quietly, keeping pace with them.

The spot where Kang and Sihyeon took them was on the other side beyond the peak.

The mountain was 125 meters above sea level. It was a little mountain that people in the neighborhood could climb with ease, morning and evening; it had a small mineral spring, and a pavilion and some plyometric exercise equipment at the top. People who lived at the foot of the mountain planted seeds in the tiny spot of land where the mountain began, to grow lettuce, peppers, spinach, and other vegetables to eat in summer.

Trash had begun to pile up where people had been. At first, it was things like support fixtures and wooden sticks that had been used for farming; later, food waste began to accumulate. In summer, watermelon rinds and kimchi that had gone bad were dumped there, causing a stench and swarms of flies to gather.

Stray cats that lived in the wild without a home flocked to the foot of the mountain for food. A few came at first, and then more and more began to appear, and even make their way down to nearby alleys and tear up trash bags, which created a problem for the people in the neighborhood.

Kang and Sihyeon thought that these stray cats had trespassed on the nature study area at school, making a mess of the birdcage.

Cats are nimble. And strays crouch down, getting ready to run, as soon as someone approaches. The kids knew that they had no chance of catching these quick and nimble cats, the way they themselves ran.

"How will you catch them?" someone asked Kang.

Kang grinned and took out a black plastic bag from his backpack. The bag held a net.

"What is that?" Kaeun asked. "How will you catch a cat with that?" she continued, doubting that this card from up his sleeve would work. The others nodded, though they didn't say anything, feeling the same way.

"Haven't you guys seen *Animal Farm* on TV? How the animal rescuer throws a net to catch a cat?" Kang asked.

"Well, that worked because people blocked up the alley and trapped the cat first. This is open space," one of the other kids said.

Kang sulked, put out by their reaction.

"How would you do it, then?" he asked, throwing out his chest.

The kids just looked at each other, unable to come up with any other ideas; it seemed that Kang was the only one who had thought of catching the cat.

"Don't you have any ideas, Sihyeon?" Kaeun asked, and Sihyeon, who had been tilting his head, opened his backpack, looking unsure.

"How about this?" he said, pulling out a slingshot—a Y-shaped branch with a yellow rubber band tied to it. Between the strands of the rubber band was a strip of leather that could hold a bullet. Sihyeon looked around on the ground, and picked up a pea-sized rock to demonstrate. The bullet flew so fast, and so far, that the kids couldn't run after it.

"Wow! That's awesome!" the kids exclaimed, and Kang looked even more sullen. Sihyeon, who hadn't been sure that his treasured slingshot would work, shrugged his shoulders, looking proud.

"How do you know the bullet will hit the mark, when you can't even see the bullet when it's flying?" Kang, who had been sulking, pointed out a problem, which called for another demonstration. Sihyeon picked up an empty can from the ground, set it down at a distance, and came back to where the rest of the kids were. Their eyes sparkled with curiosity. Sihyeon aimed carefully at the can, and pulled the rubber band. Again, the bullet couldn't be seen very well, but the can fell with a clang.

Sihyeon looked proudly over at Kang, and Kang had to acknowledge that it worked.

In the end, Sihyeon was put in charge of the important mission of catching the cat, and the kids hid where they could see the heap of trash, and waited for the cat to appear. It turned out that waiting for the cat, without budging in the sizzling heat, was not as fun as they'd expected. After ten minutes or so, beads of sweat began to form on their foreheads, and they began to complain. Swarms of flies infested the place, but the cat was nowhere to be seen. They began to wonder if it would show up at all.

Wiping the sweat off her forehead, Kaeun got to her feet.

"I'm leaving. This is no fun," she said.

"Wait a little longer, it'll be here soon," Kang said, placating her, keeping his eyes forward.

"Hayeong, let's go," Kaeun said, not wanting to leave by herself.

Hayeong stayed sitting in her spot, looking at the mountain without a word, and Kaeun began to press her, taking her arm and saying, "Come on, please? I'll buy you ice cream."

Hayeong pulled her by the arm and sat her down, and said in a low voice, "They're here."

At those words, the kids looked at her. Tension filled the air.

"Where?" Sihyeon asked, lowering his voice as well.

Hayeong raised a hand and pointed to the path that led up to the mineral spring. The path was empty, but there were two cats roaming among the trees that lined the path.

"Can you hit them from here?" Kang turned around and asked Sihyeon, who shook his head.

"Let's wait till they come closer," he said.

The kids kept their eyes fixed on the cats, not even daring to breathe. Even Kaeun, who had wanted to go home, was looking at the cats, her face full of curiosity.

One of the cats came slowly down to where the kids were. The kids gestured for Sihyeon to hurry, and he quickly raised the slingshot and aimed at the cat. But the cat must've heard the clamor of the kids, for it instantly disappeared down an alley under the mountain. Disappointed, the kids sighed.

At that moment, Kang nudged Sihyeon on the arm again.

Reflexively, Sihyeon turned his eyes to the other cat. It was a black cat, approaching the pile of food waste with caution. Anxiously, the kids looked from the cat to Sihyeon's slingshot, hoping that this time, Sihyeon would succeed.

"A little closer, just a little closer," Sihyeon mumbled quietly.

Zing! The taut rubber band was released at last. It hit something with a dull, thick sound. The cat looked up in surprise. Whooping, the kids ran over at once. The cat, dazed from the shock of the slingshot attack, sensed danger and began to run. But the shock must've been quite big—in trying to run from the kids, it ran right up to Kang.

Not missing his chance as the cat slowed down, Kang changed direction, and quickly released the net in his hand. As soon as the net was over the cat, he stepped down on it. The cat couldn't budge.

"Wow, you really did it!" said the kids, and flocked around him. Sihyeon and Kang gave each other a high five. Their joint operation had succeeded. The kids gathered around the cat, and looking at it through the net, they all had something to say.

"Is this the one that killed our birds?"

"Who cares? They won't be coming back to the school after this."

Kaeun reached out a hand to touch the cat, looking fascinated. Someone scared her from behind, and she let out a yelp.

"A lot of people pass through this way, so let's go up to the mountain," someone said, and everyone started up at once. Kang and Sihyeon carried the net together, walking side by side. The cat resisted, its feet flailing in the air; but finding it was no use, it huddled up and meowed quietly.

The kids gathered next to the pavilion at the top of the mountain, where a tree had fallen and created a little space.

"What should we do with it?" Kang asked.

"Yeah, how should we punish it?"

The kids considered the question, watching the cat in the net, looking around and trembling in fear. Before catching the cat, they'd declared that they would punish it severely once they caught it. But now that they'd caught the cat, they didn't know how they should punish it.

"Should we beat it?" Kaeun asked. The kids looked at her, aghast, and she shut her mouth, looking glum.

"You guys, take the cat out of the net," Hayeong, who had been following the kids in silence, said to Kang and Sihyeon.

"Have you come up with something?" Kang asked.

Hayeong nodded, grinning, and said, "Yeah. So take the cat out, and take one leg each."

Hayeong put her backpack down and took out her pencil case. Excited, the kids took the cat out of the net, and reached out their hands to grab its legs. But the cat wouldn't give in so easily. It resisted violently, scratching their hands.

Hayeong quickly grabbed the cat by the nape of its neck and picked it up. Unable to resist any longer, the cat waited for its fate, legs dangling in the air. Amazed, the kids stared at Hayeong and the cat.

"When you pick up a cat or a dog, grab it by the neck like this, and they can't do anything," Hayeong said, and everyone looked at her with wonder and admiration.

As Hayeong instructed, Sihyeon held the cat by the nape of its neck, and Kang and the others took hold of the legs.

The cat was hanging in front of Hayeong, with the belly—its most vulnerable part—completely exposed.

Hayeong was holding a paper knife in her hand. Looking at the cat, she slowly pushed the blade up.

Seeing the knife, the kids opened their eyes wide.

"What . . . what are you trying to do?" Sihyeon asked, his voice trembling. He knew, without hearing the answer, what she was about to do. Kaeun and Kang looked at her in horror as well.

"You're not really going to . . ."

"You said you wanted to punish the cat, didn't you?" Hayeong said.

"Yeah, but, hey. . . ," Kang began, but Hayeong's hand flew up into the air, along with the knife, then went straight for the cat's belly.

Kaeun covered her eyes with her hands. The others looked away, grimacing.

"Ow!" Kang sank to the ground, clasping his own hand. The cat had freed itself of Sihyeon's and Kang's hands, and was running away in the distance.

"Hey, what happened?" the kids asked, but Kang and Sihyeon just stood glaring at Hayeong, panting. She glared back, without blinking her eyes.

"Kang hurt his hand because of you!" Sihyeon said.

"It's not because of me. He would've been all right if he just held on to the cat," Hayeong said.

Kang had cut his hand, it seemed, as he let go of the cat and tried to get away from Hayeong's knife. Kaeun pulled out a handkerchief, and hunkered down by Kang and took his hand. She lifted his hand to see the wound, and saw blood seeping out. Fortunately, though, the wound wasn't deep; it was a light scratch.

"What are we going to do? His hand is bleeding," Kaeun said.

All eyes turned to Hayeong. But she just pulled the blade back down, and said casually, "Scaredy-cats, you should've just held on to it."

"Does it hurt, Kang?" Kaeun asked, dabbing at the blood on the back of his hand.

Hayeong started back down the mountain slope, as if to say that she was finished there.

No one called out after her. They all seemed to be thinking about the way she had so calmly wielded a knife at the cat. One of the kids, who had been staring at her, gave a sudden shiver. No one said anything, but they were all thinking the same thing.

The afternoon's play, in which they'd wanted to punish a cat, thus came to an end.

22.

A FTER HAYEONG WENT TO SCHOOL, SEONKYEONG WAS busy taking care of household chores; when she was finished, she filled a mug with coffee and headed to the study.

She began the task of transcribing Yi Byeongdo's interview, recorded the day before. Transcription was something that took longer than people generally thought, because the intonation of the interviewee, as well as the speed and the choice of the words, had to be recorded in detail.

"There was a baby monkey who lost its mother the moment it was born. The people who raised the monkey made two mothers for it: one made of wire . . ." The words flowed out.

Seonkyeong pressed the pause button. A wire mother, and a fur mother.

The mother who had brought Yi Byeongdo into this world was made of cold wire, and had poked him all over his body. A mother who was beautiful, but cold and cruel.

But Yi Byeongdo had another mother. Seonkyeong didn't know who she was, but she was someone who comforted his wounded heart and held him in a warm embrace. The day before, he had reached out a hand to this mother, invisible, beyond Seonkyeong's shoulders. He had cried, asking this mother whose name was unknown, not the mother who had died at his hands, to hug him once again. Seonkyeong wanted to know who his fur mother was.

Seonkyeong, who had guessed that he was seeing his own mother in her, thought she had been half right. She wrote "fur mother?" in her notebook, and thought she should ask him more about her during the next interview.

She was about to press the play button on the recorder, when the phone rang. It was Hayeong's homeroom teacher.

The teacher asked Seonkyeong to come see her at the school. Worried, Seonkyeong asked if Hayeong was hurt, but the answer was no. The teacher's voice was cold, saying that it wasn't something that could be discussed easily over the phone. Seonkyeong sensed that something awful was waiting for her.

Trying to push the anxiety out of her mind, Seonkyeong got ready and left the house in a hurry.

When she arrived, less than an hour had passed since the phone call.

She walked into the teachers' room and saw the teacher, whom she had met during the transfer process, sitting in her seat. The teacher led her outside to the nature study area behind the school building, saying they should talk there. The vegetable patch, which the kids tended to, seemed to have grown thick in just a few weeks.

Hayeong's teacher stood there, looking at her class's section of the garden. She didn't know where to start, it seemed, now that they were face-to-face.

"What's going on?" Seonkyeong asked, and the teacher began to speak at last, with difficulty.

"I'm not sure how you'll take this. I myself can't believe that Hayeong's done something like this, but all the kids that were with her say the same thing, so I don't know what to think."

It seemed no small matter, the way she was stalling. Seonkyeong guessed that there had been some kind of problem among the kids.

"You need to tell me what happened," Seonkyeong said.

"They say that Hayeong . . . wielded a knife at the other kids," the teacher finally said.

"What?" was all Seonkyeong could say at the unexpected words.

"Do you see the farm there? The birds there have been disappearing again and again lately, and the kids thought it was some stray cat in the neighborhood that made them disappear. So some of the kids went to catch the cat, to punish it, and Hayeong took a knife and was about to stab the cat with it," the teacher continued.

"Wait a minute, didn't you say just now that she wielded the knife at the kids?"

"Yes, but the cat ran away, and a boy was wounded by the knife."

"I think I understand the situation, but are you sure you're not exaggerating? I don't think she carries around a knife in her backpack."

"Oh, I think it was a paper knife, for sharpening pencils and stuff."

Seonkyeong felt angry. The teacher was making too much of the situation.

"So you said she wielded a knife at the kids, when in reality, she hurt someone accidentally, while trying to punish a cat with a paper knife for sharpening pencils?" Seonkyeong said.

"Huh? Oh, I guess I wasn't very precise. I was just trying to relate the kids' story, the way they told it."

"You heard about what happened in detail, so why are you exaggerating? Hayeong was going to punish a cat, not harm the children. Aren't they two different things?"

"Well, the thing is . . ." The teacher was at a loss for words for a moment, thrown off by Seonkyeong's question. She continued, however, with some difficulty, saying, "I wouldn't have called you if that's all that happened. Things felt weird in class today so I asked the kids, and . . . they told me that this wasn't the first time that Hayeong has done something violent. If someone so much as touches her desk, she'll prick their hand with a mechanical pencil, and . . ."

Hayeong had even pushed a kid at the top of a staircase. Luckily, other kids took the girl's hands and kept her from falling down the stairs, but she could've been greatly harmed, the teacher said, shaking her head.

A lot seemed to have happened. Seonkyeong was shocked by what Hayeong had done, but she was angry with herself for not noticing anything until things had gone so far. To show interest, she'd been asking Hayeong how the day had been, and if she'd made any new friends, when she came home from school. But Hayeong never really said anything. Seonkyeong had simply assumed that it must not be easy for her to make friends yet. She felt stupid for not paying real attention to the child. Then she thought of the friendly girl who said she sat next to Hayeong.

"She seemed to be good friends with the girl who sits next to her, though," she said to the teacher.

"Kaeun . . . is a very easygoing girl. It seems that she thought she should make friends with Hayeong since she was new, and since they sat together. But after what happened yesterday, her mother called and asked for a change in the seating arrangements," the teacher replied.

Seonkyeong couldn't say anything.

"She must not tell you anything at home. From what I've seen and heard, I think it might be wise for Hayeong to receive some counseling," the teacher said.

Seonkyeong thought for a moment, then told her briefly about Hayeong's situation: her parents' divorce, her mother's death, and the fire at her grandparents'. Saying that her behavior was a result of those painful experiences, Seonkyeong asked for the teacher's help, as it would take some time for Hayeong's wounds to heal.

Hearing the story, the teacher was sympathetic at once.

"I didn't know. I did guess that there was something going on, because whenever I saw her face, I felt that she didn't seem quite like a child. . . . I can see how difficult it must be for her, with the fire being so recent," she said.

"We're trying as much as we can at home to help her regain stability, but I think it'll take some time for her to recover from the shock. I'd appreciate it if you could keep a close eye on her."

"Yes, I understand. I'll explain the situation to Kaeun and her mother, and ask for their compassionate understanding as well."

The conversation ended on a good note, with the teacher being understanding. Seonkyeong's heart felt heavy, however, as she returned home.

She went to a nearby park and found a quiet spot. She took out her cell phone and called Heeju.

"I was expecting you to call. What's up?" Heeju asked.

"I'm on my way back from Hayeong's school."

"Was there a problem with her friends?"

Nodding, Seonkyeong told Heeju what the teacher had told her. Heeju remained quiet for a while after hearing the story.

"That's not good. She'll have an even harder time if she doesn't get along with kids her own age at school. . . . Has she shown such behavior at all at home?"

Hearing her say that, Seonkyeong remembered how Hayeong had torn up her teddy bear with scissors. But she'd cheered up after Seonkyeong bought her the puppy. Thinking she should tell Heeju all the facts, since she was an expert, Seonkyeong told her everything, beginning with what she knew of Hayeong's mother. Heeju was silent, so silent that Seonkyeong wondered if the line had been cut off.

"Heeju?" she said, to make sure that she was still there.

"I'm listening. If it's okay with you, I'd like you to bring her to see me as soon as you can, tomorrow if possible," Heeju said.

Feeling apprehensive, Seonkyeong asked, "Why?"

"Seonkyeong, it's just like physical illness. You know that she's sick, so why won't you get her treated? If you don't, her wounds will only deepen. Besides, Hayeong's illness began a long time ago."

Seonkyeong couldn't say anything. She understood what Heeju

was saying. But she was afraid of how Hayeong would be labeled the moment she was taken to a counseling center. More than anything, she was concerned about how the child would see herself. She felt that she should discuss it with Jaeseong first.

She hung up, saying she'd call back.

WAITING FOR HAYEONG AT HOME, Seonkyeong couldn't concentrate on her work.

With the ignored file open before her, she traced her memory back to the day when Hayeong arrived at the house.

It would be easier, she thought, if Hayeong were a newborn baby. Taking care of her would be physically exhausting, but there wouldn't be such mental strain. Living with a girl who was on the brink of adolescence was like walking in a minefield, carrying a time bomb. Every little thing Hayeong said made Seonkyeong nervous, and a look on the child's face, which she just happened to notice, troubled her heart.

When Hayeong was with her, she required attention; when she wasn't, she was still very much on Seonkyeong's mind. No matter what Seonkyeong was doing, a part of her mind was always occupied with the child.

Living with Jaeseong alone hadn't required such great attention.

When he was home, she did tend to him, of course, but when she was by herself, she could forget about him and focus solely on her work. Since they both worked, they always told each other when they were busy, and made mutual concessions. When she was tired or didn't feel like making dinner, she called him and asked him to have dinner before coming home, or if they could, they had dinner out together. She read when she wanted, and slept when she wanted. Jaeseong, too, did things as he pleased. But with a child, things were different.

On top of that, Hayeong had been through so much.

Seonkyeong felt more comfortable with her now, but the child still wasn't very easy to approach. She couldn't just leave her to herself, though, not wanting to come off cold or indifferent. Thinking about it, she realized that there wasn't a moment when she wasn't aware of Hayeong, from the moment she opened her eyes in the morning, to the moment she fell asleep.

She felt like a clown in a circus, trying to balance herself on a rolling barrel, not sure which way it would go, and moving her feet ceaselessly in the direction the barrel was going.

The puppy had made things a lot better. After the puppy came, Hayeong began to smile now and then, and even talk to Seonkyeong. So she had thought that Hayeong was getting better. She'd relaxed, thinking she was adjusting to her new home, and getting along with the kids at school.

Seonkyeong didn't know what she should say to Hayeong when she came home. She decided to prepare a snack for her.

She closed the file on the desk and was about to get up, when she remembered some things Yi Byeongdo had said, and opened the file again. She pressed the play button on the recorder, and did a fast rewind.

"Would you . . . hug a baby monkey with such bloody hands? Could you?"

She recalled the look on his face as he said these words. A little child, hungry for affection, was pleading for a hug. His face kept overlapping with Hayeong's. Two children who grew up abused by their mothers. Yi Byeongdo had driven himself to hell, to a point of no return. But Hayeong was different. She had to be treated, and her wounds healed.

HAYEONG CAME IN LOOKING unperturbed, as if nothing had happened. Without saying anything about meeting her teacher at school,

Seonkyeong handed her a cup of cold water and asked, "Would you like some cheesecake, or some fruit?"

"Some cheesecake, please," Hayeong replied.

Sitting down at the table eating the cheesecake, she glanced at Seonkyeong's face from time to time. The fact that Seonkyeong wasn't asking her any questions seemed to make her nervous.

"A new bakery has opened up near the intersection, should we try it sometime? What do you like, Hayeong?"

"Chocolate mousse cake."

"Yeah? I like sweets, too. They make me feel better when I'm feeling down."

Hayeong seemed uncomfortable sitting with Seonkyeong. She answered her questions half-heartedly, and rushed to her feet as soon as she finished eating the cake.

"Hayeong," Seonkyeong called out to her as she made her way upstairs. She looked at Seonkyeong, her face stiffening, as if she knew what was coming. Her face grew darker and darker.

Seonkyeong quickly went up to her and bent down, and took her in her arms. She felt Hayeong flinch in her embrace. She was afraid that she'd push her away, but the child remained still. She could feel her little shoulders and the warmth of her body, and she felt a pang of sympathy. She thought that perhaps the distance between the two of them had been of her own making. She could sense her gradually relax.

"Everything feels strange and difficult, doesn't it? Thank you for being so patient. Things will get better little by little. If something happens, or you're having a hard time, you can always tell me or your dad," she said with some effort, her voice hoarse. She let go and looked at Hayeong, who was standing in a daze, looking confused.

23.

BEFORE SEONKYEONG MET WITH YI BYEONGDO, THE SECURITY manager wanted to see her. He took her to his office, saying he wanted to talk to her in private. The office was in the oldest building at the prison. The battered door closed properly only after several attempts. The old-fashioned air conditioner seemed to emit dust. The room smelled musty. This setup appeared to suit the security manager, though.

"Would you like something cold to drink?" he asked as he walked toward a small fridge, sounding laid-back. He seemed to be stalling on purpose, when he knew that soon it would be time for the interview. Seonkyeong wanted him to get to the point.

"What did you want to talk about?" she asked.

"Why are you in such a rush? Let's catch our breath first," he said.

He placed a canned drink in front of her and sat down on the sofa, munching on an ice cube. He looked her up and down for a moment without saying anything, then swallowed the remaining piece of ice and opened his mouth to speak.

"I think you've done quite enough," he said.

"Excuse me?" Seonkyeong said.

"The phone calls are one thing, but . . . ," he started. Director

Han's phone call seemed to have rubbed him the wrong way. "He's been somewhat unstable these past few days," he finished.

"Somewhat unstable?" Seonkyeong asked, not knowing what he meant. She wondered if something had happened to Yi Byeongdo.

"Well, you may not have noticed, since you see him only briefly, but we watch him all day so we sense even the slightest change," he said, and went on to tell her about the changes in Yi Byeongdo's daily routine since the last interview.

"He's been having trouble sleeping lately. He often stands at the sink, staring into the mirror. He faces a wall and mumbles to himself. Sometimes he covers his ears and shakes his head frantically," he said.

From the look on his face, the security manager didn't seem to be making the details up. He was right to be concerned about Yi Byeongdo's state. After a moment of thought, Seonkyeong decided to heed his words.

She had, in fact, been having a harder time interviewing Yi Byeongdo. And she had sensed him growing more and more restless. She, too, had felt his emotions waver as she went on seeing him. But what weighed more heavily on her heart was the feeling that she was projecting the sympathy she felt for him onto Hayeong. Instead of being hardheaded, she kept being swayed. If she couldn't maintain her objectivity, it might not be a bad idea to keep her distance from him for a little while.

Director Han's face popped up in her mind for a second, but Seonkyeong knew she wasn't fully capable of handling these interviews. She had to admit that she lacked sufficient experience. It was better to stop now than to continue, feeling confused and overwhelmed by her own emotions.

When Seonkyeong told the security manager that she would do as he wished, his expression changed at once. He looked as if a load had been lifted off him. It was the first time she'd seen him look so happy since she started coming for the interviews.

"It worried me that you seemed to keep letting him take control of the situation. Anyway, this will probably be your last interview with him, so I hope you wrap it up nicely," he said.

It must have been quite troubling for him. The interviews could raise controversy regarding special favors in prison, and above all, knowing that Yi Byeongdo's psychological state was unstable as a result of the interviews, he couldn't relax his guard. The recent suicide of a prisoner, which had thrown the prison into disarray, must have added to his irritation. If the interviews came to an end without causing trouble, he would finally be able to relax.

In the visitors' room, before Yi Byeongdo came in, Seonkyeong placed an apple on the table where he'd be sitting. She would've picked one with more care if she'd known this was going to be their last meeting.

As she sat in her seat, getting ready for the interview, the door opened and Yi Byeongdo walked in. Seonkyeong got up and waited for him to sit down. Soon their eyes met, with the table between them. It had been a week.

Studying his face, Seonkyeong was surprised.

The confident—arrogant, even—look in his eyes, which had been there since the first time they met, was gone; he now looked nervous, like someone being chased. The security manager hadn't been exaggerating. Seonkyeong could feel that the last interview had brought about a change in him.

He kept dropping his gaze, unable to look her straight in the face. He kept acting strange, shaking his head as if he had bugs flying in his face, tilting his head sideways, and cupping his ears with his hands.

"What's the matter? Are you all right?" Seonkyeong asked, sounding worried, but he didn't respond.

Seonkyeong gazed at him for a moment, and then started asking, one by one, the questions she had written down in her notebook for this interview. She tried to sound businesslike, to hide the fact that she was shaking inside.

"The owners of many of the things that were found during a house search couldn't be identified. Where did you get those things?"

He made no reply.

"Are there other victims, as the investigators assume?"

Still no reply.

"Mr. Yi," Seonkyeong said, raising her voice, as he continued not to answer. Finally, he looked at her.

"Are there other victims?" she asked again.

He thought for a moment, then nodded.

"What did you do with them?"

Instead of answering, he smiled. He looked as if he were enjoying his little secret. He wouldn't open his mouth easily, it seemed. Seonkyeong didn't think she could live up to the expectations of the investigators at the Seoul Gangbuk Police Station. She waited awhile for his answer, but he seemed to have a headache, and was frowning and pressing his temples.

In the end, she gave up on asking him about his murders, and resumed the conversation they'd been having the last time. If this was to be the last interview, it seemed that it would be better to focus on him.

"Will you tell me more about the fur mother monkey you were talking about the last time?" she asked.

He stared at her, tilting his head.

"Do you have another mother, different from the one who hurt you?" Seonkyeong pressed.

"It's . . . ," he began, seeming willing to talk about his other mother when he had been so tight-lipped about the murders.

"It's probably a dream. A dream so sweet . . . that it's all the more cruel," he said.

The look of anxiety in his eyes turned into one of longing. The tone of his voice changed as well. Was he wandering in his imagination? Or was he remembering days past?

Seonkyeong wanted to know if his fur mother monkey was someone who existed in reality.

"Does she . . . look like me?" she asked.

Yi Byeongdo's gaze rested on her face. Searching his memory, he began to talk slowly.

"Maybe she did . . . it's been so long, I can't trust my memory. It could just be my imagination coloring my memories," he said.

Good memories become all the more distorted because they're good memories, and take on a rosier glow with time. Like one's first love, the mother in his memory must have been painted over.

His expression had softened as he searched his memory, but suddenly, his face stiffened and he said with a crack in his voice, "It was my one chance. My one chance . . . and I ruined everything!"

For some reason, he was angry with himself.

"Mr. Yi, what was your one chance?" Seonkyeong asked.

"I . . . ruined it. I did," he said in a faint voice, his head lowered. Then he looked up at Seonkyeong, his eyes burning.

"You'll give me another chance, won't you? Won't you?" he asked.

Seonkyeong didn't know what he was talking about, but moved by the desperation in his eyes, she nodded. His face, which had been distorted with anger, relaxed, and he heaved a sigh of relief.

Seonkyeong's unwitting answer seemed to have given him great comfort.

"Have you ever killed a cat?" Seonkyeong asked out of nowhere.

She hadn't planned on asking such a question. She'd remembered the cat his mother had loved, and how he'd been jealous of the cat; his story got mixed up together in her mind with how Hayeong and the other kids had harassed a cat, and the question just popped out.

Yi Byeongdo stared at her for a moment, looking dazed, then began to chuckle.

"You've finally figured it out, huh? All women are like cats. They run, just out of your reach . . . and reappear, when you think they're gone. All the women I killed . . . were like that. They came up to me, then they scratched me and ran. That's why I sang to them. Some of them even sang along, without even knowing what the song was," he said, and kept chuckling. He had trouble concentrating on what Seonkyeong said, and kept falling back into his own thoughts.

His story brought a lot of things to Seonkyeong's mind. The story about the day he killed his mother and the story about the women he'd killed were consistent with each other. It seemed that he wanted to kill women when he saw his mother in them. To Seonkyeong's knowledge, the victims did not have similar physical traits. Had they reminded him of his mother in psychological, emotional ways?

He kept looking around anxiously, unable to keep himself steady; in the end, he got to his feet, saying he was tired. When the guard came and took him away, Seonkyeong didn't tell him that it was their last interview.

Even if she met with him again, it didn't seem likely that he would tell her who the other victims were, or if he had committed additional murders. She didn't know why he remained silent about the other victims, but he wanted to keep his secret buried to the end. Although she hadn't been able to unearth the secret, she'd learned a lot about him through the interview. With that, she'd be able to write a report that would satisfy Director Han.

With mixed emotions, she looked around the visitors' room.

On her first day here, the room had made her feel stifled, as if she couldn't breathe. As time passed, however, and the interviews progressed, she realized that the confined space helped them focus.

She packed her bag and got to her feet, and noticed the apple on the table. She picked it up and looked at it for a moment, then took a careful bite.

The refreshing taste of the apple spread through her mouth. She put the apple back down on the table. Leaving the partly eaten apple for Yi Byeongdo to finish, she walked out of the room.

PART 4

24.

JAESEONG LEFT FOR WASHINGTON IN THE MORNING.

The previous night, Seonkyeong had told him about Heeju. He was angry when she suggested that Hayeong be examined and receive counseling.

"Why would she need something like that? She's going to school now, and adjusting fine," he said.

"You really think she's adjusting fine?"

"Do you think she has some kind of problem, then?"

Since Hayeong's arrival, Seonkyeong had learned that the child was Jaeseong's weak point. He felt guilty that he hadn't been a good father to her when they were living apart. That kept him from facing the problem head-on. Seonkyeong told him about what happened at school, and what Heeju had said to her.

"You know that something's wrong, don't you?" she asked.

He didn't say anything.

"What Hayeong's been through is different from what children normally experience. There was her mother's suicide, and then the fire. It would be strange if she wasn't scarred."

"I just thought that with time, she'd forget, and be all right."

"That's your wishful thinking."

"But she's doing well, isn't she?" he asked, standing his ground.

"Only on the surface. Which makes me even more concerned. She could be hurting inside, all alone, not being able to say that she's hurting."

Jaeseong was silent. He looked uncomfortable whenever she brought up Hayeong's problems. Not having been there to take care of her, he couldn't acknowledge that Hayeong had a problem. He must think that it was all his fault. Seonkyeong spoke as gently as she could, in a roundabout way, so that it wouldn't sound as though she were criticizing him.

"The counseling would be a sort of comprehensive medical testing. If any small symptoms show, something more serious can be prevented. You're a doctor, so you know. She's been through things that can't be handled alone. Who knows how they've injured her? Can you say that she's fine, just because you can't see the wounds? If there are any wounds, we have to find a way to heal them before they get worse," Seonkyeong continued, and at last, he gave in. He nodded, agreeing that Hayeong needed counseling, but he didn't look happy about it.

Seonkyeong let out a sigh of relief. It was a good thing he consented; if not, she might have found it necessary to be more aggressive to make him recognize that there was a problem.

He asked her to wait until he came back from his trip, saying it would be better for him to talk to Hayeong about it himself. Seonkyeong agreed. Above all, Hayeong would find it easier, hearing it from him.

He took his time saying goodbye to Hayeong. He went on and on about the things she was supposed to do. He also made extravagant promises about going to the amusement park, to the beach, and so on when he came home, since summer vacation was approaching. It seemed that he wanted to compensate for not having been very attentive to her. In contrast, Hayeong was surprisingly unruffled about him leaving. He didn't seem to think a dozen promises were enough, and added that he would buy her an even bigger teddy bear than the last one, and finally left.

With him gone, Hayeong went upstairs to get ready for school.

He would be gone for ten days.

During that time, Seonkyeong decided to focus as much on Hayeong as possible. How they spent those days would determine their relationship. After giving her a hug on the day she went to see her teacher, Seonkyeong took every opportunity to hug Hayeong and show her physical affection. They grew closer after that day. Seonkyeong felt it was because they'd had physical contact and shared warmth.

Hayeong rushed down the stairs, saying she was late. She went to the front door and was about to put on her shoes when Seonkyeong called to her; Hayeong ran quickly over and put her arms around Seonkyeong's waist. After a brief hug, Hayeong left in a hurry.

Alone at home, Seonkyeong opened both the front and back doors to the living room and began to clean the house.

Just then, her cell phone rang. The number didn't look familiar.

When she picked up, she heard a pleasantly low voice. She instantly recognized it as Sergeant Yu's. She was both glad and puzzled that he'd called out of the blue. Then it crossed her mind that the arson case might have been resolved.

Contrary to her expectations, though, he asked if they could meet, saying he had something to tell her.

She said she'd meet him at the Seoul Metropolitan Police Agency, and hung up. A chill passed through her—a kind of premonition.

IT WAS PAST LUNCH HOUR, around two o'clock, when she arrived at the Seoul Metropolitan Police Agency near Gwanghwamun.

She got off the subway at Gwanghwamun Station and took the path behind Sejong Center for the Performing Arts. The scorching midday sun was melting the asphalt. She looked for bits of shadow created by the buildings and the trees lining the street to walk in. She went to the information desk and made a confirmation call, after which she was let in, and given a visitor's badge.

When she walked in through the entrance, she saw Sergeant Yu getting off the elevator. He hurried over to her and said hello.

"Thank you for taking the trouble to come all the way here when it's so hot," he said.

"Not at all," Seonkyeong said.

Together they went into the lounge in the first-floor lobby. Watching Seonkyeong sit down, Sergeant Yu took out some coins from his pocket and went up to the vending machine.

"What would you like?" he asked.

"Some water, please," Seonkyeong replied.

Sergeant Yu got a canned coffee and a bottle of water and sat across from Seonkyeong. The water was cold enough to cool her sun-scorched body.

"I could've traveled to where you were," he said.

"No, it's fine. So what did you want to talk about?"

"The autopsy results are out."

"Huh?"

"I'm not really sure where I should begin. But since you're in this line of work, I think you'll take what I say in an objective, logical way."

Seonkyeong felt nervous listening to him stall. What was all the fuss about? What was it that he wanted to say?

"The fire in Eungam-dong was a case of arson. And the arson took place after a murder," he said.

Even as she heard the words he spoke, she couldn't make sense of them right away.

"Wait a minute, are you saying that the fire was a case of murder?" she asked.

"Yes, a case of arson to hide murder, that's what we presume," he replied.

"So when you say autopsy results . . . are you talking about Hayeong's grandparents?"

"Yes," Sergeant Yu said firmly.

Seonkyeong shook her head in spite of herself. She had thought the fire was just an accident. She could not believe that it was a result of someone's ill will. How many lives had changed because of it?

"Did you catch the culprit?" she asked.

"Let's talk about the autopsy results first," he said. It seemed that the culprit hadn't yet been caught. Seonkyeong wondered why he should be telling her, of all people.

"So these are the results. They both died before the fire broke out. There were no traces of a fire in their esophagi and lungs. If they died from the fire, there would've been traces of smoke from the fire in their esophagi and lungs," he said.

If they died from the fire, they wouldn't have been lying so still under the blanket, either. Sergeant Yu recalled for a moment how the old couple had looked at the site.

"What was the cause of death, then?" Seonkyeong asked.

The sergeant rummaged inside his jacket, and pulled out a piece of paper, folded several times over. It was an autopsy report from the National Forensic Service.

"It was death from poisoning," he said.

"Then . . . isn't there a possibility of suicide?"

"Would anyone take poison after getting ready to burn the house, with their granddaughter in the next room?"

Seonkyeong couldn't say anything.

"What's more, in cases of death from poisoning, the bodies would be contorted with pain; but both of them had their hands folded together, under the blanket. Which means that someone checked to make sure that they were dead, and set the fire after putting the bodies in order."

"If the fire took place after the murder . . . there wouldn't be any evidence at the scene."

"That's right. Almost no evidence at all, unfortunately . . . but . . ."

Seonkyeong looked at him inquiringly.

"We do have a suspect."

"Who?"

Sergeant Yu hesitated, having difficulty answering, and looked at Seonkyeong. Looking at his troubled face, Seonkyeong remembered something. They had come to the house on a hot summer day, sweating profusely, to see Hayeong. She tried to recall the questions they asked, but couldn't.

"You're not saying . . ." She trailed off.

"Yes, someone who was in the house with them, Yun Hayeong," Sergeant Yu confirmed.

"What . . . what are you saying here? Hayeong is a child. She's only eleven."

Not knowing how to respond to her protest, Sergeant Yu scratched his head for a moment, then asked, "How old is the youngest murderer in the materials you've studied?"

Seonkyeong was speechless. He was right. Age didn't matter.

Mary Bell, the most horrific underage serial killer in the history of the twentieth century, had also been eleven. Along with a friend, she strangled to death a neighbor child, not even three years old, and mutilated his body with scissors. You didn't even have to look that far—in Japan, there was an elementary school child who killed a classmate, sending shock waves around the world.

"I have several reasons for thinking that," Sergeant Yu said, and Seonkyeong listened, her entire body throbbing with the sound of her own heartbeat.

"When you go to the scene of a fire, you'll see that the victims all look similar. Taken by surprise, most of them aren't dressed properly. That morning when I saw the rescued child, something tugged at my mind, though I couldn't put my finger on it. But when I thought about it later, I realized that it was the clothes she was wearing that seemed strange," he continued.

He remembered that morning clearly. The child, even as she was being carried out by an ambulance worker, had been carrying a teddy bear. On top of that, she'd been wearing socks and shoes. How could she have been wearing her shoes, which would've been at the front door, when she went out through the window to escape the smoke? It could only mean that she'd gotten them ahead of time.

"She had her father's business card in her pocket," he added.

"Perhaps . . . she'd been planning to go see him in secret?" Seon-kyeong said, wanting to refute the evidence he had, any way she could.

He has only one piece of the puzzle, she thought. You can't judge someone with that. So many people are falsely accused through mistaken evidence. Hayeong could have been planning on leaving her grandparents' house that day to go to her father, which would explain it all.

You can't come to any conclusions based on that. You mustn't, she kept saying in her mind, but she realized that her voice was growing fainter and fainter.

"After she was rescued, the child didn't say a single word about her grandparents. An ordinary child, under similar circumstances, would ask someone to find or save her guardians if she doesn't see them. But Hayeong didn't even bother to ask if her grandparents were safe, or if they were still inside the house. Which probably means that she already understood the situation," Sergeant Yu said, and remembered something else.

The way she had looked, sleeping in the backseat of the police car. Thinking back, he realized that the look on her face hadn't shown any traces of shock or fear; it was a look of satisfaction at the thought that her father was coming.

"I don't know what to say. This is so unexpected," Seonkyeong said. She didn't think she could go on sitting there listening to him. She felt as if there were a great whirlwind in her mind.

"All this, of course, is something of my own deduction. I have no evidence to prove it. Unless the poison that was administered to the old couple is found. . . . I haven't told anyone else. None of my colleagues know," Sergeant Yu said.

"So why are you . . . ," Seonkyeong started.

"Because you, of all people, should know. You're an expert in this field, and you're also her guardian now."

Seonkyeong couldn't say anything.

"Keep a close eye on her. That's all I want to say," Sergeant Yu said, and walked away.

Alone in the lounge, Seonkyeong couldn't even think of getting up from her seat.

She couldn't think clearly, with everything mixed up in her mind—she didn't know what to make of anything, how she should take it, or what to tell Jaeseong. She finally managed to get a grip on herself, and came to one conclusion after long thought: she shouldn't say anything yet.

She couldn't let anyone accuse the child of being a murderer, when nothing had been confirmed.

There was no reason for the child to have killed her grandparents and even set the house on fire to come to her father. He was only a phone call away, so why would she have done something that would put her own life at risk?

That was what she thought in her mind, but she couldn't quite convince herself.

Yet Seonkyeong knew that many murderers killed people for absurd reasons.

Leaving the police agency, she felt afraid to go home and face Hayeong.

Heading toward the subway station, Seonkyeong changed her mind and decided to go to Eungam-dong. She couldn't go home like this. She didn't really have a plan in mind, but she wanted to see the house Hayeong had lived in. Perhaps she wanted to verify what Sergeant Yu had said.

THE HOUSE, whose address Seonkyeong got from Sergeant Yu, was quite unsightly, neglected after the fire. She could picture at once the disastrous situation that night, which she hadn't been able to do when she just listened to people talk about it. She could clearly see Hayeong, standing amid flames. The scene of the fire was overpowering in itself.

She dared not go inside, and left in haste.

A middle-aged woman walking into the alleyway noticed Seonkyeong coming out, and looked at her warily. After watching her for a while as she passed slowly by, the woman asked gruffly, "Did you come to see the house at the end?"

Seonkyeong was going to ignore the question, but then she gave a quiet nod. Seeing the mixed emotions on her face, the woman immediately dropped her guard. She seemed kindly but nosy, and looked Seonkyeong up and down, and then clicked her tongue, as if she felt sorry for her. She seemed to think that Seonkyeong was a relative who had come a little late after hearing the news.

"Those poor old people. . . . So, are you related to them?" the woman asked.

Not knowing what to say, Seonkyeong missed her opportunity to answer. But the woman nodded sympathetically, as if she understood completely.

"You must've been quite shocked. Who wouldn't be? All those

terrible things happening, as if some bad luck had fallen on them. . . .
Maybe people are right, saying that their dead daughter's spirit is still
lingering," she went on.

"Daughter? You mean, Hayeong's mother?" Seonkyeong asked.

"That's right. She took something to kill herself. I don't know what
was going on, but why would someone do that when her parents and
daughter are alive? The old woman wasn't ever the same again after
that."

"Was Hayeong happy here?" Seonkyeong asked.

"The girl? Well . . . who knows what goes on behind closed doors,"
the woman said, suddenly sounding evasive and looking flustered.
Just a moment before, she had talked as if she knew all about the
family's circumstances, but the tone of her voice was different now.
Seonkyeong wondered what was going on.

"Did something happen to Hayeong?" she asked.

"Why do you keep prying about the child? How are you related
to her?" the woman asked in return, seeming uncomfortable with
Seonkyeong's questions.

"She . . . she's in my care now," Seonkyeong said with honesty.
Hearing her words, the woman looked even more disturbed. She
began to rush into her house, looking awkward.

"Just a second, can't you tell me what happened?" Seonkyeong
pleaded.

"We just live in the neighborhood—we can't possibly know everything that happened in their house," the woman said, as if being
chased, when she'd been the one to start the whole conversation.
She seemed reluctant to even mention Hayeong. Seonkyeong was
perturbed. She had goose bumps all over, and her stomach felt tight.
Beads of sweat formed on her forehead, but the tips of her fingers
rapidly grew cold.

Without looking back, Seonkyeong hurried out of the alleyway.

25.

THE HOT, HUMID DAYS CONTINUED.
Yi Byeongdo called the prison guard and requested another interview with Seonkyeong, but all he got was a laugh in his face. After some screaming and mayhem, the security manager came to see him in his cell.

"I need another interview. I still have something to say," Yi Byeongdo said.

"The psychologist seemed to have nothing more to say or hear," said the security manager.

"I need to see her!"

"I guess you didn't know, but that was your last interview. She won't be coming to see you anymore."

"What? No. No way. Call her right now. I'm not finished telling my story!" Yi Byeongdo yelled, and the security manager came up to the steel bars and whispered in his face, "Then why didn't you do it when you had a chance? Not that what you say even matters."

"Tell her I'll let her know where the women . . . where the rest of the bodies are," Yi Byeongdo said, deciding to play his hidden card. He had meant to keep it to himself, never telling anyone. But he felt that parting with the information would be worth it, if he could see

Seonkyeong again. When you want something desperately, you become blind to everything else.

Surprised, the security manager looked at the face beyond the bars. The security manager narrowed his eyes, glaring at him, and fell into thought, as if to see if he meant what he said. But what he said next was not something Yi Byeongdo had expected.

"Hot for her, aren't you?" he said, raising one corner of his mouth and snickering.

Yi Byeongdo felt himself crushing his hidden card. This wasn't what he'd wanted; this wasn't why he'd decided to play his card. He had a grand design to complete. He couldn't let this vermin ruin it.

"I told you you had it coming," the security manager said.

"I said I'll tell her about the other murders!"

"Only the police and the prosecutors would be interested in that—I'm fine as long as you're stuck here, understand?"

"Call my lawyer. I won't stand for this."

"Whatever you want. But you know what? You've lied to the lawyer so many times, I don't know if he'll go out of his way to come see you. When the trial's over, you know."

Hearing him say that, Yi Byeongdo flushed with anger and began to scream.

"Guard! Guard! Call the chief! I need to see him!"

The guard, however, who came running from the end of the corridor, stood by the security manager without so much as a look at Yi Byeongdo.

"What do you think you're doing? Do you know who I am? I'm Yi Byeongdo! Do you think I'll just sit and do nothing?"

"Why don't you keep on screaming?" the security manager said, unperturbed by his raving.

Suddenly, the other prisoners began thumping on their doors. They swore and cursed, saying he was being too loud. They didn't want to hear him anymore, either.

Yi Byeongdo gripped the bars, trembling. He was hot with fury. Somewhere, the song started again; he had no time to waste. His mother's song that was slow, and made him crazy with suffocation. *Bang, bang . . .*

The security manager and the guard opened the middle steel-barred door, leaving him behind, glaring with bloodshot eyes.

Left alone, he sank to the floor, his back against the wall, and began to think.

He couldn't just sit helplessly. He had to find some way to see her again.

Seonkyeong was the only one who would understand his mother's song, which kept playing in his head; she was the only one who could make it stop. He wanted to tell her, just her, the old story about his mother and him.

The day he committed his first murder in the rainy yard, he checked to make sure that his mother was dead, and dug in the ground all night and buried her. The blood that reddened the ground got washed away in the rain and disappeared down the drain.

Just like his own birth, his mother's death drew no one's attention. They had kept to themselves, away from the world, so no one ever came to see them, anyway.

Several days after burying his mother in the yard, he went to the police station and reported that she had left home. She hadn't been home in days, he said. The police gave him some papers to fill out, and asked questions as a formality. He asked them if they shouldn't set out on a search, but they said that they couldn't spare their efforts on someone who had left home of her own will. They only said that he should go home and wait, since she was an adult and could come back, if she had left of her own will. He walked out of the police station, looking grim, but he hummed on his way home. His mother would never come back. She had never left in the first place.

For the first time in his life, he slept soundly, not trembling in fear.

When he thought back, he'd always leapt to his feet at the sound of footsteps, or the slightest rustle, not knowing when she would smother him with a pillow. He never slept well at the orchard house, either. When he fell asleep, his mother appeared in his dreams and pulled him by the arm, wanting to go home. He would struggle in resistance, and she would throw him into a deep tub. He woke up many times, feeling suffocated. He'd often walked through the apple trees in the orchard all night, thinking it would be better not to sleep at all.

Finding out for the first time how sweet sleep could be, he never for a moment thought about his mother.

Several years later, the police asked him to come identify a body; shocked, he ran all the way to the station. Someone had drowned in a reservoir, and the body had been discovered when the water was drained; it must have resembled the description on the papers he'd filled out. He shook his head, saying it wasn't his mother, and expressed anger at the police, who were still making scant effort to find her.

On his way back home, he even wondered where his mother had disappeared to. But although he had thought he had thus erased her completely from his mind, he'd only been fooling himself. His mother was still alive and breathing in his mind, and came to him and sang "Maxwell's Silver Hammer" in his ear when he was deep in sleep. It was fifteen years later when he realized that.

He was living among people, working at a new factory in the area and enjoying a monotonous life of going from home to work. The work was simple. He hung out with his coworkers occasionally, and even met girls. Women always smiled and came up to him when they saw him. They were all taken by his handsome and kind-looking face, but the more aggressive they were, the further he distanced himself from them. He felt more at ease without women around.

Seeing how he acted around women, his coworkers thought he

was shy. They thought he just lacked experience. Perhaps they were right. He didn't want to find out what women were like. It would be more correct to say that he was afraid.

One evening, at a get-together after work, they'd gone for a second, then a third, round of drinks, and he'd left by himself. It was quiet there, away from downtown, and after midnight there were no people around, only the glaring lights of bars and clubs. Reeling from the drinks, he began to hum a song, without being aware of it.

Bang! Bang! Maxwell's silver hammer . . .

Realizing what song he was singing, he froze on the spot, frightened. A woman he didn't know smiled and came up to him. That was when the murders began again.

He shook his head. It was no use thinking about what happened so long ago.

He thought of the apple Seonkyeong had handed him.

The woman at the orchard house used to pick big, fresh apples, hanging at the top of the tree, and put them in his hand. The apple took him back twenty years. He was once again at the orchard in June. He saw green apples swaying in the wind. He saw two older girls and a younger one. For the first time in his life, he'd felt at peace.

He thought about it. He believed that he could return to those days, if he saw Seonkyeong again. He'd thought that he had already been given the one chance in his life. But after twenty years, another chance had come his way. He couldn't let it pass. Seonkyeong said she'd give him another chance. If only he could see her again.

She would stop the song for him.

26.

THE ASHEN CLOUDS THAT HAD GATHERED SINCE THE AF-
ternoon colored the sky black. The clouds, heavy with rain,
began to get entangled and spark up. The wind smelled of
damp air.

Seonkyeong came home after meeting Sergeant Yu feeling as
bleak and gloomy as the weather.

She opened the gate, rattling in the wind, and went inside and
looked around at the house.

A gold rubber ball, which the puppy had been playing with, was
rolling around in the yard; the willow tree was swaying in the wind,
its leaves like disheveled hair. There was a little light on in the living
room, and it was quiet in the house. The light was off in Hayeong's
room upstairs. She must not have been back from school yet.

Seonkyeong still couldn't fully understand the things she had
heard.

She couldn't believe everything Sergeant Yu had said. He himself had admitted that he had no evidence, that it was only something of his own deduction. But when Seonkyeong thought back to
Hayeong's first day at the house, she couldn't completely discount
what he'd said.

Hayeong had never talked about her grandparents since she came to live with Jaeseong and Seonkyeong after the fire. That hadn't even occurred to her until Sergeant Yu pointed out the fact. She'd thought only about how the fire must have shocked Hayeong. She believed that Hayeong was making a conscious effort not to think about it because it was too hard to bear.

Considering that she'd been through a terrible fire, however, she didn't seem under much stress. She quickly adjusted to living with her father, as if she'd just been waiting for the chance.

Could she really have set the fire? Seonkyeong wondered.

It wasn't just the fire. Sergeant Yu had suggested an even more unsettling possibility.

Hayeong's grandparents died of poisoning before the fire broke out. Who could have poisoned the old couple and set the fire? Awful possibilities reared their heads, and Seonkyeong shook her head. Nothing had been confirmed. There should be no jumping to conclusions. She wished that Jaeseong was with her.

It would be at least ten days before he came home. She would be alone with Hayeong until then. The time seemed to strangle her, tightening its grip on her neck.

The wind began to pick up. Raindrops plopped down. As Seonkyeong headed toward the front door, her foot got caught on the rubber ball. She picked it up, thinking of the puppy. It couldn't be. The child, who cherished the puppy so much, couldn't have done something so horrible. The more she tried to deny it, however, the faster other memories flooded her mind, unsettling her.

She bit down on her lip. She gave the ball a gentle squeeze, then put it down. She went into the house and her eyes fell on the staircase leading up to the second floor. She wavered between going upstairs to ascertain facts, and not wanting to find out anything, for fear that she might end up seeing something beyond imagination. After some hesitation, she ended up going to Hayeong's room.

WHEN SHE OPENED THE door, the puppy ran over and greeted her. She picked it up and went into the room. She looked around, not knowing what she should be looking for.

Everything was nicely organized. The books and the pencil case were all in their proper place on the desk. Seonkyeong could see that Hayeong liked things neat and tidy. She opened the desk drawer. Notepads, notebooks, and various stationery items were neatly arranged.

The puppy in her arms whimpered, feeling stifled. She put it down and opened the wardrobe. The clothes were hanging in an orderly fashion. She ran her hands gently through the clothes, then closed the wardrobe.

She recalled how she'd slapped the child. It was possible that Sergeant Yu's words were misleading her. Hayeong must have an explanation that Seonkyeong wasn't aware of.

She would pretend she didn't know anything. She couldn't break the peace now because of a stranger's presumption. Thinking that, she couldn't stay in the room. She grasped the door handle to open the door, but at that moment, she heard the puppy whimpering somewhere. She turned her head back toward the room.

The puppy was whimpering, scratching one side of the dresser. It seemed to have smelled something that drew its attention. Reluctant to open the dresser, she just stared at it for a while. Then, finally making up her mind, she opened it.

There was an extra blanket inside.

She heaved a sigh without realizing it. The puppy whimpered even more. She was about to shut the drawer, but she carefully lifted the blanket. There was a little box underneath. She had an ominous feeling about it. A faint, strange odor seemed to emanate from it.

She had come this far. There was no turning back now. She took the box out and sat on the bed. The box was the size of a tissue box. It wasn't heavy. Opening it with caution, she nearly dropped it in astonishment.

The things that fell out of the box got scattered all around. Looking at those things, Seonkyeong felt aghast. She couldn't believe her own eyes. There were several stiff, dead birds in the box. Some with the feathers plucked, and the bellies cut open. There was a bloody paper knife in the box as well, probably used to cut the birds.

Seonkyeong's blood froze.

She recalled how, on the day they went to the school for the transfer procedures, Hayeong had tried to catch birds at the nature study area.

Seonkyeong now also pictured Hayeong thrusting a knife at a cat. Hayeong had followed the other kids to look for the cat, knowing full well who had taken the birds but feigning ignorance. She was probably curious as to what they were going to do. What would have happened if they hadn't been startled into letting the cat escape?

Just thinking about it made Seonkyeong's hair stand on end.

She quickly picked up the puppy as it began to sniff at the dead birds on the floor. She got some tissues, picked up the birds, and put them back in the box. All kinds of information flashed through her mind. She gripped her forehead and flopped down on the bed.

Unaware of what was going on, the puppy jumped onto her lap. Holding the puppy and stroking it, Seonkyeong wondered what she should do. She decided that for now, she would wait for Jaeseong to come home.

She stared at the floor for a while, then closed the box full of birds that had died in pain.

SEONKYEONG WAS SITTING in the living room, deep in thought, unaware of the rain that was pouring down. She didn't even notice Hayeong, drenched from the rain, come in through the front door. She came to herself only when Hayeong called out to her. Seeing Hayeong, she finally turned her gaze out the window and saw that it was raining.

"Oh, I didn't know it was raining," she said.

"Could you get me a towel?" Hayeong asked.

"Oh . . . yes, just a minute," she said, finally getting to her feet after sitting in a daze, just staring at Hayeong as she stood there wet. She felt stifled and uncomfortable, as if her head were stuffed full of crumpled up rubbish.

She brought a large towel from the bathroom at once, and dried off Hayeong's hair and body. She was completely wet, and her clothes had to be taken off. Her body was cold—she must have been in the rain for a long time. Her little shoulders were shivering.

"Why didn't you call me from school?" Seonkyeong asked.

"It's okay, I like it when it rains," Hayeong said.

"Go to the bathroom and take a hot shower. I'll bring you some clothes."

"No, I will," Hayeong said and went upstairs, still dripping, without waiting for Seonkyeong's reply.

Seonkyeong boiled water while Hayeong took a shower. She prepared some hot milk and chocolate mousse cake. Hayeong's cheeks were flushed from the shower. She seemed to be feeling better, too. She came into the kitchen and saw the snack laid out on the table, and put her arms tightly around Seonkyeong's waist.

Seonkyeong held her breath. She barely managed to keep herself from shoving the child away.

Sitting down, Hayeong told her about her walk in the rain. She chattered in a cheerful voice, sounding happy. Normally, Seonkyeong would've been quite responsive. But she pretended she was busy putting dishes away, avoiding Hayeong's eyes.

"What kind of weather do you like?" Hayeong asked.

"Me? Sunny spring weather, I guess," she said, without really giving it a thought. She wished that Hayeong would finish eating quickly and go upstairs. She didn't want to sit face-to-face with her, pretending nothing was wrong, nor did she think she could. She needed time to pull herself together.

Hayeong was unusually talkative. She went on and on about the things that happened at school. She talked about how she had tended to the vegetable patch with her friends. Everything she said grated on Seonkyeong's nerves. Hayeong's teacher had sent her a text message, worried that the other kids were avoiding her after the incident with the cat. And here she was, lying with a straight face when it was so easy to catch her in a lie if you paid just a little attention. Seonkyeong wondered if she was doing it to show that she wasn't having any problems at school, or if there was another reason.

Noticing that Seonkyeong was different from usual, Hayeong stopped in the middle of talking and looked at her.

"What's wrong?" she asked.

"Oh, um . . . I have a little headache," Seonkyeong said. Her temples really were beginning to throb. No, her entire body was beginning to throb.

"Are you very sick?" Hayeong asked.

"No, I'll be all right after I take some medicine and get some sleep," Seonkyeong said.

Hayeong just sat there blinking, trying to read her face.

Lightning suddenly flashed. Soon it began to thunder. Even Hayeong, who said she liked rainy days, flinched and looked out at the yard.

Staring at the rain striking the window, she whispered, "This is like the day my mom died."

Seonkyeong felt alarmed.

"There was a storm, just like this," Hayeong said, sounding gloomy. Memories of her mother seemed to have put her in low spirits. She appeared to have lost her appetite as well—she put her fork down, and went up to her room.

Seonkyeong went into her own bedroom. She felt heavy, and had a hard time standing on her feet. She put a hand to her forehead—it was hot. She had caught a cold, it seemed.

She got some cold medicine from the cabinet and lay down on the bed. Her head was pounding. Her mind kept darting to the second floor, but there was no sound other than that of the rain, and the rattling windows.

As the medicine began to take effect, she dozed off.

27.

I N HER ROOM, HAYEONG LOOKED OUT THE WINDOW FOR A MO-
ment, then climbed onto the bed. There was a flash of light, and
then the window began to rattle. She hid under the blanket and
squeezed her eyes shut. There, her fear lifted somewhat.

The reason why she'd kept talking to Seonkyeong after coming
home was that she didn't want to be alone.

The whole way home, walking in the rain, she'd felt strange—as
if someone were following her. She wanted to turn around and look
but couldn't. She was afraid that her dead mom would be there if she
did. Her dream had made her think of her mom.

The night before, her dad had come to talk to her in her room.

He said he was going away on a business trip for ten days, and
told her to have a good time with Seonkyeong. Hayeong nodded.
She hadn't liked her at first. Her mom had told her that she was a bad
person—a wicked woman who had taken her dad away, someone
who was very selfish, and destroyed other people's family. But as time
passed, Hayeong realized that her mom had lied. Her dad seemed
much happier when he was with Seonkyeong than when he'd been
with her mom. Seonkyeong didn't yell, or drink, or curse.

She'd slapped her on the cheek, but it hadn't really hurt. She said
she was sorry. Hayeong's mom never did.

Hayeong found it strange that her dad had made her promise, again and again, that she would be obedient to Seonkyeong. She wondered if it was because Seonkyeong didn't like her. She thought that was why her dad was telling her to be careful. But when she thought about it, that didn't seem true. Seonkyeong held her gently in her arms now. When Hayeong was in Seonkyeong's arms, she wanted to close her eyes and go to sleep. She felt comfortable. Her mom hadn't liked hugging. Her mom hugged her only when there were other people around.

After her dad went downstairs, Hayeong lay in bed, thinking about her mom and Seonkyeong. She thought she was happier now, living with Seonkyeong. And then she fell asleep. Hayeong met her mom in her dream. Her mom was very angry. Just like that day.

Get your father here, right now!

Hayeong covered her ears. She could hear her mom's sharp voice. Her mom grabbed her arm and twisted it, and she opened her eyes in pain. She felt relieved, realizing it was a dream.

Lightning struck again. The rain fell and the wind blew. Her mom had wanted to see her dad even more on days like this. Hayeong wanted to stop thinking about her.

She's dead. She's dead, so stop thinking about her, she said to herself in her mind.

On days like this, however, she felt afraid that her mom would come out from somewhere and start yelling. Hayeong got up off the bed, carrying her pillow. She felt that she wouldn't be afraid if she slept in Seonkyeong's arms, even if her mom appeared. She was about to leave the room, when her foot caught on the puppy.

Startled, the puppy hid under the bed and wouldn't come out, no matter how many times Hayeong called. Finally, she reached under the bed. She felt something—something icky.

What came out from under the bed was a feather. Seeing the feather, she immediately opened the dresser drawer. She looked under the blanket, and the box that should've been there was gone. She could guess who had taken the box. She began to pout. It was a habit she had when she got angry.

She had to go demand an answer. But first, she decided to take the puppy out from under the bed. It must have been the puppy that told Seonkyeong where the box was. It was supposed to be a secret between just the two of them. The puppy must've done something wrong, to hide like this.

A puppy that doesn't keep secrets must be punished.

Her hand caught the puppy. She dragged it out from under the bed, and looked it in the eye. With the puppy struggling in one arm, she looked for the brown bottle she'd hidden somewhere deep.

SEONKYEONG WAS IN A HUGE MANSION, looking around. She was wearing a black dress, and walking through an endlessly long corridor with a high ceiling, checking the open rooms one by one, looking for something.

Someone was standing in the sunlight at the end of the corridor. Seonkyeong ran toward the light. The moment she realized that the person standing there was Hayeong, the child ran into another room, as if playing hide-and-seek. The sound of her laughter rang through the space and spread to the ceiling.

Seonkyeong wanted to cover her ears. A rope fell on the floor in front of her as she ran away from the laughter. The rope was in the form of a noose, as if to say that she should hang herself with it. Startled, Seonkyeong pushed the rope away and ran. She turned a corner, and saw that there was a door at a dead end.

When she opened the door, Hayeong was standing there, waiting, and offered her a handful of cold medicine. Seonkyeong refused, shaking her head, and Hayeong became furious and pounced on her, and was about to force the medicine down her throat.

Seonkyeong shook Hayeong's arms off and shoved her with all her might. Her eyes wide open in surprise, Hayeong fell down and down, her hands waving in the air. Standing at the railing, Seonkyeong looked down in shock and saw Hayeong lying still on the floor, her legs bent out of shape. Hayeong cried and reached out toward her.

Somehow, Hayeong's arms stretched out longer and longer and reached Seonkyeong's neck. The child clung to her. The warmth of her tender skin gave Seonkyeong goose bumps.

Seonkyeong's eyes flew open. Her body was drenched in sweat. It was a dream, but she could still feel Hayeong's little hands that had just been clinging to her neck. She felt her neck. There was nothing there, of course.

At that moment, she saw Hayeong standing before her. Goose bumps rose all over her body. It seemed that the touch of the hands hadn't been a dream after all.

"What's the matter?" Seonkyeong asked.

Hayeong was carrying a pillow. She must have come down, not wanting to be alone in the storm. The child stretched out a hand. She felt Seonkyeong's forehead, and then her own.

"Your head feels hot," she said.

"Yes, I'm not feeling well. Will you go upstairs to your room?" Seonkyeong asked.

"No, I'll stay with you."

Seonkyeong wanted to keep her eyes open, but the medicine made her drowsy. She fell back into a deep slumber. She wasn't even aware of Hayeong slipping into the bed next to her and putting her arms around her waist.

28.

S PARKS FLEW UP IN THE DARKENED SKY; A VIOLENT GUST OF wind blew, and heavy rain began to fall.

Yi Byeongdo was tearing his hair out, with the song going around in his head again. It would never go away, even if he gouged out a part of his brain. The notes of pain had been carved into his cells through his whole life.

She grabbed me by my throat and shoved me into the tub, he thought. I saw her distorted face through the lapping water. She looked so sad, as if she were crying and laughing at the same time, and I cried as I drank the water. Maybe I cried because my lungs hurt so much, it felt like they would burst.

Yi Byeongdo continued to replay the scene in his mind: Her eyes were on me, but she wasn't looking at me. I think maybe she was seeing the traces of him that were somewhere on my face. I'd never heard anything about my father. I knew enough not to ask.

Once, just once, she did say something about him. She said he deserved to die.

She said not to even say the word "father." That's when I learned for the first time. That I'd been born through the violence of a man. I didn't even know what it meant, but I could guess, seeing the look on her face, that it was a terrible, painful, cruel thing.

You should never have been born. I think of that moment whenever I see you.

She was screaming with rage and pain that wouldn't go away even when she shoved my head into the bathtub, he thought. Why didn't she kill me then? Or if she had me removed before I was born, neither of us would've had to go through such painful times.

Sounds and light hit the prison simultaneously. Lightning seemed to have struck somewhere close.

Seeing the blinding light, he thought he couldn't stay in prison like this. He looked at the CCTV camera in the corner.

They must be watching me through the monitor, he thought, and looked at the cuffs on his hands and feet. He had wanted to end it, even if this was what it took. And being in prison, he'd thought for a while that it was really over.

The more he killed, the emptier he felt. He killed to make the song in his head go away, but it always came back. It didn't come back after he had killed twenty people. But now, other things tormented him.

There never had been a song.

After he killed his mother, he led an ordinary life. When he began to kill again, he knew.

From now on, I'll be frantically roaming the streets at night, he thought. Whenever I see someone, I'll try to find a way to get to them, and picture myself killing them. Then one day, I'll commit murder, craving blood, just as people go to bars, craving a drink. My hands are already wet with blood. So are my feet. I . . . I've just been looking for an excuse to kill.

When I came to myself, I was strangling a woman, singing a song. Mom came alive in me like that. I thought I was killing people to make the song go away, but now I know. I kept killing because I wanted to hear it again.

I didn't kill her because I hated her, Yi Byeongdo thought. I wanted desperately for her to love me. I was so thirsty for love, that I got jealous over her showing a cat the slightest bit of affection.

I wanted her to look at me with affection. I wanted to feel the warmth of her hand, stroking my head. I wanted to go to sleep in her arms, listening to her sing me a lullaby, he thought.

His soul was like a worm-eaten leaf, with holes everywhere. Whenever he felt the wind blow through the holes, he killed someone. But killing didn't fill the emptiness.

It isn't over yet, he thought.

The emptiness would fill, he thought, if he saw Seonkyeong again. She could make the emptiness, which had eaten away at his soul, go away. If only he could see her again.

Looking at the camera in the corner, he fell into thought.

How would he break through these impenetrable walls, and see her again? Security had been maximized after the suicide of an inmate. It would be impossible for a condemned criminal like him to get out, unless he was dead.

Another flash of lightning struck. Heavy rain was falling. It sounded as if the storm would sweep the world away.

He finally came upon an answer. He began to get ready to break free.

A GUARD, WHO HAD BEEN WATCHING the monitor in the security office, jumped to his feet. Another guard, who had been dozing with his legs stretched out on a chair, opened his eyes in surprise.

"What's the matter?" he asked.

"The . . . the crazy son of a bitch slit his throat!"

Shocked, the guard who had been dozing quickly looked at the monitor. Most of the other condemned criminals were in bed. Only Yi Byeongdo's room looked different.

Standing in the middle of the room, he was looking at the camera, as if he wanted someone to see him. He seemed out of his mind, baring his teeth and grinning. Dark blood was dripping down his throat. The blood wet his body and pooled on the floor. He couldn't be left to go on bleeding in that way. He would die in no time.

"Call the manager. Announce it's an emergency."

The security manager picked up the phone and ordered the guards to go immediately to Yi Byeongdo's cell with a medic, and transfer him to a nearby hospital if things were critical. His voice was trembling with rage.

The medic on duty answered the guard's call and came running. Accompanied by the medic, the guards ran to the condemned criminals' section of the prison. They opened the door in haste and went inside. Yi Byeongdo was lying on the floor, his hands clutching his neck. The floor was slippery with blood.

The medic rushed to get a look at the neck, but Yi Byeongdo was groaning, struggling in pain. The medic tried to pry his hands off, to see the wound and stop the bleeding, but it was no use.

"He's bleeding severely. He could die if it's the carotid. We need to get him to the hospital, now," said the medic to the guards. They hesitated, not quite knowing what to do, but in the end they got the key and unlocked the cuffs on Yi Byeongdo's hands and feet.

"Tell them to park the ambulance inside. And call the manager," said one of the guards.

An ambulance from a designated hospital nearby arrived, making it through the torrential rain.

Yi Byeongdo was placed on a stretcher brought by the medical team, and transferred to the ambulance. The two guards got in the ambulance with him. In great haste, the ambulance headed to the hospital on the rainy night street.

29.

SEONKYEONG OPENED HER EYES AND SAW THE CHILD SLEEPING next to her.

She shivered without realizing it, and turned over. She couldn't bring herself to look at Hayeong's face as if nothing were wrong. At that moment, lightning flashed, and the little lamp on the nightstand went out. The lightning had struck somewhere nearby and caused a power failure, it seemed.

Hayeong felt around with her hands, then clung to Seonkyeong's waist, afraid even in her sleep.

Seonkyeong wanted to push away the little hands at her waist. She wanted to scream that she wanted the hands off her, that she didn't want to be touched at all. But she couldn't. She turned back over and put her arms around the child's head. Her head felt hot, as did her body. Her hair, wet with perspiration, dampened Seonkyeong's hands. The sleeping child smacked her lips and said something incoherent. She seemed to be saying that she was scared.

"Don't worry. The light will be back on soon," Seonkyeong said in a low voice. But the power didn't come back, even after a while.

Seonkyeong had indescribably complicated feelings about the child.

She recalled her brief dream. She thought of Hayeong, handing her the medicine. What Sergeant Yu had said must have triggered the strange dream. Thanks to it, one of her questions was resolved. Poison. She had refused to believe what Sergeant Yu said, thinking that a child couldn't have gotten her hands on poison. But the answer was simple.

Hayeong's mother took something to kill herself. What if Hayeong found the poison in her mother's room, and kept it hidden until now? It was likely enough. Seonkyeong was leaning more and more toward Sergeant Yu's deduction.

Hayeong was asleep, taking shallow breaths. Her cheeks, still plump with baby fat, were so cute that Seonkyeong wanted to bite them. Hayeong seemed to be dreaming, furrowing her brow and whimpering now and then. She whimpered again. Seonkyeong patted her on the chest, and Hayeong fell back into deep sleep.

Looking at the child, Seonkyeong felt as if there were a storm raging in her heart, just as there was outside the window.

Listening to Yi Byeongdo tell his story and seeing the wounds deep in his consciousness was different from seeing Hayeong's shattered heart.

Yi Byeongdo was a stranger, and a part of her job. Once the job was finished, there would be no point of contact between them. But Hayeong was Jaeseong's daughter, and someone she'd consented to living with. Hayeong wasn't a job; she was part of Seonkyeong's daily life, someone who slept and ate in the same house, someone she saw every day.

If Yi Byeongdo was a dark soul, deep in a bottomless pit, Hayeong still had a chance. She had a chance to remove her festering wound and live a good, ordinary life like other people—if things were set right now.

Seonkyeong patted the child's head. She wondered how deep a shadow the past events had cast on her soul. Even if the scars remained forever, Seonkyeong believed that things could change, depending on how much of the wound was healed. Seonkyeong saw herself as an optimistic person. She believed there was hope for everything. She believed that there was hope for Hayeong as well.

But was there really? She was starting to have doubts. She wondered if it wasn't too late.

Imagine someone keeping for over a year the poison that had killed her mother, giving it to her grandparents to make them die, and setting a fire to hide the act. It was a cold-blooded method that only criminals like Yi Byeongdo would employ. It wasn't something that an eleven-year-old child, with big eyes and peachy cheeks, still plump with baby fat, would do.

What was in Hayeong's heart?

Seonkyeong remembered Hayeong's face when the child shook the scissors at her. For the first time, she'd felt afraid of her. In the girl's heart was something she couldn't imagine. Age didn't matter.

The left side of her head was aching terribly from waking up after sleeping under the influence of the medicine. She glanced at the clock and saw that it was past one in the morning. She didn't want to stay in bed, lying next to Hayeong. It wouldn't be easy to fall back asleep. She got up quietly and stepped out of the bedroom.

30.

T HE SECURITY MANAGER, WHO HAD BEEN ALERTED, WAS
standing at the entrance of the hospital's emergency room.
He looked pitiful, almost, drenched in the rain.

He frowned, watching Yi Byeongdo being carried out of the ambulance. His prison garb was bloody; so was his face.

Moved to a hospital stretcher that had been waiting for him, Yi
Byeongdo was soon taken into the emergency room.

"What the hell happened? Why does he look like that?" demanded the security manager, upset, grabbing one of the guards who
had come in the ambulance.

"I'm not sure. I was looking at the monitor, and saw him slit his
throat with something," the guard said.

The security manager rubbed his face with a hand, and heaved a
sigh

"He wants to screw us over. Why the hell is he doing this, when
there's been a suicide so recently?" he said.

He didn't know how much blood Yi Byeongdo had lost, but things
didn't look good if he had slit his throat.

The security manager really didn't want things to get messy again.
It wasn't long ago that he'd been summoned here and there to

handle all sorts of trouble because of Seong Kicheol's suicide. If word spread that something like that had happened again, he might really have to take responsibility and step down. Yi Byeongdo had to be revived.

Swallowing back curses, the security manager went into the emergency center.

Yi Byeongdo, transferred to an operating room, was given a blood transfusion and stitches. The medical team informed the security manager that fortunately, the cut on the throat had missed the artery, and Yi Byeongdo would be stable after the stitches and the blood transfusion. The loss of blood was mostly from a head wound, not the throat. In any case, the security manager could relax a bit.

After the surgery, Yi Byeongdo was quarantined in a recovery room. Seeing the transfusion continue and Yi Byeongdo sleeping, breathing evenly, the security manager finally looked at his watch and yawned.

He wanted to strangle him, thinking about how he'd had to wake up in the middle of the night and drive frantically to the hospital in the rain, and worried himself sick. Thinking he would make Yi Byeongdo pay for the disturbance, the security manager walked out of the recovery room.

He instructed the two guards to keep watch, one in the room, the other in the corridor. With the wound on his neck, and the loss of blood, Yi Byeongdo would have difficulty even sitting up. Running away was unthinkable.

Back home in bed, however, trying to make up for lost sleep, the security manager had a gloomy foreboding.

From his first day at the prison, Yi Byeongdo had jarred him. He was just as ostentatious as Yu Yeongcheol, and wanted special treatment. He had often caused problems with his excessive demands, and irritated the guards by filing complaints.

He thought about the woman, the criminal psychologist.

Thinking about it, he realized that Yi Byeongdo had changed since his interviews with her. He was quiet in his cell, perhaps because he had someone new to play with. As the interviews progressed, however, he became noticeably anxious. When he found out that she was no longer coming, his anxiety reached its peak. His attempt at suicide must have had something to do with her.

Was it so unbearable for him not to see her? the security manager wondered.

He had never liked the idea of the interviews, which had been Yi Byeongdo's to begin with. He could not understand why so many people had to go about accommodating him, so that he could be interviewed when he wished—why all the fuss about finding out what was in the brain of someone like him?

He wanted Yi Seonkyeong and no one else.

Even in his cell, he could see whom he wished, when he wished. In a way, he possessed great power. The woman didn't seem to know why he'd chosen her. There was no telling what he wanted to get out of the interviews, but things must have been absolutely to his advantage. It must've satisfied his ego. But the woman was no pushover.

The security manager was shocked by the fact that she refused Yi Byeongdo and put a stop to the interviews. The sense of loss Yi Byeongdo suffered seemed to be as great as what he felt on the day he was sentenced to death. The desperation of not being able to see her again had made him do this. Was this indeed the end?

That was what made the security manager uneasy. No one knew what Yi Byeongdo might do now. The thoughts followed, one after another, and sleep fled him; his uneasiness grew so much that he couldn't lie still.

In the end, he got up, thinking he should go back to the hospital. At that moment, the phone rang. The call was from one of the guards there. He said Yi Byeongdo had disappeared. What the security manager had been dreading had come true. He felt drained of all hope.

Finally coming to himself, he spat curses into the phone.

How had Yi Byeongdo escaped, in a condition like that?

31.

FOR YI BYEONGDO, FINDING OUT SEONKYEONG'S ADDRESS was a cinch.

He looked around, standing in front of her house. There was no trace of anyone in the alley, it being late, with a heavy downpour and strong wind. He swiftly jumped over the wall by the gate. The wound on his neck felt hot, but it was bearable. When he was strangling the guard with the IV tubing, he thought the sutured wound would burst open again. With any further exertion, hot blood would've dripped down his neck.

He had learned many useful things during his several stays in jail. Those who had come before him taught him how to find out someone's address, and how to make it look as if you were bleeding a lot when the wound wasn't deep.

There was no hesitation in his steps as he walked through the yard.

The torrential rain hushed up all the sounds he was making. He went up to the front door and put his hand gently on the doorknob, and turned it. The door was locked. He moved to the right and went to the window. Faint light leaked out through the curtains. The light swayed—it must be candlelight. He finally understood why all the streetlamps were out. The weather had caused a blackout. It was a good omen for him.

There must be someone inside, if there was a lit candle.

He turned back around and saw a little window. He guessed from the gas pipe passing through that it was the window to the kitchen. He went carefully up to the window, and checked to see if the door to the kitchen would open. The knob turned and he was about to open the door, when he saw through the window someone walking into the kitchen.

He quickly leaned flat against the outside wall. The footsteps came closer.

He heard the sound of dishes clinking, and the gas stove being turned on. He turned his head slightly and peeked out of the corner of his eye, and saw a woman standing in front of the stove. It was Seonkyeong.

She was looking at the kettle on the stove. She seemed to be boiling some water for coffee. The blue flames lit up her face in the darkness. She was deep in thought. A strand of hair fell over her face, hiding it from view.

He wanted to reach out a hand and brush back the fallen strand of hair. He wanted to drink the coffee she made, and talk about the days he had lived through. There was so much he wanted to say, but she didn't want to listen. He suddenly remembered how cold she'd been with him.

She was lying when she said she was giving me a chance. She's going to pay for it, he thought.

He began to hum a song in a low voice. It had begun once again. But this time, it really was going to be the last.

A whistle came from the kettle. Seonkyeong, who had been staring at the kettle, got a coffee cup and poured water in it. She didn't know that he was there. She wasn't even interested in him.

It had been that way from the beginning. She only wanted to know how he'd killed the women. She pretended otherwise, but he knew very well that she was deceiving him. That was why he'd ended the first interview so abruptly. He didn't really have much to tell her. He didn't want her to find that out.

He wanted to see her face.

He wanted her to look at him, smiling. He wanted her to listen to what he said, and understand his loneliness. The moment Seonkyeong talked about her first childhood memory, his expectations were shattered. Why did all the women he met start their lives with such trivial memories?

He had hoped that Seonkyeong would be different. He'd thought that she was someone who would take a more serious look into his soul. He'd believed, just as the woman at the orchard house had taken home a child who had woken up in a hospital and accepted him without a word, that at least one other person in the world would see the emptiness inside him and sympathize with him. He'd thought that Seonkyeong was that person. But she only brought him disappointment.

He saw her walk away with the cup in her hand. He watched to see which room she went into. Even after the door closed, he waited in the rain for a while.

Cautiously, he began to walk again. He saw a door past the kitchen.

He turned the doorknob, and the door opened without a sound. He hurried inside, afraid that the sound of rain would enter through the open door. It was dark, but his eyes had already grown used to the darkness. He could vaguely make out the contours of the objects. It seemed that he was in a utility room, with a boiler and a washing machine.

He took out a towel from a laundry basket next to the washing machine, and carefully mopped his hair dry and wiped off his clothes. Water pooled on the floor.

He threw the towel back into the basket and opened the door

connecting the utility room to the rest of the house. He saw the kitchen where Seonkyeong had been a moment before.

Walking toward the kitchen, he turned his head and looked at the sink for a moment, then began walking again.

He noticed a knife block on a shelf. The wooden block held a number of efficient-looking knives. He pulled out a few and checked the blades, and took a sharp one. The handle fit snugly into his palm, as if it had been waiting for him. His grip on the knife tightened automatically.

He turned around again, and walked cautiously toward the room she was in.

WAKING UP, HAYEONG REALIZED that she was alone. She was lying by herself in the big bed. She looked around the unfamiliar room.

Where was Seonkyeong?

A black shadow swayed outside the window. She looked up and gazed out the window. She felt afraid, but as she looked carefully, she saw that it was the shadow of tree branches swaying.

She sat up and fell into thought.

She remembered the way Seonkyeong had looked at her. The kids who caught the cat had the same look on their faces when she wielded her knife at them. No one talked to her after that. They all avoided her. Seonkyeong, too, would turn away, with a cold expression on her face. Hayeong's stomach felt cold. She didn't feel good. She was obedient to Seonkyeong at first because she wanted to live with her dad, but now Hayeong wanted to live with her, too. But Seonkyeong wouldn't want to live with her anymore.

She couldn't ask her dad what she should do, because he was away on a business trip, at a time like this. She had to think and decide for herself.

She hadn't expected Seonkyeong to find out about it. The problem was the fire fighter.

When she came into Seonkyeong's room to lie down next to her, Seonkyeong's cell phone made an alert sound. A text message had arrived. Seonkyeong was knocked out from the medicine. Thinking it might be her dad, Hayeong flipped the cell phone open. But the words on the screen took her by surprise.

Reinvestigation of the Pak Eunju suicide confirms the same poison was used in the Eungam-dong fire. Yu Dongsik

The message was from the fire fighter whose name she'd seen on a card. Pak Eunju was her mom's name. Hayeong took a long look at the message. She didn't understand what it meant, but it felt strange to see her mom's name. The fire fighter seemed to have found out about her mom. And since he texted Seonkyeong about it, they both seemed to know Hayeong's secret.

She deleted the message and put the cell phone back down on the table.

What should I do? I made up my mind not to tell anyone about this, not even Dad, but now Seonkyeong knows. Will she tell him? What would he say if he found out that I set the house on fire? Hayeong thought, trying to picture how her dad would look.

She was afraid of how angry he would be. She didn't want to think about anything at the moment. She wanted to get some sleep first, next to Seonkyeong. That was what she was thinking. Then Seonkyeong groaned in pain, looking sick. Hayeong felt her head. It was hot. She seemed very sick. She woke up. Hayeong stayed lying by her side, even when she told her to go upstairs.

Hayeong fell asleep, and then woke up; Seonkyeong was gone.

Hayeong was afraid that she'd gone to call her dad already. She saw that the cell phone was still on the table, however, so maybe Seonkyeong hadn't gone to make a phone call.

I should be the one to tell him, Hayeong thought, and began to think about what she'd say to him.

It was certain that he wouldn't like the fact that she had set fire to her grandparents' house. On top of that, she'd kept the thing she had promised him to throw away. He would remember, and be angry. When he came back from his trip, Seonkyeong would tell on her for sure.

Seonkyeong knew too many of her secrets. She even found out about the birds Hayeong had kept hidden in the dresser. Thinking about it, Hayeong grew anxious. She wondered what Seonkyeong was doing.

Hayeong opened the bedroom door and began to walk carefully. She went up to the study door with muffled steps. She must be inside, Hayeong thought. She put her ear to the door and waited to see if there was any sound. What she heard was a man's voice. Hayeong nearly yelped. Dad isn't back yet—who is this man? she wondered. Again, she pressed her face against the door and listened.

Hayeong's curiosity intensified.

A MAN'S LARGE HAND CLAMPED over Seonkyeong's mouth.

Seonkyeong, who had been sitting in a chair, lost in thought, hadn't even heard someone come in. A man suddenly lunged at her, held her tight with one hand, and put his other hand over her mouth, throwing her into utter confusion. The hand that held her had a knife in it. Fear and dread washed over her.

A strange man had entered the house, probably climbing over the wall, taking advantage of the rainy night. Every cell in her body felt frozen. Then she heard the man's voice. It was a familiar voice.

"I came to see you . . . because you wouldn't come see me," the voice said.

Yi Byeongdo. He had come. She felt momentary relief that it was someone she knew, but then her blood ran cold.

He had escaped from prison.

There was no telling how he'd escaped and made it to her house, but the boldness of the act and lack of reserve hinted at his mental state. He'd come to this dead end on his own two feet, with no hesitation whatsoever, which meant that he didn't care if he died; he had nothing to fear.

His body felt cold and damp, probably from having been in the cold rain for a long time. Seonkyeong felt goose bumps rise as his cold skin touched her cheek. She felt his cold body against her back. She relaxed her own body, to hide the fact that she was recoiling in fear, and to appear calm.

Yi Byeongdo sensed her relax, and his arms loosened their grip.

"Promise me you won't scream, even if I take my hands off you," he said, his breath on her cheek. His face was right next to hers.

Seonkyeong nodded quietly, and he slowly took his hand off her mouth.

"Why don't you . . . take the knife away, too? If you're not here to kill me, that is," she said.

"Well . . . I haven't made up my mind yet," he replied.

Seonkyeong waited without saying anything. He buried his nose in her hair for a moment, sniffing it, and then let her go. Seonkyeong, who had been nervous with tension, gave a light sigh, and turned around and looked at him. He scratched his head, then took a step back and put the knife on a corner of the table.

Seeing him shiver all of a sudden from the cold, Seonkyeong handed him Jaeseong's shirt from a chair. He declined, shaking his head.

"You'll catch a cold," she said, at which he began to chuckle. He took a deliberate look around the study.

"So this is . . . your world?" he said.

Seonkyeong couldn't answer; she couldn't believe her eyes. Why was he standing here before her, when he should be sleeping in his solitary cell? She must be dreaming, no matter how she thought about it.

"Will you tell me what happened?" she asked.

Yi Byeongdo, who had been looking at the books on the bookshelves, turned around to look at her and smiled.

"Does it matter where I am? What matters to me is that I'm with you right now," he said.

Seonkyeong thought of the security manager. He was the one who, more than anyone else, must have wanted Yi Byeongdo to be in his place. She wondered if he knew what was going on.

"It's finally time to answer your first question," Yi Byeongdo said.

He thought back to the day he first saw her.

For the first time, he told her about the orchard house. It was the answer to her question about the fur mother monkey. Looking at her face as she listened earnestly, he felt as though he were once again back at the orchard house.

He wanted to end the long journey.

No one is born through his own will. But living, or putting an end to living, can be your choice.

He'd felt relieved that he no longer heard the song in his head. He hadn't murdered of his own will. He'd had no other choice. It didn't matter that he was caught and taken to prison. All he wanted was for the song, which had tormented him relentlessly, to come to an end. No matter how hard he listened, he didn't hear it again. He'd felt that he could finally sleep in peace. It didn't matter that he was in prison. He was even grateful for a solitary cell, where only condemned criminals stayed. He'd thought that his mother's ghost had finally left him.

That's what he'd thought, until he saw Seonkyeong's face. After he saw her, he fell into confusion again. He felt that he'd run into someone he had so longed for; on the other hand, he didn't want to show himself to her. He couldn't see her, looking the way he did. But he couldn't give up this opportunity that had come to him after twenty years. In the end, his desire to see her triumphed.

Seonkyeong, however, was not the woman at the orchard house. He ate the first apple Seonkyeong brought, but it didn't taste sweet. The apples he had tasted in his paradise felt like an unattainable dream now.

"How could you do this to me? How could you leave without even saying goodbye?" he asked.

"I thought it would be better for you not to know" was Seonkyeong's reply.

He shook his head.

"No, you lied to me. You were supposed to give me a chance, but didn't. The song was driving me insane, but you didn't give a damn about me. You're just like her. I thought you were the woman at the orchard house, but you're just like my mom," he went on.

"I'm neither of them. There are other people in the world besides your mother and the woman at the orchard house," Seonkyeong said.

She had more to say, but he wouldn't listen. He pounced on her. He looked into her eyes while strangling her. He no longer heard her voice. The song was thumping in his head.

Humming the song for the last time, he thought, was the only way to make it stop.

"If you'd only . . . only told me one thing, I would've been happy. Was I really so awful to you, Mom? Did I never bring you happiness? Could I never make you smile?" he asked.

Sensing danger in his eyes, Seonkyeong began to fiercely resist. But her resistance was something he could easily suppress. Strangling her and feeling the tendons standing out in his arms, he counted in his mind.

When he shoved her against a wall and tightened his grip on her neck, her violent struggle began to subside and so did her panting. Her breath touched his cheek. He squeezed with all the strength left in his hands. Her hands, which had been scratching his arms, dropped and dangled limply in the air.

Dying was so simple.

He lifted one hand and pushed back the strands of hair covering her face. He leaned against her head and closed his eyes for a moment. The tears filling his eyes trickled down his cheeks.

At that moment, he felt a severe pain at his side. He looked down and saw a knife stuck there.

How strange, he thought, the knife should be on the table. He looked up, and saw a little girl, looking at him from a few feet away. Unruffled, she was watching with serene eyes to see how things unfolded.

So this is your cat? Yi Byeongdo thought, and removed one hand from Seonkyeong's neck and felt his side where the knife stabbed him. He wasn't bleeding much. But he didn't like the peculiar sensation of the knife piercing his body. Clenching his teeth, he pulled it out. Blood gushed from the wound.

The knife must have somehow pierced through his ribs and stabbed his lung. He wheezed whenever he exhaled. His hands went limp. Seonkyeong, held only by one of his hands, came to and shoved his arm away, freeing herself.

As a result, Yi Byeongdo fell to the floor.

He wasn't feeling right. His mind seemed to be separating from his body. He knew instinctively that he was going to die soon. Whenever he breathed, blood came from deep within his lungs. He burst into coughs. He threw up blood. He had difficulty breathing. The blood that flowed from his body spread out under him as he lay on the floor.

He felt a fog coming on, but he struggled to keep his eyes open.

He saw the little girl approaching him, her eyes full of curiosity. His blood spread toward her feet. Feeling himself lying there helplessly, he smiled hollowly.

Suddenly, bright light flooded Yi Byeongdo's vision. He lay on the floor, looking at the dazzling light. The power must be back on; the fluorescent light blinded his eyes.

He saw Seonkyeong stop the little girl from approaching him, then take her hand and step back. He tried to reach out a hand and take hers, but he didn't even have the strength to push back his eyelids.

He'd believed that dying was nothing—that it just meant everything came to an end, that it was darkness, disappearance. That was what he'd thought. But as death approached, he realized at last that death was not an endless darkness, but a momentary blackout. It was not disappearance, but displacement into another world.

He felt afraid that he had to go, with his consciousness and memories intact. It frightened him that he had to move on to another life, with the same consciousness, the same soul. He'd thought that afterlife was an illusion, concocted to overcome fear. But it was not an illusion; it was another universe that was present in human consciousness. His only consolation was that his mother's song, which had inflicted pain on him all his life, was now comforting him, embracing him.

Yi Byeongdo closed his eyes and listened to the song.

Unlike in the version of the song in his first memory, now his mother's voice sounded cheerful and warm. He waited for his mother's hand to touch him. Her big, warm hand, which he had waited for all his life, stroked his head and caressed his eyes, nose, and cheeks. Finally, he felt the deep, dark hole inside him, which had been empty all his life, fill up. The song that had tormented him all his life vanished after that.

"Is he dead?" asked the little girl, but her voice, too, grew more and more distant.

SEONKYEONG TOOK HAYEONG, WHO kept craning her neck to see the dead man, out of the study. She turned around to look, afraid that he might come back to life, but she saw his eyes close, his face relax, and a smile spread across his face. Death seemed to have brought him rest.

As they entered the living room, Seonkyeong's cell phone rang in the bedroom. She rushed over to it and took the call. It was the security manager at the Seoul Detention Center. The call had come much too late. But she didn't have the energy to blame him for neglecting his duty.

Without even listening to him, she said briefly, "He's here. Come . . . take him away."

Not explaining further, she gave him her address and hung up.

She sank into the sofa. She couldn't remain standing up, as she was trembling all over. Hayeong stood a little way off, staring blankly at her. She must be in shock from what had just happened.

If not for Hayeong, Seonkyeong would have died at Yi Byeong-do's hands. She felt grateful to be alive, but she also felt some mixed emotions.

"Are you all right?" Seonkyeong asked, but the child just stared at her, without answering. Seonkyeong wondered if she was hurt, and hurried over to her. She felt the child's head, arms, and legs, and asked if she was hurting anywhere.

Hayeong, who had been silent, showed Seonkyeong her palms. Blood. Her hands were wet with blood.

She seemed to be in shock from seeing the blood on her hands. She was showing them to Seonkyeong because she didn't know what to do with them. Her eyes, looking at Seonkyeong, were as deep and tranquil as the cold night sea. Seonkyeong could not fathom what was swirling in her heart. Hayeong opened and closed her palms, feeling the congealing blood.

Alarmed, Seonkyeong took Hayeong by the arm and hastened to the bathroom.

She turned on the faucet and thrust Hayeong's hands underneath. The blood washed down the drain. Seonkyeong put soap on Hayeong's hands and worked up a lather, so that not a drop of blood would remain. She scrubbed and scrubbed her hands until they were red. She felt that if she didn't, Yi Byeongdo's blood would seep into Hayeong's body, tainting her young soul.

It sickened her to imagine it.

"Stop, it hurts," Hayeong said, drawing her hands back, and Seonkyeong came to herself. Hayeong drifted away, sensing something strange as Seonkyeong scrubbed frantically at her hands.

Seonkyeong got a towel from a bin and handed it to her. But Hayeong wouldn't take it. After she went out of the bathroom, Seonkyeong washed her face with cold water. She felt more herself.

She looked up and saw herself in the mirror. She looked awful. She raised her head and checked her neck. There were vivid red handprints there. Her muscles ached dully from the shock.

She went to the living room and saw Hayeong sitting on the sofa. She was looking out the window at the yard, just as she had on the day she arrived. She seemed lost in thought, which for some reason made Seonkyeong nervous.

"Hayeong, are you all right?" she asked, sitting down next to her.

Hayeong pointed with a finger out the window.

"The wind has stopped," she said.

Seonkyeong turned her head and looked at the yard as well. The fierce rain had calmed its rage and quieted down. The branches of the willow tree, which had been swaying in the wind, were hanging low, drenched by the rain.

Having said that, Hayeong went on looking out the window in

silence. Fearing the silence, Seonkyeong looked intently at her face. Her face revealed nothing, which made Seonkyeong uneasy. She couldn't bear it any longer, and turned her head away.

"You don't . . . want to live with me anymore, do you?" Hayeong asked.

Startled, Seonkyeong looked at her once again. Meeting her eyes, Seonkyeong fumbled for words. The child waited quietly for her answer.

Looking into Hayeong's eyes, Seonkyeong said after some hesitation, "Let's talk when your father comes home."

A look of disappointment crossed Hayeong's face. She got up and went upstairs.

Left alone, Seonkyeong waited for the police to come, biting her lip in anxiety.

As she thought about Hayeong, something hot rose in her throat. She tried to swallow it back, but it wouldn't go down. In the end, she began to sob loudly.

It wasn't the child's fault. She had been abused by a mother, who, starved for love, did things to her child without even really knowing what she was doing. If that fractured Hayeong's soul, what effect would the night's incident have on it? Although it wasn't her fault, Seonkyeong realized that she'd done something even more terrible than what Hayeong's mother had done.

Would the child have experienced something like this if she hadn't been living with her? Seonkyeong felt afraid. She wanted to ask someone, anyone, why things like this kept happening to Hayeong. It seemed as if her fate were leading her down a path prepared for her. Seonkyeong feared finding out what lay at the end of that path.

She wanted to deny it. She shook her head violently at some unknown being.

No. This can't be. This is impossible. Stop it, stop it!

Stop tormenting this child.

32.

THE POLICE WOULDN'T LET THE SECURITY MANAGER OF the Seoul Detention Center in the study, in order to preserve the scene of the crime.

The manager, who had been standing in front of the study door peeping inside, waiting for the crime scene investigators to finish the primary investigation, approached Seonkyeong and paced around her. Seonkyeong, who was discussing the situation with the investigators, glanced at him out of the corner of her eye.

He actually looked relieved. It must be something of a solace to him that Yi Byeongdo had come here, of all places, and died. He would be reprimanded, but the escape had been handled with alacrity, so things could've been worse for him.

"So he was strangling you, but hesitated when the light came on, and that's when you stabbed him with the knife he'd brought into the study from the kitchen?" an investigator asked.

"That's right," Seonkyeong said, lowering her eyes. She held her neck with a hand, grimacing. The investigators would not miss the marks on her neck. One of them craned his neck to get a close look at them, and scribbled something in his notebook. Another investigator took one picture after another of Seonkyeong's neck.

She had decided to lie to the investigators for Hayeong's sake.

If they found out that Hayeong was the one who killed Yi Byeongdo, they'd press her about what happened at the time. In the end, they'd conclude that it was self-defense, but considering how they would harass the child in the meantime, it would be better, she thought, to make some changes to the story.

Besides, there was the arson case. If the child said something wrong in answer to the investigators' questions, things could take an unexpected turn. Seonkyeong's sole concern was to protect the child until Jaeseong came home.

She would discuss the problem with him when he returned.

"Will you be all right without going the hospital?" asked the investigators, as they closed their notebooks. It seemed that the scenario she'd prepared satisfied them.

Besides, the knife that had been found at the scene had Seonkyeong's fingerprints on it. The only other person in the house was the child who was sleeping in her room upstairs. And she'd slept soundly despite the fierce rainstorm. There was no room for suspicion.

The investigators seemed, in fact, to sympathize with Seonkyeong, who had escaped a life-threatening situation with a convict she'd interviewed at the prison. When they were finished talking, the investigators got up from their seats and headed to the study.

The security manager, who had been waiting for a chance to talk to Seonkyeong, came to sit down as soon as the investigators left.

"What happened?" he asked.

"That's what I want to ask you," Seonkyeong said.

The security manager's face stiffened for a moment, then relaxed. In a way, he was to blame for what happened. He should offer profuse apologies, no matter what Seonkyeong said. Taking on a submissive attitude, he tried to placate her.

"I was deceived by the act he put on, just like you were. Who could've known that he would escape from the hospital after all that bleeding?" he asked.

Seonkyeong could guess what happened. It was impossible to break through the tight security at the prison. If you wanted to escape, the sensible thing would be to seek an opportunity after making it out of the prison somehow. Chances were that in a hospital, the security wouldn't be as tight.

"What did he say?" the security manager asked, his eyes gleaming.

He was surprised that Yi Byeongdo had taken such a great risk to escape. It had seemed strange from the beginning that he'd wanted to be interviewed by her and no one else. The manager knew that he'd decided to escape because of her.

Although he knew that Seonkyeong was special to Yi Byeongdo, he didn't know what it was about her that made her special. The manager wanted to know what had shaken him up so.

"He said he could come see me anytime, if he had a mind to," Seonkyeong snapped at the manager. Attack was the best defense.

She didn't want to hear him say this and that about Yi Byeongdo. She could never explain to anyone what she'd seen in his eyes in his last moment. His eyes said everything—more than a thousand words could. She didn't want to turn his loneliness, which must have chilled him to the bone, into idle talk for the security manager to indulge in.

Some people wounded their own souls with inherent sensitivity. Seonkyeong, too, had lived with the loneliness that came from having no siblings, and the emptiness that came from her mother's death early on. Yi Byeongdo's words had penetrated deep into her heart, where no one had been able to reach. She didn't want to try to explain the sense of kinship she'd felt for him, which no one would understand.

The security manager looked at Seonkyeong, offended, but when he saw the body being brought out of the study, he quickly got up and followed the others. As he went out through the front door, he turned around and said to Seonkyeong, "I told you, didn't I? That no good would come of getting involved with him."

He gave her a light nod, and went outside.

Seonkyeong got up from the sofa and went toward the study; the investigator she'd talked to earlier was on his way out.

"You'd better keep the door closed tonight. We'll call the criminal victim support center and request cleaning service in the morning," he said.

Seonkyeong nodded and took a look at the study.

Dark blood stained the floor where Yi Byeongdo had lain.

The detective closed the door to the study and looked for a uniformed officer. One came with yellow tape for marking limited access, and taped it across the door.

Once the final investigator had left, the house was quiet.

Seonkyeong looked around inside the house, unfamiliar after the tornado that had swept through, and went upstairs.

Hayeong was sleeping in her bed. Seonkyeong pulled up the blanket, which the child had kicked off, and tucked her back in and left the room.

She went downstairs and checked the lock on the glass door. The rain had almost ceased. She realized that her headache was gone, too.

Sleep overwhelmed her. She felt drained of all energy. She turned off the living room light and went into the bedroom.

As soon as she slipped under the blanket, she fell deep into sleep.

It was a dreamless slumber.

33.

SEONKYEONG OPENED HER EYES, FEELING AS THOUGH SHE had slept for a week, but the clock said eight o'clock. She thought she'd slept quite long, exhausted from all the commotion, but it had been less than three hours.

She slipped out of bed and pushed the curtains back. A clear sky, and sunlight that had just begun to spread, filled her view. The frenzied hours of the night before seemed like a dream. But the traces that remained in the yard proved that it hadn't been.

The yard was a mess after the storm. Seonkyeong felt rather relieved that there was a lot to do. As she moved her body, her mind would slowly work out what was to be done next.

She was making the bed when she heard footsteps outside her bedroom. The sound came from the living room. Thinking Hayeong must be awake, she was about to step out from the room when the door opened.

Hayeong came in, with a cup of milk on a tray.

Seonkyeong was astonished at the fact that the child looked fine, even after what happened the night before. She wondered if Hayeong was used to death by now.

Hayeong's calm face disturbed Seonkyeong even more. Washing

the blood off the child's hands the night before, Seonkyeong had realized something awful: she was scrubbing and scrubbing her hands, until they turned red, but in the end, it was she herself who had put the blood on Hayeong's hands. She had shattered the soul that had barely been kept intact.

Would such a thing have happened if Seonkyeong had been an ordinary housewife? The child had already killed someone before. Now she had killed again. What did she think, looking down at the blood on her hands? Just thinking about it sent chills up Seonkyeong's spine.

Perhaps she and Hayeong should never have met.

"Are you okay now?" asked the child, putting the tray down on the table. She was making an effort, in her own way, to show that she cared. Seonkyeong stared at the cup of milk she'd brought, then looked away with mixed emotions.

"There's something I want to ask you," Hayeong said, perching on a corner of the bed.

"What is it?" Seonkyeong asked.

"Are you . . . going to tell my dad about it?"

She seemed to be referring to the fire incident, in which she'd killed her grandparents and set the house on fire. She was more afraid than anything of her father finding out about it. Or perhaps she was afraid that she might no longer be able to live with him because of it—she'd done such a terrible thing, because she wanted to live with him.

"I won't tell him," she said.

A look of relief flooded the child's face. But when she heard what Seonkyeong said next, her face hardened.

"I want you to tell him yourself. If you don't, then I will have to tell him."

"Do I . . . really have to tell him?" Hayeong asked.

Seonkyeong looked quietly into her eyes. Seeing the look in Seonkyeong's eyes, Hayeong lowered her head, as though to say she knew she had no choice.

"All right," Hayeong said quietly, and fell into thought for a moment. But she perked up soon enough, and looking at Seonkyeong, held out the cup of milk as though she'd just remembered it.

Seonkyeong shook her head, not wanting anything. Hayeong looked disappointed. Seeing her like that, she realized she couldn't refuse the milk. Reluctantly, she took the cup from the child's hand.

Hayeong wouldn't leave, but kept staring at her and then said, "You don't like me, do you?"

"Yes, I do like you," Seonkyeong said.

"You're lying. You don't even know me that well," Hayeong said, her voice growing croaky.

"You can like someone, even if you don't know them very well. I really wanted to get along with you," Seonkyeong said in honesty. The change had been sudden, but living with the child, she had been learning what it was like to raise a family.

"My dad likes you. But . . . I don't," the child said coldly, which hurt Seonkyeong's feelings. She felt a lump in her throat. Not knowing what to say, she took a sip of the milk.

"All I wanted was to live with my dad," Hayeong mumbled, sounding distressed.

"You'll live with your dad. But first, you have to tell him," Seonkyeong said, and drank some more milk. She wanted to send Hayeong out of the room as soon as possible.

Hayeong, who had been quietly watching her drink the milk, smiled suddenly and whispered, "Do you want me to tell you a secret?"

Seonkyeong felt afraid for some reason to see Hayeong smile, her eyes gleaming, looking completely different from the way she had a moment before. Seonkyeong felt stifled. She wanted to go to the bathroom and throw up.

"Do you know how my mom died?" Hayeong asked.

She had died, supposedly after taking something. But Hayeong's smiling face seemed to say something different. Seonkyeong felt sick with an ominous dread.

"How . . . how did she die?" she asked.

"She died after drinking some milk, like you just did" was Hayeong's reply.

Seonkyeong looked at her in trepidation.

"My dad told me to put it in the milk and give it to her, if she hurt me really, really bad."

"The medicine, then?"

"He gave it to me. He said it would make her fall asleep. I think she died because I put too much in."

Seonkyeong's mind went blank. Her hands and feet felt numb, and she kept rubbing her hands. Her head felt heavy, too.

"It's a secret between just my dad and me. He told me to throw away the rest of the medicine, but I didn't," Hayeong said, and took something out of her pocket and held it out to Seonkyeong. A dainty little medicine bottle lay in the palm of her hand.

Why hadn't Seonkyeong thought of it? It would've been so easy for him, a doctor, to get his hands on medicine. She remembered his sensitive reaction whenever she brought up his ex-wife. Seonkyeong had thought it was because of the wounds the woman had inflicted on him, but there seemed to have been another reason.

She wondered what his true intention had been in handing Hayeong the poison.

Had he given it to her because he couldn't bear to see his daughter being abused by her mother? Or had it been a plan, to free himself of his ex-wife? There was no telling why he had really given Hayeong the poison, but it had killed them all—Hayeong's mother, grandmother, and grandfather. Now it was Seonkyeong's turn.

Seonkyeong smiled in spite of herself. Hayeong tilted her head, unable to understand why she was smiling. Seonkyeong had re-proached herself again and again for the horrible experience the child had gone through the night before. But the child was far beyond the point where her concern could do any good.

With deep, large eyes, Hayeong was looking at the changes taking place in Seonkyeong. Her eyes shone with anticipation.

Seonkyeong feared how the child would grow up. What lay in her future?

She wondered who had turned her into a monster. Was it her mother, who abused her, or her father, who gave her the poison? Or was it Seonkyeong herself, who had made her commit another murder? Sleep washed over her and interfered with her thoughts. How strange. She thought she had slept well; why was she so drowsy?

Seonkyeong tottered, and Hayeong rushed over and took the cup from her.

Seonkyeong fell limply onto the bed. Hayeong covered her expertly with a blanket, as if she had just been waiting to do that. She put her arms tightly around Seonkyeong's waist and said, "Do you know something? I liked you till just yesterday."

Seonkyeong couldn't say a word.

"I wished that you were my mom."

Seonkyeong couldn't see her face very well, because her eyelids kept drooping. She recalled Yi Byeongdo's face.

She felt that the devil had played with their fates, by putting him into her hands.

The devil had killed Yi Byeongdo, and created another monster in his place. A new devil that came to completion when Yi Byeongdo was dead.

Hayeong, who was still so young, was smiling innocently, unaware of the devil's scheme. Or perhaps Hayeong was evil itself. But it was everyone—her mother, her father, and everyone else—who had brought this evil into being.

Seonkyeong knew the end Hayeong was to meet.

Yi Byeongdo had shown that to her through his own death.

She wondered how Hayeong would look, when one day, far in the future, she realized that she was at the end of her life.

As her consciousness slipped into deep slumber, Seonkyeong heard the child's clear voice in her ear, saying, "Good night . . . Mom."

ABOUT THE AUTHOR

Mi-ae Seo was born in 1965 and studied Korean literature in college.

She made her literary debut in the spring of 1994 when she won a contest held by *Sports Seoul* with her short story "Thirty Ways to Kill Your Husband."

Her works include the novels *The Only Child, The Doll's Garden, Arin's Gaze,* and *The Night Your Star Disappeared,* and the short-story collections *Thirty Ways to Kill Your Husband, The Murderer I'd Like to Meet,* and *Trajectory of the Star.* She won the Grand Prize for Korean Detective Literature in 2009 for *The Doll's Garden.*

She wrote the screenplays for *My Beautiful Girl, Mari,* which won the Grand Prix at Annecy International Animation Film Festival, as well as *Temptation of Eve: Kiss* and *Temptation of Eve: Her Own Technique.*

In television, she's written for *Please Don't on Sundays, Into the Storm, Detective Q, Thirty Ways to Kill Your Husband,* and *The Murderer I'd Like to Meet.*

Currently, she is working on the sequel to *The Only Child* and on a script for a television drama about a criminal profiler.